The Million Dollar Deception

Do You Take This Woman?

The Million Dollar Divorce

Dating Games

Love Frustration

The Harris Family

Father Found

The Harris Men

Stacie & Cole

THE
MILLION
DOLLAR
DEMISE

RM JOHNSON

Simon & Schuster
New York London Toronto Sydney

Simon & Schuster
1230 Avenue of the Americas
New York, NY 10020

First Simon & Schuster hardcover edition September 2009

SIMON & SCHUSTER and colophon are registered trademarks of Simon & Schuster, Inc.

For information about special discounts for bulk purchases, please contact Simon & Schuster Special Sales at 1-866-506-1949 or business@simonandschuster.com.

The Simon & Schuster Speakers Bureau can bring authors to your live event. For more information or to book an event contact the Simon & Schuster Speakers Bureau at 1-866-248-3049 or visit our website at www.simonspeakers.com.

Designed by Nancy Singer

Manufactured in the United States of America

10 9 8 7 6 5 4 3

Library of Congress Cataloging-in-Publication Data
Johnson, RM (Rodney Marcus)
The million dollar demise : a novel / RM Johnson.
      p. cm.
Sequel to: The million dollar deception.
1. African Americans—Fiction. 2. Triangles (Interpersonal relations)—Fiction.
3. Revenge—Fiction. I. Title.
PS3560.03834M545 2009
813'.54—dc22   2009004615

ISBN 978-1-4165-9626-4
ISBN 978-1-4165-9992-0 (ebook)

To my niece Portia, and Jeremy.
Congratulations on your new life together.

THE
MILLION
DOLLAR
DEMISE

Since he had been thrown out of his house, Freddy Ford had barely been able to hold anything in his stomach. He had lost almost ten pounds off of his already thin frame. The T-shirt he wore now hung loosely on him. His jeans dropped from his narrow hips, and his hair had grown long and unruly.

He looked over his shoulder again after ringing Nate Kenny's doorbell. None of Mr. Kenny's neighbors were around.

Freddy heard the door unlock.

He quickly reached behind him, pulled the gun from the waist of his jeans, and pointed it at the door. When it opened, Mr. Kenny stared straight into the barrel of the weapon.

"Freddy," Mr. Kenny said, all cool, like there was nothing wrong. "Our business is done. I told you that three weeks ago."

"Step into the motherfucking house," Freddy said.

"Freddy—"

Freddy cocked the gun.

"Fine." Mr. Kenny turned, walked back into the house.

Freddy walked behind him, the gun pointed between his shoulder blades.

Images popped into Freddy's head. He shut his eyes, trying to black out those images. He saw his mother crying, as the sheriffs had all their furniture dragged from the house and thrown to the curb. An image of his girlfriend raced through his head, her feet in stirrups, an overworked doctor in the middle of performing the abortion, slicing his unborn baby into pieces and sucking it out of her.

When Freddy opened his eyes, the stain of those images still soiled his thoughts.

It was this man's fault, Freddy told himself, the gun shaking in his hand. He had to pay.

All of a sudden Mr. Kenny spun around. He was smiling. "I tell you what I'm gonna do."

Without a thought, Freddy squeezed the trigger of his gun and shot Mr. Kenny in the chest.

Then he shot him again, in the stomach. There was something comforting about the gun going off in Freddy's hand, something calming. Freddy fired two more times, his arms absorbing the shock of the small piece's kick, a lifeless expression on his face— once in the thigh, and again in the chest.

Mr. Kenny staggered back, horror in his eyes, bloodstains blooming large on his white shirt.

There was a scream.

Mr. Kenny turned and yelled, "Monica, no!"

Freddy whirled around and blindly fired the gun.

A single bullet tore into the side of the forehead of the woman who was standing by the bedroom door wearing only a bath towel.

It was Monica, Lewis's old girlfriend.

The towel fell, leaving Monica naked—her body dropped to its knees, then fell flat on its belly.

By then Mr. Kenny had fallen across the sofa. Freddy could see they were both dead.

Freddy hadn't meant to kill the woman, but maybe it was for the best. After another moment, he turned and was about to walk out of the house when he heard movement behind him.

Freddy turned again, the gun pointed in front of him.

"Mommy. Daddy." There was a small boy standing in the entrance of the kitchen. The child ran to his father and pulled on his bloody arm.

Freddy walked over to the boy, stood over him, and pointed the gun into the child's face.

This must be Mr. Kenny's boy.

The nagging image of Freddy's unborn child forced its way into his brain again. If it wasn't for Mr. Kenny, Kia never would've aborted their child.

Freddy moved the gun closer to the little boy's face. The child was bawling and seemed oblivious to the gun.

An eye for an eye, a child for a child, Freddy thought, applying pressure to the trigger.

Freddy envisioned the bullet ripping through the child's neck, dropping him to squirm in his own blood and die. He pulled on the trigger a little harder, but hesitated slightly.

"Do it, dammit!" Freddy grunted.

But he could not.

He lowered the gun, shoved it back into his jeans, then turned and walked out the door, hearing the sound of the wailing boy.

Again, Brownie knocked at Daphanie's bathroom door.

"Girl, if you don't tell me what it says, I'm gonna kick this damn door down. Are you pregnant or not?"

Inside the bathroom, Daphanie stood with her back pressed against the wall. She stared down at the pregnancy test wand sitting on the edge of the sink, but she had not read the results yet. Daphanie let her mind wander back to a month ago.

She had arrived in Chicago late, on a weeknight. She rented a car, drove over to her boyfriend Nate's house, and, using her key, let herself in. Daphanie didn't know what it was, but the moment she softly closed the front door behind her, she knew something was terribly wrong. Most of the lights were out in the house, save for the lamp in the front room.

She climbed the stairs, wanting nothing more than to take off all her clothes, climb in bed, and just be with her man. But when Daphanie gently pushed the bedroom door open, the faint moonlight that filtered in through the bedroom drapes exposed another woman's body in the bed.

She knew her eyes were deceiving her. It was the flight home.

She walked farther in, stood in the center of the room at the foot of the bed, and saw, for sure, there was another woman sleeping beside Nate. Tears came to her eyes. Daphanie was about to leave when all of a sudden he rose in bed. She froze. Nate said nothing. He wiped at his eyes with his fist, then lay back down as if he were not awake at all. He probably had no idea that Daphanie was even there.

That's what Daphanie banked on when she saw Nate the next day.

When she returned, he hugged her, told her how beautiful she looked, and that he liked her new hairstyle.

Daphanie told herself that the woman he had been in bed with could've been a one-night stand, an old acquaintance— anything. She'd been gone for two weeks. What man can go without sex for two weeks? She told herself if that was all it was, then she would never mention it to him, and things could go on as before.

But Nate had realized that she'd been there. He said he thought he'd been dreaming. He admitted that he was just as much asleep as he was awake that night, but the perfume, one that she had never worn before, that she had actually bought in Europe, he could not forget.

"Who is she?" Daphanie asked.

"My ex-wife."

Daphanie told Nate that if it was just the one time, if he could promise never to see her again, then they could forget it ever happened.

He looked as though he were considering saying what she wanted to hear. She truly hoped he would. But he did not.

"I still love her," Nate said. "We should end this."

Daphanie couldn't believe what had happened. Only the day before she'd thought she was in a beautiful relationship, one in which she had allowed herself to fall in love. Not only with Nate but with his adopted three-year-old son, Nathaniel. And she fell hard, telling Nate that she loved him after only a month. She wasn't lying. She sincerely loved him, and she could tell, when he told her back, he felt the same.

They even talked about having a child together, had unprotected sex several times, telling themselves that if they were blessed enough to get pregnant, then they'd happily welcome the child into their lives.

A child that he had fathered—it was what Nate said he had always wanted, ever since he was a child himself. Each time after they made love, Nate would lie in bed with Daphanie, gently smoothing his palm over her belly. He never spoke a word about the possibility of her getting pregnant on those nights, as though it made no difference, but he always seemed disappointed when Daphanie told him her period had come.

Everything that was happening had led Daphanie to believe they would marry somewhere down the line. The rest of her life was written, and she was overjoyed at what lay before her.

And then Nate told her he was still in love with his ex-wife.

Tears running down her cheeks, she threw what few garments she kept at Nate's house in a bag and rushed out of there. Driving much faster than she should have, Daphanie dialed the last man she had been intimate with before Nate. His name was Trevor. He was an attractive man—tall, brown-skinned, black wavy hair, and a perfect smile. He and Nate bore an uncanny resemblance. After two months of dating and having sex, Trevor had told Daphanie how much he wanted her to have his child. She would've agreed, considering how much she liked Trevor and how much she wanted children. That was until, almost in the same breath, Trevor told Daphanie he was married.

"My wife doesn't want children. She never has. I thought I could deal with that, but I can't," Trevor admitted.

"And if you got me pregnant, then what the hell would happen?" Daphanie asked, just to see what ridiculous plan he had in mind.

Trevor hunched his shoulders and said, "I don't know. We'd work it out. But I really want a child."

Daphanie had four words for Trevor: "Get the fuck out!"

But that day a month ago, when Daphanie had gotten her heart broken by Nate, she was speed-dialing Trevor. "Meet me at my place," she ordered when she got him on the phone.

Daphanie wanted sex. She needed to be wanted, to be loved. And she wanted everything Nate had promised her. She wanted that child. She wasn't thinking about what Trevor's wife would think in nine months. She just wanted to be pregnant.

Now, a month later, Daphanie snatched the wand off the edge of the sink, opened the bathroom door, and held it out to her best friend of nearly twenty years, Brownie.

"Well, what does it say?" Brownie asked.

"I'm scared to read it. You do it."

Brownie squinted, looking at the tiny box in the wand, then said, "Girrrlllllll, you are prego."

As Freddy stood outside the house, the gun was still warm in his fist. He wasn't shaking anymore. A strange calm fell over him. He was surprised that it was just as calm outside. None of Mr. Kenny's neighbors were wandering among the mansions wondering where the gunshots had come from. There were no police sirens in the distance. Nothing.

It was late evening. The sun was down as Freddy gazed up the block.

Not four weeks ago, Freddy had been just trying to do right by his pregnant girlfriend Kia and his moms. He was working on getting them out of the ratty old house they lived in. He was trying to move them from that horrible, crime-ridden neighborhood. And he had been on his way to achieving all of that.

He'd had a plan. The house that he and his best friend, Lewis, had rehabbed was going to sell. The two of them would make a nice little penny, and continue to flip houses till they were wealthy. But that bastard Mr. Kenny had his investigator, some lady named Abbey Kurt, act like she was going to buy the house.

Abbey Kurt had Freddy go to Mr. Kenny's office, thinking

he was about to make a real sale, when all Freddy got was a proposition—help Mr. Kenny blackmail his best friend, Lewis, or Mr. Kenny would take away the very house Freddy and his family were living in, that he had lived in all his life. Mr. Kenny informed Freddy that his mother had not paid the taxes on the house in years. Mr. Kenny had bought those taxes out from under them. That gave him ownership of the house, and he was threatening to have it demolished.

But even knowing this, Freddy stood defiantly in Mr. Kenny's office that day and said, "Fuck you! Lewis is my best friend."

Days later, Mr. Kenny walked Freddy through a brand-new town home. "Do what I ask and this house is yours."

The house was beautiful. It was just finished, in a quiet neighborhood. There were no gunshots, no car alarms going off, no people being killed two doors away. Freddy could raise his new child there and not worry about her being hit by a stray bullet. Freddy's mother had been mugged not long before then, only a block away from their house. If he lived in the new neighborhood, he wouldn't have to risk that again.

He had no choice. Freddy did what Mr. Kenny asked of him.

The plan worked as Mr. Kenny had wanted it to. Lewis lost Monica and was even taken off to jail. The only problem was that, before his arrest, Lewis caught on to the fact that Freddy had betrayed him. Lewis cornered Freddy in an alley and beat him until Freddy told him everything.

Because of Freddy's admission, Mr. Kenny reneged on the deal he had made to give Freddy the new house. He didn't even give Freddy the old house back. Mr. Kenny had Freddy and his mother evicted and demolished their house. But what hurt even more was what Kia had done after Freddy told her he was going to set Lewis up in exchange for the new home. She had left, and then she had aborted their unborn child.

—

Standing on Mr. Kenny's porch now, Freddy realized he had nothing. Kia, the woman he loved dearly, the would-be mother of his child, was gone. Freddy and his mother had no home and now he didn't even have his childhood best friend, Lewis. This was the reason Freddy had come to kill Mr. Kenny. This was the reason he felt no remorse now. But as Freddy was about to walk away, he felt Mr. Kenny's and Monica's deaths weren't enough. Freddy turned back and pushed through the door. He walked down the hall, into the living room. The boy was still standing over his dead father, pulling at his shirt, trying to wake him. Freddy walked over, reached down, and grabbed the child by his arm. The little boy screamed and clung tighter to his father's blood-soaked shirt.

"Come here!" Freddy yelled, snatching the kicking and screaming child off the floor, pressing the boy close to his chest, wrapping his arm tight around his little legs.

Freddy looked one last time at the destruction he had caused, then stepped over Mr. Kenny's lifeless body and walked out of the house.

Lewis Waters stood from the jail cell floor, stretched his arms. They were tight from the two hundred push-ups he had just finished. He grabbed his faded brown uniform shirt from his bunk, slipped his chiseled arms through the short sleeves, and buttoned it up.

A metal mirror hung over the metal sink and toilet in the nine-by-ten-foot cell. Lewis walked over to the mirror, stared at himself. His hair had grown long, as well as the whiskers on his face. Over the three weeks that he had been locked up, he no longer cared about his appearance. He would shave tomorrow for his court date.

"I spoke to their attorney last week, and he said they still plan on pressing the charges," a short, boyish-faced, red-haired public defender had told Lewis earlier today. "So I figure you'll probably get three to five years. Parole after two."

Slumped in his chair, Lewis had just looked at the man. When Lewis didn't respond, the public defender—his name was Larry Charles—grabbed his briefcase, stood from his chair, and said, "Well, tomorrow. Bright and early. Any questions?"

Lewis knew he was doomed. "There's nothing more that you can do? You can't get me parole now?" he asked anyway.

"They have video of you striking that Kenny guy over the head with your gun. Tape of you taking fifty thousand dollars from his safe. No," Larry had said. "It's pretty open-and-shut. The only way you don't do time is if the charges get dropped."

Half an hour later, Tim Kenny, Nate's younger brother, pulled his Saab to the curb outside Nate's house. He had tried ringing Nate a couple of times to tell him that he was in the neighborhood, but Nate had been hard to get hold of.

Tim shut the car off and stepped outside.

He walked up the path and climbed the three steps up to the porch. He was about to ring the doorbell when he noticed that the door was ajar.

He nudged it open a little more and said, "Hey. Anyone in there?"

When no answer came, Tim pushed the door open all the way and walked into the hallway leading to the living room.

"Hello," Tim said again. No answer.

He stepped into the living room and gasped. He almost choked from what he saw.

"No!" he cried when he saw his brother's body lying across the sofa, his legs kicked out to the floor in front of him, covered in blood. As Tim ran to Nate, he saw Monica's naked body by the bedroom, face down. He halted, not knowing who to check on first.

He forced himself to move, hurried to Nate, and dropped to his knees. Tim leaned over his brother and pressed an ear to his face, trying to determine if he was breathing. He couldn't tell. Tim quickly slapped Nate a half dozen times across the cheek, trying to wake him.

"Nate. Nate! Please! Wake up!"

No response.

Tim whipped his head back and forth, as if looking for assistance. Where is Mrs. Weatherly? Where are the children? Are they in bed? Did they see this? Are they hiding in a closet? Were they victims? No! He could not think like that now.

Tim dug into his pocket, yanked out his cell, stabbed 911, pushed Speaker, then dropped the open phone to the floor. As it rang, Tim pulled his brother's body from the sofa, laying him flat across the carpet. Tears spilling from his eyes, he tilted his brother's head back, pinched his nose closed, opened his mouth, and blew heavily two times into Nate's mouth.

"Nine-one-one. What is your emergency?" a voice asked from the phone.

Tim was centering his interlaced hands on Nate's sternum, preparing to start heart compressions, when he yelled, "Please, please!" Tears were falling from his face. "My brother and his wife have been shot. Please send an ambulance now!"

Freddy's right hand rested on the open trunk lid as he looked down sadly into the cramped compartment. In it was the boy he had taken from Mr. Kenny's house about an hour ago. Freddy looked up at the house he was parked in front of.

It was the huge brick house with the long front yard that Kia's father owned.

About an hour ago, Freddy had thrown the boy in the front seat with him, the boy wailing, tears practically squirting from his eyes. Freddy had to decide where he would go, what he would do.

"Would you just shut up?" he'd yelled. "Just for one minute. Shut up!"

Freddy had been parked in front of Kenny's mansion, still surprised that he saw no police lights in his rearview. He sank the key in the ignition, deciding he had to go home. He had to tell his mother that he had done something bad, and that he wouldn't be seeing her for a while.

Freddy threw the car in gear and slowly pulled from the curb.

But he needed to make a detour. He had to see his girl, warn her about what was coming. He pulled off into a dark alley, left the car running. Tears had stopped flowing from the boy's eyes, but he was still making crying noises, his chest heaving as he took deep breaths. Freddy climbed out of his seat, quickly crossed in front of the car, threw open the passenger door, and snatched the boy. Luckily, there was a roll of old duct tape in the trunk of the car, which Freddy used to cinch the boy's ankles, fasten his wrists behind his back, and tape his mouth shut.

Afterward, he hoisted the child up and lowered him into the trunk.

Freddy had driven on to Kia's house, jumped out of the car, and had just now opened the trunk to see the boy still squirming around, but not as much as before.

The boy's eyes were wide with fright.

"Don't worry, kid. I know you scared. But I ain't gonna hurt you. Just chill right here a little longer, and I'll be right back."

Freddy shut the trunk, heard the boy moving around in the car, heard his faint moans as he walked toward the house. Freddy guessed that at this time of night Kia would be home. But there was a good chance her father would be, too. The man hated Freddy. Called him every derogatory name in the book. He was the one who had pushed Kia to have an abortion. She had never listened to him before. Kia had loved Freddy then, trusted him, knew that he'd make something of himself. But after Freddy betrayed Lewis, all of Kia's hope and love seemed lost.

Freddy swallowed hard, patted his unruly hair down, and wished that he didn't look like a bum at this moment. If Kia's father came to the door, Freddy would simply tell him that he needed desperately to talk to his daughter. If he would not allow that, Freddy would politely ask him one more time. And if the man still wouldn't budge, Freddy had already killed two people tonight, what difference would one more really make? He saw the curtain sway back behind the small square of window in the door. Someone peeked out, but Freddy could not tell who. He heard the locks on the door come undone, and then the big wooden door swung open. Thankfully, it was Kia that Freddy saw standing behind the screened security door. She was as beautiful as ever. She seemed to have lost weight, but she didn't look unhealthy.

Freddy smiled sadly, knowing that she had already gone on with her life without him.

Kia did not look happy to see him. "What are you doing here, Freddy? You know my father—"

"I don't give a fuck about—" Freddy stopped, shook his head, waved his hands. "I'm sorry. Look. I just needed to talk to you for a minute. Can you open the door, or at least come out on the porch?"

"No, Freddy. You got something to say, just say it."

Freddy looked into Kia's eyes, and asked himself how the two of them had gotten here. This woman used to love him. They were going to have a baby, spend the rest of their lives together. "You know that's all I ever wanted, right?" Freddy said.

"What are you talking about?"

"All I ever wanted was to be married to someone I loved, have a kid or two, and be a better father than my old man was to me."

Kia didn't respond, just looked at Freddy with little compassion.

"But all that's gone now," Freddy said. "That wasn't my fault. Somebody else is to blame for that. You know that 'cause I told you. I told you, right?"

"Yes, Freddy. You told me," Kia said, losing her patience.

Freddy looked down at his dirty sneakers, then up again.

He turned, looked out on the street. It was such a quiet, beautiful warm night. He caught sight of his car, envisioned the boy inside, and forced himself to come out with his admission.

"I took care of that, though. That man who was blackmailing me, I took care of that."

That got Kia's attention. Her face filled with concern. She pressed closer to the door. "What are you talking about, you took care of that?"

"I just did. And I had to come by here and tell you that, because you're gonna be hearing about it. I don't know when, but you're gonna be hearing. And I didn't want you to think that I did it for nothing. That I'm just evil or something."

"Did what, Freddy?" Kia said, raising her voice.

"I did it because I love you. I loved our baby, and . . ." Freddy choked up a little, almost unable to finish. "I knew if it wasn't for him, we would still be together. But we ain't. And he had to pay."

"Freddy," Kia said. "You're scaring me. Please just—"

"Kia," Freddy stopped her, his palm up. "I'm sorry things turned out the way they did. But when you find out what I did, try to remember me the way you saw me when you still loved me, when you was gonna have my baby and we were gonna be a family. Okay?"

Kia's fingers were latched onto the door. She tried to swallow the lump in her throat, and as two tears slid down her cheeks, she said, "Okay."

"Moms," Freddy called, his voice a whisper. When she didn't respond, he called again, giving her a gentle shake. "Moms!"

Freddy was standing over his mother's twin bed. It was one of two small beds that sat in the small guest bedroom in Uncle Henry's house.

His mother stirred, then slowly opened her eyes, squinting a bit at the bright light from the TV. "Fred, what's wrong? Is everything all right?"

"I ain't got much time to talk, Moms, so I just need to say what I gotta say."

"What is it?" his mother said, worry now on her face. She propped herself up on an elbow.

Freddy sat down beside her, taking her hand.

"Moms, I did something. Something I'm gonna be in trouble for."

Freddy heard his mother sigh deeply, dreadfully. "Freddy, no."

"Moms, I know all I've been is trouble to you. I'm the reason why Pops is gone, the reason why we've been poor all our lives.

All I was trying to do was make things better, fix what I had messed up. And I was gonna do it, too. You know I had gotten that real estate license."

"I know, Fred," his mother said sympathetically.

"But that man. He lied to me. He said he was gonna give us that new house if I just . . ." Freddy ground his teeth, frowned, turned away from his mother a moment. When he turned back, he squeezed his mother's hand and said, "But he didn't. He lied to me. He got us living up in here. The two of us in this little room. And then my child is gone."

"Freddy, please say you didn't—" his mother said, drawing close to him, placing a hand on his back.

"I'm sorry, Moms, but I did what needed to be done . . . what that man deserved."

"What did you do, Freddy?" Tears came to his mother's eyes, falling one after the other. "What?"

Freddy didn't speak at first, then said, "I don't know if nobody knows yet, but it's gonna get out. And when it does, they . . . the police gonna come looking for me."

Freddy's mother lowered her head, brought her hands to her face, sobbing. He reached out to her shoulder.

"Moms, I'm sorry, but I ain't going to jail for this. I wasn't wrong about this, and I ain't going to jail for it. So I'm leaving. I'm going—"

His mother grabbed Freddy's arm. She looked up at him and said, "Don't. If they ask me where you are, I don't want to lie when I tell them I don't know."

Four hours later, the sound came from far away, as if from down a long tunnel, echoing.

Beep! Then a pause. *Beep!* Pause. *Beep!*

Everything was black, but Nate was aware of himself—the weight of his body, the pain in his chest, his gut, his thigh. His leg throbbed. He thought he moved it, but didn't know for sure. He tried to wiggle the toes on that foot, but he was still in darkness, still unaware if he was awake—he could not tell if he was successful. He felt more of his body. He tried to move his left arm, his hand. He felt his fingertips graze over cold linen. Then he heard a voice. It was distant, but Nate heard it.

"He moved. I think I saw him move his hand!"

That sounded like his brother, Tim, Nate thought, but he still could not open his eyes. He wasn't sure if he was dreaming or if he was—

"Nate. Can you hear me?"

Tim's voice was louder now, as if he were leaning right over Nate, his mouth practically to Nate's ear. "Nate, if you can hear me, open your eyes."

"I don't think he can hear you," Nate heard another man say. He was not familiar with that voice.

"Wake up, Nate," Tim's voice pleaded.

Nate felt his eyelids now. He slowly raised them. All he could see was white space, and three dark fuzzy images standing somewhere in the near distance. Nate didn't know where he was, what had happened. With effort, he blinked four times, bringing into focus his brother and two men standing on either side of him wearing suits. Badges were clipped to their suit pockets. Nate saw a smile spread across Tim's face.

"Nate, how you feelin'?" Tim said.

Nate wondered who the men were. He slowly turned his head from side to side on the pillow, looking around the room. "Where am I?"

But before Tim even had a chance to answer him, all that had happened rushed back to Nate's memory. Freddy marching Nate into the living room, the gun going off, the sizzling metal tearing through his flesh, Monica falling to the floor, his son's scream, then blackness. Horror immediately covered his face and seized his body. Nate latched onto his brother's wrist. His throat painfully dry, Nate begged, "Where's Monica? Where's Nathaniel and Layla?"

"Mr. Kenny," one of the other men said. He had a goatee, was broad-shouldered, and was the shorter of the two. "My name is Detective Davis. This is my partner, Detective Martins." A shaved-headed, medium-brown-skinned man stood on the other side of Tim. "We're investigating this case. Can you tell me who shot you?"

"Where's Monica?" Nate said to Tim.

"Nate," Tim said, holding firmly to his brother's hand now. "I want you to calm—"

"Mr. Kenny," Davis interrupted. "If I could just ask you—"

"I want to know where my wife is, where my son is!" Nate yelled as loud as his weakened lungs would allow. He coughed behind the pain in his throat. The image of Monica falling to the floor kept replaying mercilessly in his head. "Where is my wife?"

"She was shot, Nate," Tim said. "In the head."

"I know that," Nate said, his voice a whisper now. "Is she—"

"No. I found the two of you, called for an ambulance. They brought you both here, did surgery." Tim tightened his grip a little, smiled as best he could. "Nate, you're gonna be fine. The doctor said—"

"I want to know how Monica's going to be," Nate insisted.

"She's in a coma, Nate. They don't know when she's going to wake up."

Nate jerked forward in bed, trying to get up. Only then did he became aware of the hard plastic oxygen mask over his nose and mouth, and the countless tubes inserted into his arms. Tim eased him back onto his pillow.

"I need to see her."

"There will be time for that. She's just down the hall. But now you need to get your rest."

Nate let his head fall to the side, feeling helpless.

"Can we ask you a few questions now, Mr. Kenny?" the clean-shaven man, Detective Martins, asked.

"Where's Nathaniel and Layla?" Nate said, ignoring the detective's question. "Layla was napping. But I know before I blacked out I heard Nathaniel calling me. Did you bring him here?"

Tim didn't answer, but Nate could tell by the pained look in his brother's eyes that something was terribly wrong.

"Tim, where's Nathaniel?"

"They found Layla still sleeping upstairs. But Nathaniel . . . he wasn't there, Nate."

"What do you mean, he wasn't there? Where is he? Does Mrs. Weatherly have him?"

"No."

"Was the entire . . ." Nate gasped, out of breath. "Was the entire house checked?"

"Yes."

"Did he wander off?"

"He could've," Tim answered sadly. "But they don't think so."

"We believe," said Detective Davis, stepping forward, "that he was taken by whoever shot you and your wife, Mr. Kenny. Now, if you could help us find out who that was, we can start looking for your son."

Nate looked up at the ceiling, locking his jaw, trying to fight back the single tear that defiantly rolled down the side of his face.

"Can you give us a description of the—"

"I know who it was," Nate said, still looking upward.

"Who?"

"Freddy Ford." Nate paused, rage in his eyes. "The man's name is Freddy Ford."

9

Freddy had been on the road for four hours since he had left his uncle's house. He sipped from a bottle of Coke he had just bought from some hick-town gas station five minutes back. Now he was driving down a dark two-lane road, looking for his way back to the interstate. He looked into the rearview mirror at the boy.

He had no idea what he was going to do with him. But Freddy had to admit, he was a good-looking boy, and he always had wanted a son.

Freddy blindly reached for his cell phone in the passenger seat and flipped it open. One eye on the dark road before him, one eye on the phone, he scrolled through the directory and stopped on the name *JONI*.

He punched Talk, and waited while the phone rang.

Freddy glanced at the clock on his radio: 4:13 A.M.

It was very early in the morning, but if he remembered Joni correctly, she probably hadn't even gone to bed yet.

"Hello," Freddy heard a voice answer.

"Joni. This is Freddy."

"Do you know what time it is?" Her voice was sweet, like music. "I haven't heard from you in damn near a year, and you call me at—"

"Were you asleep?" Freddy asked.

"No."

"Then why you bitchin'?" Freddy smiled a little to himself.

"Because I was watchin' a DVD, and you interruptin' the best part. I should hang up on your ass."

"Don't," Freddy said, the smile disappearing. "I need to come to Atlanta, stay with you awhile."

"Why?"

"I just do."

"You in trouble again?"

Freddy paused a long moment. "What if I said I was?"

"Then I'd say ain't shit changed, and come on down. I miss you," Joni said, laughing.

Freddy let her have her moment, then after she quieted he said, "This time it's serious."

"Whatever, Freddy," Joni said in a way that made Freddy know she had his back regardless. "Get here when you get here. I'll be waiting."

"Cool," Freddy said, disconnecting the call. Just then he saw the blue/red flash of police lights in his rearview mirror.

"Fuck!" he said, slowing the car and easing it toward the shoulder. Before he came to a halt, he leaned over, unlatched the glove box. Freddy grabbed his gun. He set it down near his hip, covering it with his right hand.

Looking up in the rearview, he had no idea why in the hell he was being stopped. Had they already found out about the bodies in Chicago? Against the glare of the bright police lights, Freddy saw the silhouette as an officer got out of the car and started walking toward him.

There's just one man, Freddy told himself. He shouldn't be much trouble. But Freddy would have to act quick, catch him by surprise. And most important of all, not miss.

The officer sidled up cautiously beside Freddy's door. His hand was on his gun, but it was not drawn.

"Put your hands where I can see them, sir," the officer said, a twang in his voice. "I'll need to see your license and registration."

Freddy didn't look at the officer. His eyes were still directed out the front window. "Can you tell me why you stopped me, Officer?"

"I'm asking the questions here, son. License and registration."

"They're in the glove box. Can I get them?"

"Slowly," the officer said.

With one seamless motion, Freddy lifted the gun, whirled it in the direction of the officer, aimed at the man's head, and fired off a single shot. The bullet bore through the front of the officer's wide-brimmed hat, then tore through his skull, exploding out the back of his head. Freddy's victim stood on his feet for a moment longer, his eyes wide, his mouth hanging open, then he fell slowly backward.

Freddy's feet were on the ground before the man hit the pavement.

He checked the backseat to see if the boy had been awakened. Of course he had been. Nathaniel was looking around and starting to cry. But Freddy had to move quickly. He didn't need a car driving by and spotting him.

Freddy stepped over the officer's body and ran back to the police cruiser. He pulled his sleeve over his hand, careful not to leave his prints, then whipped open the driver's-side door. He climbed into the car, scanned the dash for a camera of some sort. He knew that a lot of police cars had video these days to tape the stops.

Freddy didn't see anything of the sort. He checked again, just in case. Satisfied, he climbed out of the car. He stopped, looked down at the officer. His skull was haloed by a circle of blood. Freddy kicked him hard to make sure he was indeed dead. The man didn't move.

Freddy jumped back in his car, slammed the door, and brought the engine to life.

As he sped onto the dark road, he told himself he hadn't wanted that to happen. After killing his own father, Freddy had told himself he never wanted to kill again. But Mr. Kenny had forced him down this path with all the evil things that man had done to him. No, he hadn't wanted to kill the officer. So this body belonged to Nate Kenny, not Freddy.

Lewis Waters sat in the courtroom wearing the faded gray trou-sers and DOC collared shirt the jail provided him. It was a small, cheaply wood-paneled room, filled with other inmates and their family members. It was seven-thirty A.M. Lewis looked over his shoulder. He had expected to see Nate and Monica sitting some-where in the room. They hadn't arrived.

"Where are they? Aren't they supposed to be here?" Lewis said to his public defender, Larry Charles.

"Yeah." Larry glanced down at his watch. He looked over at the opposing attorney, stood, then leaned over to Lewis and whispered, "I'll be back."

Lewis watched Larry as he stepped across the aisle. He spoke to a man Lewis assumed was Monica's attorney—distinguished, slightly wrinkled, graying around the temples. The man hunched his shoulders at a question Larry asked, then Larry turned back and walked toward Lewis, smiling.

"What happened?" Lewis said. No, he was in no rush to sit while Monica practically slammed the gate shut on his cell, but he was bothered by the fact that she wasn't here yet. And even under these jacked-up circumstances, he was kind of looking forward to seeing her.

"Give me a minute," Larry said, still smiling, holding a finger up before Lewis.

He turned to face the judge at the front of the room and said, "Your Honor, my client sits here, patiently awaiting his day in court, but if his accusers do not show, shouldn't he be set free?"

"Judge—" Monica's attorney began, leaning forward on the desk before him.

"Hold on, Mr. Charles," the judge, a heavy brown man with curly hair and a trimmed beard, said. "Do we know where your clients are?" he asked, speaking to the opposing attorney.

Mr. Kennedy smiled thinly. "I've tried reaching them at their numbers, but I can't get hold of them."

"Your Honor, if no one is here to press charges, then there is nothing more to do but release my client," Lewis's attorney said.

The judge narrowed his eyes on Larry, then said, "Nice try, Mr. Charles. What I'll do," he continued, speaking to Mr. Kennedy now, "is I'll give your clients till tomorrow to appear. If there is no one here by then to bring charges against this man, then all charges will be dropped."

Freddy stood outside on a slope of grass, staring out on a small, man-made body of water surrounded by trees. It was morning. The sun had come up some time ago, and it was already warm out. He guessed it was because he was so far south, about half-way through Tennessee. The shit was beautiful. That moment Freddy felt at peace. He knew in the near future all hell was going to let loose on him, but at that moment, staring out at those trees, hearing the birds chirping in the branches overhead, he felt more at peace than he had in years. The moment was ruined by Nathaniel's whining.

"I want my daddy," the boy said.

"You're gonna see your daddy. That's where we're going."

"But you hurt my daddy," the boy said, looking up at Freddy with huge tear-shiny black eyes.

Damn, Freddy thought. He remembered hearing that some-times when kids saw something tragic, it messed with their brains so much that they just forgot it. He had been hoping that that had happened to this boy, because although Freddy had wanted Nate dead, he'd had no intention of doing it right there in front of his kid.

"Don't you worry," Freddy said, rubbing a hand across the child's curly hair, and with the other pulling a candy bar out of his jeans pocket. "Your daddy is gonna be fine, as long as you stop crying. You hear me?"

Freddy held the candy bar out in front of the boy's face. Little Nathaniel wiped his cheeks with his fingertips, nodded his head, and reached for the candy bar.

"Good," Freddy said. "Now eat that, and don't start crying, 'cause I got to make a phone call."

After dialing the number, Freddy took a few steps away from the child, who was so involved with his candy bar that he didn't seem to mind.

"Cook County Department of Corrections. This is Officer Hardimon. Can I help you?"

"Yeah," Freddy said, now ten feet away from Nathaniel but keeping an eye on him. "I need to speak to an inmate."

"Name?" the officer said, her tone curt.

"Waters. First name Lewis."

"Your name?"

"Freddy Ford."

Freddy was placed on hold. Almost a full five minutes later, he heard Lewis come on the line and say, "I thought I told you not to contact me no more."

It pained Freddy to hear Lewis speak like that to him. They had been so tight for so long. Not anymore.

"Don't hang up on me, man. I got something to say."

"I already heard all you gotta say."

"Just hear me out."

"Fuck you, Freddy. Don't call—"

Freddy knew Lewis was going to hang up and never take another one of his calls, so he blurted out, "I took care of him for you."

There was a moment of silence.

"Took care of who?" Lewis finally said.

"That motherfucker who did this to us."

"The only motherfucker that did anything to me was you. Who you talking about, and what did you do?"

Freddy glanced at Nathaniel. The boy was still into that chocolate bar. It was all over his face and hands.

"Nate," Freddy said, his voice lowered. "I told you I was gonna take care of him, and I did."

"What did you do?" Lewis said, seriousness in his voice.

"What you think?"

"Tell me, or I'm hangin' up this—"

"Shot him, man," Freddy said. "I killed him."

Inside that jail, Lewis was staring right in the face of a guard when he heard what Freddy said. He turned his back to the big man, lowered his voice. "You ain't do that, Freddy. Say that you ain't do it."

"We used to be best friends. He used me against you, and now—I had to," Freddy said, the slightest bit of regret in his voice.

Lewis all of a sudden felt sick. He didn't like Nate, couldn't stand the man, actually. But to think that he was dead, gunned down by the man Lewis used to love as a brother . . . He felt sorry for Nate. A second later, Lewis's heart was racing.

"Where did you do it?" Lewis asked urgently.

"At his house."

The phone was now wet in Lewis's hand as he prepared to ask the next question. He closed his eyes, prayed as the words left his lips.

"Where was Monica?"

Freddy said nothing. He wondered just how to go about this. Tell him the truth and Lewis would be pissed. But they weren't friends anymore anyway. Besides, lying was what had gotten him into this with Lewis in the first place, so might as well just tell him the truth. "I ain't know she was there, man."

"What are you talking about?" Lewis said, the phone tight in his grip, pressed tight to his face.

"The gun was in my hand. My adrenaline was up and shit, and she pop out of nowhere, scare me, and—"

"And what? You did what?" Lewis said, now yelling into the phone. The guard was in his face, told him something about how he would have to quiet down or else. But Lewis barely heard him, he was listening so intently for Freddy's next words.

"I ain't mean to, Lewis. But I shot her, too."

Freddy heard loud yelling as he pulled the phone from his ear and pushed the End button.

"C'mon, boy," he said to Nathaniel, walking over, placing his palm to the back of the boy's head, and directing him toward the car.

Daphanie was a slender woman, with brown hair she'd recently had cut to shoulder-length. Men called her beautiful, but she considered herself just cute. In her opinion, her eyes were a little too narrow, her lips a little too big. But she did what she could by dressing nicely when she was out, or at work, which was where she was now.

She worked at Reese Pharmaceuticals. She'd been there for five years. Daphanie had made the transition from being a nurse, working in the ER and on countless intensive care units with her best friend Brownie. She'd gotten burned out on the whole care-giving thing, while Brownie had learned to love it more, then got promoted to nursing supervisor.

This morning Daphanie sat in Parker's office. Parker was a couple of years younger than she was. He was good-natured and happy-spirited. He had a boyish haircut and a freckled face on which there always seemed to be a smile. For some reason, though, he wasn't smiling right now.

"So what's up, Parker?"

Parker took a long moment to answer, anguish now on his face.

"Remember three and a half months ago, when I told you that this branch might close?"

Daphanie remembered. Parker had called her into his office, as he had just done, and informed her of the possibility. There had been three positions open in the south suburban branch, and he had suggested that Daphanie transfer into one of them.

"I already spoke to the manager over there, and he said he'd look out for your papers," Parker had said back then.

"Well, how likely is it that this branch will close?"

"Not very, I don't think. But to be safe, I think I'd transfer if I were you. This is not the time to be without a job, Daphanie."

Daphanie didn't want to transfer. She didn't know anyone over there, and the morning drive would be at least an hour.

"I don't think I'm interested."

"Think it over, okay?" Parker said. "Talk to whoever you need to talk to, and let me know by the end of the week."

Daphanie went home and had the conversation with Nate that night.

"If you don't want to go, don't," Nate said, peeling back the blankets and climbing into bed with her.

"And what if they actually close my branch, and it's too late to transfer?"

"Then you can stay at home if you want. Be a housewife," Nate said, giving Daphanie a peck on the lips, then sliding under the blankets. "Or you'll find a new job. It's not like there'll be a rush. It's not like we're hurting for money."

So Daphanie hadn't taken the transfer, and now, three and a half months later, she sat before Parker, waiting to hear what her future would be.

"Yeah, I remember," Daphanie said.

"Well, I got finalization today. We're closing, Daphanie."

"Are there still any positions at the south suburban branch?" Daphanie asked, worried.

"I'm sorry. Those were filled more than a month ago. I'm really sorry, Daphanie, but you're gonna have to be gone in two weeks."

13

Nate sat in a wheelchair, staring sadly at Monica. His IV pole stood beside him on small wheels. He wore a hospital gown. He had stitches from his surgery, and they throbbed each time he took a breath. His surgeon, a balding Asian man named Dr. Kim, told him not to get out of bed for any reason.

Nate had demanded to see his ex-wife several times hours ago. His doctor and the staff refused him. They gave him pain medication, which he desperately needed. It put him into a deep sleep.

Upon waking this morning, Nate did not take no for an answer, and two nurses came to his room, helped him into a wheelchair, and pushed him in to see Monica in the ICU down the hall.

The blinds were pulled in her room. As he sat in his chair beside Monica, the room was only minimally lit by a fluorescent light just over the bed. Her head was heavily bandaged, a tube snaked up one of her nostrils, and a needle was lodged in her arm, connected to an IV unit similar to the one Nate had beside him.

"There is good news and bad," Monica's doctor had said, before Nate was taken out of bed and moved to the wheelchair. Her name was Dr. Beck. She was a middle-aged woman with short blond hair.

"The good first," Nate grunted.

"The are a number of factors working in Monica's favor. The bullet was from a small-caliber weapon. A twenty-two. She was struck here." The doctor pointed to just above the outer corner of her left eye. "It penetrated the frontal bone, and the bullet shattered, much of it exiting the parietal bone without doing serious damage to any of Monica's brain tissue."

Nate pulled himself up in bed. He winced against a sharp pain in his gut.

"There were fragments lodged in the superficial tissue of her brain. We believe we were able to remove those without causing any permanent damage. So the good news is your wife should wake up, Mr. Kenny."

"But you said there is bad news," Nate said, bracing himself.

"Yes. Although the injury was not lethal, the bullet fragments did cause Monica's brain to swell. The minutes immediately after a head injury are crucial. It was a good thing your brother found you when he did. But a great deal of time passed before we were able to relieve the pressure." Dr. Beck looked at Nate, sympathy in her eyes. "The swelling is the reason for the coma, and unfortunately we don't know when she will wake up."

"But you said she'll wake up. When she does, she'll be fine, right?"

"I'm sorry, Mr. Kenny," Dr. Beck had said. "We won't know that till she regains consciousness."

Nate shifted himself in the wheelchair, feeling the pain in his thigh become unbearable. His chest ached, his gut felt as though it were on fire. But he was out of bed. He could sit up in a chair, and was even able to stand for a short period. He was conscious. His doctor had told Nate he'd make a full recovery if he just allowed his body to properly heal. That could not be said for Monica, and this tore at Nate to no end.

Nate reached out, grabbed Monica's hand. He shut his eyes to the image of her standing in their bedroom doorway; to the bullet tearing into her skull. If he could've only done something then. God, he had tried. Earlier this morning, Nate had told the two detectives, Davis and Martins, everything he knew about Freddy—from when he was born, to who his friends were, to where he last lived.

"How did you come to know this Freddy Ford?" the clean-shaven Detective Martins asked.

"He worked for me." Nate told them in exactly what capacity. He withheld nothing. "We had a deal, and he didn't keep his end."

Detective Davis scribbled some of what Nate said on a pad. There was a look of disapproval on his face.

"Since you took his home from him, do you know where he'd be now?" Davis said.

Nate didn't appreciate how that question was phrased. "No. That's your job. And you better do it," Nate said. "He tried to kill us, and there's a good chance he has my son. You better—"

"We understand, Mr. Kenny," Martins said. "I guarantee you, we will find this man."

Davis had slid his pad into the inside pocket of his suit jacket. He'd looked at Nate as though he couldn't stand him. "We'll be in touch, Mr. Kenny," he had said.

As he looked at Monica now, tears came to Nate's eyes. His body was wracked with pain, but gingerly he leaned out of his chair and onto Monica's bed as much as he could, placing an arm across her chest. He held her, pressed his tear-streaked face to hers.

"Monica, I promise, I will get him for doing this to you, baby," Nate said, unable to control his anguish and his tears. "I will get our son back, and I will get that man for doing this if I have to give my life to do it!"

14

Freddy sat slumped low in the cracked vinyl seat, behind the steering wheel of his car. He stared at the small brick middle-class home in front of him. He had pulled up not five minutes ago, but had not moved an inch since then.

It was approaching two P.M. He was surprised Joni had not called to find out where he was. But then again, Joni wasn't that type. She was an easygoing woman. She didn't trip over foolishness, and Freddy thought back to when they had dated—if he said he didn't want to be sweated about this or that, Joni would say, "Whatever. Fine, I won't sweat you."

She had been that way since Freddy had first met her in high school. Joni was cool, but Joni was trouble.

It seemed she was in detention as much as Freddy. Either she had beaten up some chick, tried to beat up some dude, or stolen something that wasn't hers. Back then, Joni wasn't big into work, into putting forth the effort it took to earn things herself. The only reason she had a house was because her father died and left the Atlanta crib to her. It was the reason she left Chicago. That and the fact that she had gotten the idea that Freddy's interest in her had disappeared. Freddy had dated Joni for thirteen months. They had everything in common. They both had fuck-the-world attitudes, got high together, spent what money they had, and didn't sweat over what they didn't have. And they had sex constantly.

"Come in me, baby," Joni would breath into Freddy's ear whenever she felt him reaching orgasm. "Come in me," she'd plead. "I want some babies."

What the hell? Freddy always thought, making no effort to withdraw, even though he wasn't wearing a condom. Every time they would screw, he would bust in her, always expecting some night she'd come to him, grinning wide, talking about how she had missed her period. Freddy would've had no problem with that. He always wanted kids. And seeing as how they got along so well, knowing that no woman loved him or had his back like Joni did, he figured why not have kids with her? He figured maybe one day they'd even get married.

But that all changed one night while Freddy was out at some college party. He had no business there—was probably drunk and just stumbled in. But while he was there, he met Kia. In Freddy's opinion, Joni was a decent-looking girl. She had the Afro-centric thing down pat, with her short-cut natural hair and the tiny diamond in her nose. The girl had a body, too. A tiny waist that flowed into some ridiculous curvy hips and the roundest ass Freddy ever saw fill a pair of jeans.

Yeah, Joni was tight, but Kia was beautiful. Kia was sophisti-cated. Kia was a law student.

Freddy didn't know why, but the woman gave him play. And from the moment he walked away with her phone number, he felt like a better, more important man. As he became closer with Kia, he lost more and more interest in Joni. Being with Kia made him want to do more for himself, for his mother, and possibly for Kia, if his dreams came true and they ended up together.

A month after Freddy started kicking it with Kia, Joni came to him and said, "I seen you with that girl. Is that why you haven't been coming by?"

Freddy didn't want to hurt Joni, but they had always been honest with each other. "Yeah. I think we need to call it quits, Joni."

Joni didn't blow up in his face, try to fight him, or beg him to come back. Freddy knew she wouldn't. Joni was too cool for that. But she did stare right into his eyes for a moment. Her lip quivered, and she looked to have blinked away a tear or two, then said, "If that's how you want it. I ain't gonna be living here much longer anyway. My father died, and I got to move to Atlanta to take over his house."

"I'm sorry," Freddy said sincerely.

"It's okay. But I'm not gonna change my cell number, so . . . so . . ." Joni said, blinking back tears. "If things don't . . . you know, work out, give me a ring."

Things didn't work out, Freddy thought now, still staring up at Joni's house. Things were fucked up, and if Freddy didn't come up with some sort of plan, his ass would be going to jail, might even get the damn death penalty. Freddy quickly shook that thought out of his head. It was still too early in the game to think about dying.

Bottom line was, the shootings were in Chicago, and Freddy was in Atlanta now. Hopefully none of that would ever follow him here.

Freddy saw the curtains in the front window move. They parted for a second, then fell closed. It was Joni checking to see if Freddy had arrived. A moment later, the curtains were opened wider, Joni stepping between them.

Behind that window, she didn't mouth any words to him, didn't motion with a curled finger for him to come in. She just stood there, watching Freddy. Something told him she knew he was considering driving off. She knew him *that* well. They were close, and if she had gotten pregnant, they would've probably been married by now. Freddy's hand was on the keys. Yeah, he could go. He actually was thinking about it. He didn't want to heighten his risk of getting caught by trusting Joni. But not just that. He didn't want to run the risk of her getting into serious trouble just by being involved with him. But where else would he go? He was going to leave in a day or two, after he came up with a plan. But right now, where would he go? He had no answer. Freddy pulled the keys from the ignition and climbed out of the car. He opened the back door, reached in, and pulled Nathaniel out, carrying him in his arms. He closed both doors with his hip, then started around the car and walked up the steps to the front door.

15

That evening, Daphanie lay across Brownie's sofa. The flat-panel TV was on above the mantel, but Daphanie just stared up at the ceiling, thinking about the news she had gotten earlier.

When she heard the locks being undone on the front door, she didn't even look up to see her friend enter her house. Brownie walked in looking worn out. She was five-foot-three and had a small upper body, but her hips and thighs were so curvy, men often stopped her on the street, trying to get her number. Her skin was fair, and she most often wore her blond-streaked brown hair in a ponytail. Wearing hospital scrubs, as usual, Brownie kicked off her Crocs at the door and said, "You're at my place more than me. Cook dinner, by chance?"

"I'm getting fired," Daphanie said to the ceiling.

"What?" Brownie said, hurrying around the corner and sitting beside Daphanie. "What are you talking about?"

"Remember a few of months ago I told you Parker was trying to get me to transfer, because there was a chance they were closing our branch?"

"Yeah."

"Well, they're closing it."

"Aw, I'm so sorry," Brownie said, giving Daphanie a hug.

Daphanie stood, took a couple of steps from the sofa. "The only reason I didn't transfer is because that motherfucker said I had nothing to worry about."

"And which motherfucker are we talking about?"

"Nate."

"Oh, yeah. *That* motherfucker," Brownie said.

"He said I'd be a housewife, or I could take my time looking for a new job if I lost this one, because he would have my back. Now look what's happened. This is all his fault."

"Uh, Daph . . . I don't know if it's *all* his fault."

"Trust me, it is," Daphanie said. "I can't stand him!"

"I don't know if I agree with you."

"Then you don't know what you're talking about," Daphanie said, walking back to the sofa and having a seat. "What am I supposed to do about a job? You know what the unemployment rate is now? You know how many drug reps keep asking me if Reese is hiring?"

"Please, Daphanie, you have nothing to worry about. You were a nurse first. Nurses are never out of work. Dust off the old license and—"

"The old license expired three years ago. So now do I need to worry?"

Brownie dropped her head. "Damn, girl. Now you might be in a bit of a fix."

"Yeah, in a fix with a baby on the way."

"And what did you decide to do about that?"

"What do you mean?" Daphanie said, standing again. "I'm having it. I didn't fuck Trevor because I was horny, I fucked him because I wanted a baby. Why would that change now?"

"Well . . ." Brownie said.

"I'm not gonna worry about that. I'll find a job, and if not, I'll find some creative way to pay for this child. How many sisters been in the same situation and just make it work?"

"I feel ya," Brownie said, not seeming very certain.

"Till then," Daphanie said, "I think it's time to call Trevor and tell him what he's gotten himself into."

16

Nate sat in his wheelchair in his hospital room, brooding, deter-
mining if he had missed absolutely any information at all. His
private investigator, Abbey Kurt, stood on the other side of the
room, holding a pen and a pad, taking down everything Nate
said. She was a small, muscular woman. She wore a dark pantsuit, her gun and holster undetectable beneath the jacket. Her
hair was pulled back into a bun, and she wore no jewelry, save
for the watch on her right wrist. Abbey had been working with
Nate for five years. He trusted her with his life. She was the first
person he called once he gained access to a phone.

"Did you follow up with those detectives, see if they found
out anything?" Nate asked. "What were their names?"

"Detectives Martins and Davis," Abbey said. "And no, they
have no new information, Mr. Kenny."

"Did they activate the AMBER Alert?"

"I've called them, and it's already been activated, sir."

"Good," Nate said, glancing over at his nightstand. His pain
medication sat on top of it in a little plastic cup. He was in ago-
nizing pain. He knew the meds would knock him out, and he

needed to be awake to plan how he would go about finding that bastard Freddy Ford. "You will get the contact information for everyone Ford knows."

"Yes, sir. I will get the information for his ex-girlfriend Kia Martin, for her father, for Freddy's mother, and for his uncle, Henry Ford—the man Freddy used to work for."

"Do the police have a photo of Ford?" Nate asked.

"I e-mailed one to them immediately after you asked me to."

"Good," Nate said, his voice soft. He was not satisfied, though. He knew, regardless of what the police did, Ford had the upper hand because of his head start. He could be anywhere, doing who knows what to Nathaniel. That is, if Nathaniel was even still alive.

Nate leaned over and locked the wheels on his chair. He pressed his palms onto the arms, and with everything he had tried to lift himself from the chair.

Abbey rushed over to him. "Mr. Kenny, what are you doing? Do you want me to call a nurse?"

Nate fell back into the chair. "No. They don't even want me in this chair. They want me to remain in bed. I can't do that," Nate said. "Now help me."

Abbey stood at Nate's side, grabbing him by his arm. He pressed his hands onto the arms of the chair again. With all of his strength, Nate grunted and pushed, and with Abbey's help, he stood from the chair.

"Now let go of me," Nate directed.

"Sir, maybe this isn't such a—"

"I said release me!"

Abbey cautiously let go of Nate's arm and took a step back. Wobbling on his legs, his arms spread out to his sides like a blind man, Nate stood. His surgical incisions that had been sewn up felt as though they might rip open. He told himself they wouldn't. He needed to do this to accelerate his recovery. While Ford was still out there, while he still had Nathaniel. Nate could not afford to be a patient, lying drugged and helpless in a hospital bed. He had to find Ford.

The door to Nate's room opened.

"What are you doing?" Tim said, stepping in, seeing Nate appearing as though he were about to fall. Layla was in Tim's arms. He rushed over, gave Layla to Abbey, then grabbed Nate by his elbow and carefully lowered his brother back into his wheelchair.

"Nate, what the hell?" Tim said.

"None of your business."

"Nate, you can't—"

"Tim," Nate said, reaching his arms out toward Layla, a smile now on his face. "It's over. You brought Layla like I asked, and that's all I care about right now. Abbey, bring her to me."

Abbey carried Layla over to Nate and set her down to stand on the floor in front of him. Nate grabbed her little hands.

"Uncle Nate would love to pick you up, but he's in a little bit of pain right now. But I would like a kiss."

Nate leaned down as well as he could. Layla stood on her tippy toes and gave Nate a peck on the cheek. He took her hand and held it.

"How is she?" Nate asked Tim.

"She's fine."

"Does it seem as though she might've heard any of . . . you know?" Nate said, referring to the shooting he hoped the child had slept through.

"If she did, she's not showing any signs, or saying anything about it."

"Okay," Nate said, smiling down at the little girl.

"So . . . if you don't mind me asking," Tim said, his voice hushed, "what are you going to do with her?"

"While I'm in here, I'd appreciate it if you continue to keep her."

"You know that's not a problem, Nate," Tim said.

"But I won't be staying in here for much longer."

"And what about after you're out?"

As Layla played with one end of his robe belt, Nate lowered his voice.

"I'll do what Monica wanted. I'll adopt her, and we'll raise her like our own, since her father is in jail."

17

Earlier that afternoon, when Freddy walked into Joni's house with Nathaniel, the first thing she said was, "Who's the little shit?"

"His name is Nathaniel," Freddy said, giving Joni a long once-over. "I'll tell you more about him later. Right now he and I both need to get some sleep. You got a bed?"

"Yeah. Two. They're upstairs, already made up. I'll show you."

Joni looked good, like always. She was still in crazy shape. She still had those hips, those thighs, and that flat belly. She was showing it off in cut-off shorts and a halter top. Joni walked in front of Freddy up the stairs. When they reached the second floor, she turned to him. "This is your room right here. You can put the boy in there."

"Yeah, thanks," Freddy said, staring at Joni again. "What happened to your face?"

Her left eye was swollen, bruised purple, and her lip was cut down the middle. It looked as though it had been healing for about a day.

"I'll tell you later. Like you said, ya'll need to get some sleep," Joni said.

—

After climbing out of bed, Freddy pulled on his T-shirt and slid back into his jeans. He looked at himself in the mirror above the dresser. The five hours' sleep he had just gotten did him some good. He felt better, but still looked like hell.

The room he was in was small. He walked over the old, creaking hardwood floor back to the bed and pulled the blanket up over the pillows.

The house Joni's father had left her was an ancient, wood-paneled thing. The white paint outside was dirty and peeling. The lawn was unkempt, mostly weeds. It was in Fairburn, a city outside of Atlanta.

On her particular street, the houses were spaced wide apart. They had big yards. Old trucks were parked on front lawns. Some folks even had a chicken or two running around. It was country as hell for Freddy's taste, even though it was only twenty-five minutes outside of Atlanta.

Still looking at his face in the mirror, staring into his thoughts, Freddy wondered what was going on in Chicago. Had anyone found the bodies yet? He walked across the room and cracked the bedroom door. He smelled food cooking. He opened the door all the way and walked to the next door over. It was the third bedroom, where Joni had made the bed for the boy.

Freddy opened the door, saw Nathaniel sleeping on the twin bed. The child jerked every now and then, his facial muscles twisting into expressions of fear, then anger, then sadness. He was reliving what he had seen the day of the shooting, Freddy told himself. It was a shame the child had to deal with that, but shit happened to everybody. He would get over it, or at least learn how to deal with it, Freddy thought, closing the door.

Approaching the stairs, Freddy heard Joni's voice. She was

arguing with someone on the phone. As Freddy descended the steps, he was better able to make out what was being said.

"I told you, I'm done. No! Don't be coming around here no more. I'm serious. Good-bye!"

By the time the conversation ended, Freddy was downstairs, standing in the kitchen. Joni's back was to him.

When she turned around, Freddy could tell that she was startled by him. She smiled, played it off. "Hey sleepyhead," she said, a plate of fried chicken sausage in her hand. "Just in time. Have a seat."

Freddy told himself since he had just gotten there, he had no right poking in her business. At least not yet.

The kitchen was the biggest room in the house. Freddy pulled out a chair at the head of the old painted wooden table, and sat before the plate and silverware already set.

"Hope you don't mind breakfast food at night. It was all I had," Joni said, scooping eggs onto Freddy's plate, along with two sausage patties, toast, grits, and sliced cantaloupe. She served herself half as much food, then sat next to him, opening a napkin and smoothing it over her lap.

She stabbed one of the sausage patties with her fork and was about to take a bite when she said, "What you waiting for? Eat."

He wanted to mention what he had just heard, but he again told himself it wasn't his business. He ate.

Halfway through the meal, Freddy said, "You call off from work today?"

"I don't work," Joni said, chewing. "When you ever known me to?"

"I know that. But seeing as you have this house, how you pay for it? How you live?"

"The last scam was a good one. I knew a guy who worked at Home Depot. He said if I let him push a box on me from a shelf thirty feet up, I could sue and we'd split the money. I wasn't hurt. Just pretended."

Freddy laughed. "And ya'll did it?"

"Yup. It took them a year to settle out of court, but we split two hundred and fifty thousand dollars. It's almost gone, but I been living off that for three years now."

"Girl." Freddy shook his head. "You don't change."

"Gotta live, but that don't mean you gotta work."

Freddy took a sip from his orange juice. Joni did the same, eyeing Freddy from over the rim of the glass.

After a moment, Joni cautiously said, "What did you do in Chicago?"

"It's best you don't know that."

"Okay. Fine. What happened to Kia, the girl you left me for?"

"It's best you don't—"

"Un-uh," Joni said, waving a finger. "You in my house, I'm serving you eggs and shit, I think I need to know at least that much."

Freddy looked down at his food. "She thought she was too good for me. She left."

"I'm sorry."

"It's cool."

Joni picked at her food some more.

"Why you bring that little boy? He yours? You know how much I wanted a baby with you. You throwing that child in my face, trying to make me feel bad?"

"He ain't mine."

"Oh."

Joni balled up her napkin, set it on the food that she hadn't been eating. She reached for Freddy's plate. "You through eating?"

"Yeah," Freddy said, stopping her hand with his own. "Leave it. I ain't done talking."

"Talking about what?"

"I heard your phone conversation."

Joni snatched her hand back. "So what?"

"That fool on the other end of the phone got anything to do with why your face looking like that?"

Joni turned her black eye away from Freddy. "Don't worry about that. It's under control."

"Is it?" Freddy said, grabbing Joni, this time by the forearm.

"Yeah," Joni said, trying to pull away.

"No. Is it?" Freddy said, squeezing her a little to emphasize the question.

Joni stared into Freddy's eyes for a long moment, as if she wanted to confess something, but was afraid. "Yeah."

Freddy let Joni go. "Make sure. I know I don't live here, and I ain't your man no more, but I ain't gonna sit here like no punk and see you done wrong. Make sure whoever he is know that."

18

The next morning, Lewis leaned over in his chair, staring at the entrance to the courtroom. He had been watching it for the last fifteen minutes straight. This was his follow-up court appearance from yesterday, and he knew that Nate and Monica would not walk through that door, but Lewis still stared unblinkingly, hoping and praying they would.

Monica's attorney was seated. He anxiously glanced down at his watch for what seemed the twentieth time, then looked over his shoulder at the door. Lewis's attorney sat beside him, a suppressed smile on his face. Above and in front of them, the judge looked irritated, as if counting the seconds off in his head till he would let the attorneys know that he was tired of waiting.

This moment was torture for Lewis, but not nearly as bad as last night had been. Yesterday after Freddy had called him, told him that he had shot both Nate and Monica, Lewis stumbled backward, almost fell from shock.

If any other man had told him that, he would've had to ask him if he was serious. But he knew Freddy. He had been standing just outside Freddy's father's bedroom the afternoon

Freddy stepped out of it, blood covering his face, hands, arms, and T-shirt. He held the baseball bat, shiny with blood, that he had used to kill the man in his sleep. If Freddy said he had shot Monica and Nate, Lewis knew that he had.

After Freddy's admission, he hung up. But Lewis dialed him right back, because he didn't just have questions about Monica and Nate. His little girl had been there, too. What the fuck had Freddy done with Layla?

Lewis got Freddy's voice mail. Angrily, he slammed the phone into the cradle, rang him again. Voice mail. With no other options, Lewis left a message.

"Freddy, call me back. Where the fuck is my little girl? You need to be calling me!"

Enraged, Lewis was escorted back to his cell. He threw himself onto his bunk as the cell door slid closed in front of him. The guard, a black man the same age as Lewis, stared at him through the bars for a moment, as though he thought Lewis had something to tell him.

There was something, Lewis thought. He had just found out that his onetime best friend had possibly murdered the woman Lewis loved, and her ex-husband. Lewis should've been up off that bunk, at those bars, demanding that the guard do something. Call the police. Tell them to go to Nate's house. Lewis knew where the bodies were. He could give them directions. But Lewis did nothing, just sat there staring up at the guard, hating himself for not doing more.

Freddy said he shot Monica and Nate, but that didn't mean they were dead, Lewis hoped. And Layla could've been up in her room asleep. Maybe she slept through the entire ordeal. And Monica and Nate could've been alive, could've been sprawled out on that living room floor, bleeding but still breathing, hanging on to dear life with the hopes that someone might find them.

The guard walked away, and Lewis pulled his feet into the bunk, rolled on his side, brought his knees toward his chest. For the entire night he could not sleep—could not get rid of the image of Monica covered in blood, bullet holes riddling her body.

During the night, Lewis prayed that the gunshots had been heard. That neighbors had called the police. Then he kept telling himself that's what had to have happened. An ambulance came, Monica and Nate were rescued, taken to a hospital, and were being worked on at that moment as Lewis suffered. And his daughter was found upstairs sleeping. And now she was being held somewhere safe and sound.

He had to believe that. That was the only way withholding this information would make sense. If Lewis had told that guard what he had known, that Freddy had shot Monica and Nate, the next day for Lewis's court appearance Monica's attorney would've said that Lewis had put Freddy up to it. They might try to charge Lewis with that crime. There was no telling how long his sentence would be then.

Lewis needed to be out. That would allow him to go to Monica—that is, if she was still alive. He could be with her, help nurse her back to health. But his freedom would also allow him to track down Freddy. Lewis knew no one would have a better chance of finding Freddy than he would. His being locked up in jail would only make things worse for everyone involved.

So for the entire night Lewis sweated and rolled on that bunk mattress till the lights came on this morning. A different guard appeared at Lewis's cell door and told him it was time for him to be taken across the street for his court appearance.

Now Lewis looked up as he heard the judge clear his throat, and watched him shift around in his chair.

"Mr. Kennedy," the judge said. "Are your clients going to make an appearance today or not?"

Mr. Kennedy stood, looked over his shoulder one more time. "They're going to come, Your Honor."

Lewis's heart skipped. Had Mr. Kennedy spoken to them?

It was the exact question the judge now asked of Mr. Kennedy.

"No, not exactly, Your Honor. But I left several messages on both their voice mails, and—"

"So you have not spoken with either them, seen them face-to-face, possibly gone by their house to ask them why they did not show yesterday and ensure they come today?"

Mr. Kennedy lowered his eyes a moment, then looked back at the judge and said apologetically, "Judge, I've been very busy. They are not my only clients. I—"

"Understood, Mr. Kennedy," the judge said, raising his gavel, pounding it once. "As of today, Mr. Lewis Waters will be released from custody, due to failure of . . ."

The judge went on, but Lewis could not hear him for the noise his attorney, Larry Charles, was making beside him, grabbing Lewis's hand, pumping it excitedly, saying something about how they had done it.

"We won, man. You're free!"

19

Daphanie sat in her car in the downtown parking garage off
Wacker Drive. The bank Trevor managed was around the corner
and down the block. Daphanie had called him from work and
told him she had to see him during her lunch hour.

"What do you mean, you have to see me? I haven't spoken to
you in a month. You don't return any of my phone calls, texts, or
e-mails. What's going on?"

"Just what I said, Trevor," Daphanie said, impatient. "Can I
come by there at lunch or not?"

"Yeah. Come by."

Daphanie sat staring at her cell phone call list. Nate's number
was highlighted, her thumb hovering over the Call button.

She could place the call—tell him that she just wanted to see
how he was doing. Yeah, she would hope that he would tell her
that he decided he no longer wanted to reunite with his ex-wife
after all. That he had kicked her to the curb and wanted Daphanie back. But if that had been the case, wouldn't Nate already
have called and told her that?

She could call him and let him know that, if things did go

sour between the two of them, he could always call Daphanie and she would come back to him. But then again, how would that look, her stepping back into Nate's life while carrying another man's child?

No. There was no going back, Daphanie thought, stuffing the phone back in her purse. She threw her car door open, stepped out, and slammed the door shut.

She would not call him and beg him to take her back, Daphanie told herself. She would simply have to forget about him. Stepping through Trevor's office door, Daphanie noticed how nice he looked in his suit and tie.

"Have a seat," he said, gesturing toward the chair. He walked back around his desk, took a seat, folded his hands in front of him, smiled, and said, "I almost forgot how beautiful you are. How are you?"

"I'm fine, Trevor. How are you?"

"I'm good. Better now."

"How about the wife? How is she?" Daphanie asked, regretting the question the moment it left her lips.

Trevor didn't answer. "What is it you want, Daphanie?"

Without ceremony, Daphanie said, "The last time we had sex, you know, a month ago . . . You're going to be a father."

A wide smile appeared on Trevor's face. He shot up from his chair, ran from behind his desk to Daphanie, and wrapped his arms around her.

"Oh-ho!" he said, staring her in the face. "You're pregnant?"

"Yeah," Daphanie said, her face emotionless, even though she was somewhat pleased at how excited Trevor was. She just wished that he was Nate instead.

"Congratulations. Wow!" Trevor said, releasing her, quickly pacing the floor. "I wish I had a cigar or something, you know?"

"No, I don't know."

Trevor leaned against the front of his desk, slightly winded. He was still elated. "So, what do we do next?"

"I'm glad you asked. I wanted to tell you about the baby, because it is only right. But why don't we just end things right now? I appreciate your contribution, but I can take it from here. We never need to speak again, and you can trust that this child will be cared for."

"What?" Trevor said. "No."

"What do you mean, no?"

"I fucking mean no. That's my child, too. You can't decide to cut me out of its life."

"You have a wife, Trevor. You're married. If the fucking wedding ring on your finger isn't enough to remind you, maybe the wife in your bed every night will do the trick," Daphanie spat, standing from her chair.

"I'll work around that."

"Huh." Daphanie chuckled cynically, walking toward the door. "There is no working around it. This child won't be your dirty little secret. You're not sneaking around to see it whenever you can steal an hour. My child won't be used by you like that."

"It's my child, too."

"Right now I don't really care about that," Daphanie said, opening the door. "Why don't you tell your wife the same thing and see what she thinks?"

20

Lewis stood outside the glass door of AERO, the men's clothing store that Monica owned and operated. He had been released from jail this morning and given back the clothes he had walked in with, as well as the few belongings he had.

Standing outside the jail's gate, Lewis had counted the money in his wallet. Forty-two dollars. He stared down at his cell phone. He pressed the On button, but nothing happened. Of course, the battery had died long ago. Lewis couldn't be concerned about that now. He needed to find his daughter, find out what happened to Monica. He thought of going back to her house, where he and Monica used to live. But what good would that do him?

She would probably be living at Nate's house by now, Lewis had thought, and immediately started walking quickly toward the street, looking for a bus stop. He slowed some when he realized that someone had to have found their bodies by now. It had been enough time since Freddy had shot them.

Lewis could only think of one place to go, and he hoped when he got there Tabatha would be able to give him the information he so desperately needed.

Lewis pushed his way into the store, looking around. Half a dozen customers milled about, some looking at suits, some at shoes and shirts. He walked slowly through the store as though he were being watched. When he turned to see who was behind the elevated counter, he saw Roland, Monica's floor manager. Roland was a thin, feminine-looking man. He wore a lavender V-neck sweater. He stared at Lewis wide-eyed, almost fearfully.

Lewis walked over to him. "Is Tabatha here, Roland?"

Roland froze, looking even more startled. He glanced left and right as if for assistance. When no one came to his rescue, he reached for the phone.

Lewis grabbed Roland's hand before he could lift the receiver. "Roland, I asked you a question. Is Tabatha here?"

"I ... I ... ." Roland stuttered.

Lewis was beginning to lose his patience when he noticed Roland's eyes focus on something behind him. Lewis spun and saw Tabatha, who was tall and thin, standing in the hallway that led from the back office. She appeared as shocked as Roland when she saw him.

"Tabatha," Lewis said, taking steps toward her.

"What are you doing here? You're supposed to be—"

"They let me out," Lewis said, urgently taking Tabatha by the arm. "I need to talk to you."

"Miss Tabatha," Roland called from behind the counter, fright on his face. The phone was to his ear, his finger poised to dial 911. "Should I call the police?"

"No," Lewis said.

Tabatha didn't respond.

"Tabatha, tell him no," Lewis said. "If you think I had anything to do with what happened to Monica, you're wrong. I love her. You know that."

She turned to look Lewis in the eyes, trying to determine if he was sincere. Tabatha said, "No, Roland, don't call."

In her office, Tabatha closed the door, turned to Lewis. Only now did he notice how exhausted she looked. "So how do I know you had nothing to do with Monica and Nate getting shot?" Tabatha asked.

"So it's true," Lewis said, feeling what little hope he had left seep out of him.

"Yes, Lewis. They could've died."

"So they're not dead?" Lewis stepped closer to Tabatha.

"No. I've been to see them."

"And how is she?" Lewis asked, afraid to know the answer.

"She's in a coma, Lewis."

Lewis couldn't speak for a moment, could barely breath.

"When will she wake up?"

"They don't know."

"I'm so sorry."

"You should be," Tabatha said, spite in her voice.

"Do you know what happened to my daughter? Is she okay?"

"Layla's fine. She was upstairs asleep when it happened. She's at Tim's house now. She's fine."

"And Monica? Where is she? I need to see her."

Tabatha didn't answer.

"Don't keep this from me," Lewis begged. "Not a month ago, me and Monica were supposed to be married. She was gonna adopt Layla. You can't keep this from me."

"That was a month ago. You aren't about to marry her anymore. She's going to marry Nate, and something tells me you had something to do with them getting shot. Tell me you didn't, Lewis."

Lewis lowered his head, looked back up at Tabatha. "It's complicated, but you know I'd never hurt her like that. I just wanna be there for her, make sure she's all right."

Tabatha walked away from Lewis, then turned and looked back at him sadly. "If she had never met you, you wouldn't have to make sure she's all right. But whether or not she still does, I know she loved you once and would probably want you to know where she is, so I'll tell you."

With the aid of a walker, Nate stood beside Monica's bed. On the other side of the bed stood Dr. Brooks. He was a short, clean-shaven man with a head full of unruly graying hair. He was considered a coma specialist by all the doctors in the hospital. Dr. Brooks looked up from Monica's chart.

"It seems to me they're doing all that can be done, Mr. Kenny. I have every reason to believe that she should wake from this."

"When?" Nate said, his arms trembling to hold his own body weight.

"I'm sure her doctor told you we can't predict—"

"Exactly. That's why I'm asking you. You're supposed to be the specialist, isn't that true?" Nate said.

"Yes, but—"

"Money is not an issue. I can pay whatever it will take to wake her."

"Mr. Kenny . . ." Dr. Brooks chuckled.

"Is there something funny?" Nate said, taking offense at what he considered to be Dr. Brooks's lack of concern.

"No. And I do apologize. I'm not making light of this situation. But comas have to run their course. No amount of money will change that."

"So you're telling me there is absolutely nothing that can be done? Nothing that has ever been done, been tried before? I will not believe that, Doctor."

"Okay, Mr. Kenny," Dr. Brooks said. "Yes, there was a man, trapped in a comalike state for six years. He was brought back to consciousness by doctors who planted electrodes deep inside his brain. The method is called deep brain stimulation, or DBS. It successfully roused communication, complex movement, and eating ability in the man, but there was resulting brain damage."

Dr. Brooks closed Monica's file, hung it back on the foot of her bed.

"Monica's case is not that serious. It's only been a couple days. I strongly urge you to not consider that treatment, or any other at this time. I do believe she will wake from this."

Nate stared helplessly at the man. He felt a bead of sweat roll down the side of his face. Nate wished this doctor could guarantee his beliefs, because without that, they meant nothing.

"So," Dr. Brooks said. "If you have any other questions or concerns, you have my pager and cell number. Call me anytime, okay?"

"I'll do that," Nate grunted.

"And, Mr. Kenny," Dr. Brooks said, before stepping out of the room. "You've had surgery just days ago. You really shouldn't be on your feet like this."

Nate didn't tell the doctor what he could do with his last remark. He let him walk out of the room, then Nate walked to the chair that sat in the corner of Monica's room and gingerly lowered himself into it. He let out a long sigh. There was pain, but not nearly as much as yesterday. And he was able to stand for a longer period, even without the walker. A knock came at the open door. Nate looked up to see Abbey there.

"Come in. Did you contact Ford's people?"

"I was able to speak to the ex-girlfriend and the mother. The uncle is out of town on business."

"And?"

"Both the girlfriend and the mother hold you responsible for what happened to Ford and refuse to talk to us. The girlfriend said she would tell the father not to speak to you, either."

Nate angrily slapped his palm down on the arm of the chair. "Have they at least been interviewed by the police?"

"I assume they would have been," Abbey said. "But neither they nor the police will confirm that. I spoke to Detective Davis today, and he told me to, quote, butt out, end quote."

"Abbey, I don't have to tell you how important it is that we speak to these people. The police have not found anything out, and with each day, each hour that passes, the chance of me seeing my son, of catching this maniac, becomes smaller and smaller."

"I know, sir," Abbey said. "So what do we do now?"

"Dammit!" Nate said, striking the chair again, this time with the side of his fist. "I can't think of anything else."

In the next moment, Nate was shocked to see Lewis Waters standing just inside the hospital room door.

"What are you doing here?" Nate said, not fully believing his eyes. "You're supposed to be in jail."

"Sir, shall I—" Abbey began, taking a step toward Lewis.

"No! Let him answer."

"I came to see Monica," Lewis said, looking over at her.

"Why aren't you in prison?"

Before Nate had even finished speaking the question, it all came back to him. The day after they had gotten shot, he and Monica were supposed to show up at court to press charges against Lewis. Nate figured the judge had probably given them another day to appear, and when they didn't show, Lewis was released. And then there were the countless voice mail messages on his cell phone. Nate was sure his attorney had called several times, trying to inform him of Lewis's release. Nate just hadn't had the time to check those messages.

"No one to press charges," Lewis said, answering Nate's question.

"So they let you go," Nate said.

"That's right," Lewis said, starting toward Monica's bedside.

"Don't you go over there," Nate warned.

Lewis halted. "Is she okay?"

"Does she look okay?" Nate said. "She's in a coma, and even though they believe she'll wake up, they don't know when."

"I guess it could be worse," Lewis said. "You have Layla. I'm gonna need for you to give her back."

"No."

"What do you mean, no?" Lewis said, starting toward Nate.

Abbey stood in his way, her hand sliding into her jacket. Lewis froze.

"I mean, this is all your fault," Nate said. "Because of you, that psychopath tried to kill me and my wife."

"She's not your wife."

"And he's taken my son. You won't get your daughter till I get my son."

"Fuck that!" Lewis said, starting toward Nate again.

This time Abby threw back her jacket, revealing the 9mm weapon, her hand wrapped around it. "Mr. Waters, I wouldn't if I were you," she warned.

"It seems as though we have a situation, Waters," Nate said. "I could call my attorney right now and tell him what's happened and get you back in court, have you convicted and sentenced."

"Try it. I'm not a fool. It's too late. You can't do that."

Nate nodded. "Maybe not. But I could try, and you'd be surprised what a very well-paid lawyer can pull off. I could at least have you taken back into custody under suspicion of having something to do with the shooting."

"I didn't have anything to do with this! I would never hurt Monica!" Lewis shouted. "I ain't going back in there!"

"Fine. Then you and I make a little deal. I need help finding your friend Ford. You help me find him and get my son back, you stay out of jail, and you get Layla. Will you help me?" Nate said, extending a hand to Lewis.

Lewis hesitated.

After a moment he took Nate's hand and said, "Yeah, okay. I'll help."

22

Daphanie and Brownie roamed leisurely through the aisles of Best Buy looking for the new Me'shell CD.

They had wandered over to the flat-panel TVs and were both standing in front of a fifty-inch Samsung LCD model.

"See, that's what you need," Brownie said.

"Exactly," Daphanie said. "One more welfare mama with a fifty-inch flat-panel sitting in her living room on a milk crate."

"Please. You're not gonna be a welfare mama."

"I know," Daphanie said, stepping away toward the Toshibas. "Because I made an appointment for an abortion."

Brownie froze, staring at Daphanie, her mouth hanging open. "What did you say?"

Daphanie walked back to her friend, stood right in front of her, and whispered, "I said, I'm getting an abortion."

"Why?" Brownie said, grabbing Daphanie by the wrist. "You said—"

"Because it's my right."

"Besides that?"

"I thought about it and I'm about to be out of a job. And my child will be a bastard, with a father who's married to another woman. And because I love another man."

"You aren't talking about that motherfucker Nate—" Brownie said.

"Yes, I still love that motherfucker Nate. And the plan is—"

"Wait. You have a plan?"

"And the plan is," Daphanie said, continuing, "to get rid of this baby and go to Nate and tell him that I understand that he might have missed his wife, but that he divorced her for a reason. It was the right decision, and he should come back to me."

"You're joking, right?"

"Yeah. And me getting an abortion is the punch line," Daphanie said. "No. I'm dead-ass serious."

"He's not worth it, Daph."

"Really," Daphanie said, raising a finger to Brownie. "Let me tell you why you say that."

"Please do."

"You've been in a monogamist relationship with John for three years. He loves your dirty bathwater, and you're only thirty-two years old, so you still have time to have a baby. Me, I'm thirty-seven. I need to get pregnant now."

"Hello! You are!"

"I'm not talking by anyone. It's not just about having a baby. It's also about getting a good man. Nate is the man I want. A handsome millionaire who I've fallen in love with, and who I know loves me," Daphanie said. "That's what I want. And I know he ain't gonna go for that with me carrying some other fool's baby."

"So Trevor's a fool now?"

"Okay, no. I'm the fool for getting pregnant by the wrong guy. That's why I'm getting the procedure. When I'm done, I'm going to get my man back."

"Daphanie, sometimes you don't make a lick of sense," Brownie said, raising a finger back at her friend. "Right now I need distance from your ass."

She walked away, leaving Daphanie standing in front of the wall of flat-panel televisions.

Brownie had everything just the way she wanted things in her life, so Daphanie's opinion didn't mean squat. Daphanie turned to face the screens in front of her, when she realized she recognized the scene that was on the TVs.

It was a house roped off by yellow police tape, with squad cars out in front of it and detectives and uniformed officers milling about. Only after staring glossy-eyed at the screens for ten seconds did Daphanie finally realize it was Nate's house she was looking at.

"Brownie," Daphanie called, her voice barely audible.

Brownie heard her. She turned and waved Daphanie off, still angered by their conversation.

"Brownie!" Daphanie screamed this time. "Come here!"

Brownie ran to Daphanie's side.

Daphanie had thumbed up the volume on the closest TV. She felt light-headed, like she was about to faint listening to what she was hearing.

A thin woman in a purple pantsuit, holding a microphone was in midsentence. ". . . shooting occurred two days ago, and only now the names of the victims have been released. Monica Kenny and ex-husband Nate Kenny have been taken to a local area hospital. Both are in critical condition. There are still no suspects in the shooting, but we'll keep you up to date as we get more information."

Daphanie, her face covered with tears, turned to Brownie and said, "Nate. He's been shot. I've got to see him."

23

Lewis stood at the front door of Freddy's uncle's home. Freddy's mother had to be here, Lewis figured. There was nowhere else she could go.

After Lewis left the hospital, he had taken the bus to Freddy's house, hoping Freddy's mother would let him stay there. When he got off the bus and walked down the street to the house, Lewis was shocked to see what lay before him. What once was a house was now just a huge pile of old splintered wood. A giant metal dumpster sat to one side of the mess. The entire site was encircled by a temporary chain-link fence. Fastened to it, a yellow sign read DANTE DEMOLITION.

So Freddy hadn't been lying. Nate really had used him. Lewis felt a moment of sympathy for his onetime friend, because he knew how evil Nate could be. Lewis shook that emotion. Freddy should've come to him. They could've worked against Nate. But Freddy chose to do things his way, and now Monica and Nate were in the hospital.

—

Lewis knocked on Freddy's uncle's door, hoping that Henry wasn't there. He didn't know how happy the man would be to see Lewis, considering all that had happened. Lewis saw someone peek out from behind the curtain shading the front door's window. The locks were undone, then the door opened. Freddy's mother, a big brown woman in her sixties, stood there, a sad smile on her face. Her graying hair was tied in a scarf. "Lewis, is that you?" She pushed open the screen door and opened her arms. "Come here, child."

Lewis stepped forward, allowing her to embrace him. He hugged her back, almost wanting to cry, considering what they had both gone through—what they were now going through.

Moms was what Freddy called her. It was what Lewis had been calling her for almost twenty years as well. She asked Lewis into the house. Lewis hesitated.

"Don't worry. Freddy's uncle is out of town. Won't be back for a week."

Inside, Moms insisted that Lewis have a seat in the living room. She brought him a cold glass of lemonade and sat on the couch before him.

Lewis guzzled half the glass down before saying, "Moms, you know why I'm here?"

"I thought you was in jail."

"I was, but they had to let me go. It's a long story. But you know why I'm here, right?"

Moms dropped her face in her hands.

"Moms, Freddy—"

"No!" Moms said, looking frightened, her palm up. "Fred was here. He said he did something horrible. The police came for him. I ain't have to lie to them, and I don't want to start."

"But—"

"I said I don't want to hear it!" Moms cried, her hands covering her ears.

Lewis stood from the sofa and sat on the couch next to her. He put his arm around her broad back. "Can you tell me where he is, Moms?"

Her hands still to her ears, her eyes closed now, she said, "I don't know. I told him not to tell me that, too."

Lewis pulled his arm away, stood. He looked down at Moms. She was devastated. This was one more reason to hate Freddy, Lewis thought. He had to have known this moment would happen, had to have known the grief he would cause everyone who loved him, but obviously he didn't give a damn.

Lewis glanced down at the home phone sitting on the end table. "Can I use the phone, Moms?"

"Do whatever you like, Lewis."

Lewis picked up the phone, dialed Freddy's cell number. Without a single ring, the call went straight to voice mail. Lewis hung up. He sat back down.

"Moms, Freddy did something bad. Really bad. He's hurt a lot of people because of it, including you, and I don't like that. I'm gonna have to find him." Lewis took Moms's hand, squeezed it. "I just want you to know. You understand?"

Moms nodded. A tear ran quickly down her wrinkled bronze skin.

Lewis embraced her, then stood. "I'll let you know everything that happens, but I gotta go now." Lewis walked toward the front door.

"Where?"

Lewis turned around to see Moms standing, wiping her face dry.

"Um . . ."

"Have you eaten?" Moms asked.

"No."

"You got a place to stay?"

"No, Moms, I don't."

"Then I'll fix you a meal. And like I said, my brother won't be back for a week. You stay, do what you got to do from here till you find Freddy."

24

After Daphanie had seen the report of Nate's shooting, she was so distraught, Brownie had to help her out of the store and into her car.

Instead of taking Daphanie home, Brownie drove her back to her house.

Inside Brownie's town home, slumped low in an armchair, Daphanie looked up from her damp Kleenex. "We have to find out what hospital Nate's in. I have to see him. Can you call around?"

Brownie stood in front of her friend, staring down at her without saying a word.

"Brownie, can you call around, find out where he is?"

Sadly Brownie said, "I can't, Daph. I know it hurts, but that man is no longer your responsibility. He's out of your life."

Daphanie shot up from the chair. "I don't care. I still love him!"

"But he doesn't love you!" Brownie took Daphanie by the shoulders. With concern in her eyes, she said, "He told you that. The two of you are finished. You're free, girl."

"I don't want to be free. I want to be with him."

"And what if he dies?" Brownie said. "Ever thought of that? Maybe it's not even your choice whether or not the two of you are together. You have enough on your damn plate already. Can you just deal with that?" Brownie released Daphanie.

"I need to see him," Daphanie said, her voice low.

Brownie stepped away from Daphanie, then turned back to face her. "Your car is at home, and I'm not taking you back till you promise me that you won't go looking for him."

Daphanie fell back into the chair, dropped her face in her hands, knowing her best friend was right.

Two hours later, Brownie was dropping Daphanie off in front of her building.

"You sure you're okay?" Brownie said from her side of the car. "You want me to come up?"

Daphanie smiled as best as she could, shook her head. "I'll be fine."

"No calling, looking around for Nate. This is killing you, I'm sure, but you know I'm right about this."

Daphanie nodded. "Yeah, I know."

An hour later, Daphanie had found the hospital where Nate was taken. It just happened to be where Brownie worked. After hanging up the phone and writing down some information, Daphanie quickly threw on a jacket, grabbed her keys, and hurried out the door.

Daphanie exited the elevator on level three. She was excited to see Nate, but nervous about the condition he might be in. She pushed that out of her mind as she walked quickly down the carpeted hall. She told herself that he was fine. And even if he wasn't, she would sit by his side until he was. Daphanie eyed the numbers on the doors as they passed: 328, 324, 322. She stopped when she saw a man walking toward her. He did not look at her, seemed to have a lot on his mind. He walked past her.

"Tim," Daphanie called.

The man stopped and turned around. It was Nate's brother. He walked back to Daphanie, a look of mild surprise on his face. "Daphanie. Um, what are you doing here?"

"I came to see Nate. Is he alright? I saw on the news that—"

"He's fine, Daphanie. Did you speak to him? Does he know that you're coming?"

"No. I didn't even know if he was in any condition to talk. I just came by. Is there a problem?"

Tim looked as though he really had an issue with her being there.

"Uh, no. I just really wish you had called first." He looked back in the direction from which he had come. "You're here now, so I might as well walk you down to see him."

Daphanie walked beside Tim. He didn't say a word to her. At room 312, Tim knocked lightly on the door, pushed it open only enough to stick his head in.

Daphanie heard Tim say, "Nate, you have a visitor."

"Who is it?"

Daphanie didn't hear Tim answer, which led her to believe he probably mouthed her name to him.

"Let her in," Daphanie heard Nate say.

Tim pushed the door completely open and stood aside. When Daphanie walked through the door, a huge smile spread across her face when she saw that Nate was not only in one piece but standing. She rushed over to him, threw her arms around him, and squeezed.

"Oh, no, no, no. Ouch!" Nate said. "Surgery. I'm still healing."

Daphanie pulled away from him. "I'm so sorry." She took a step back. It was so good to see him. She felt a tear coming, and wiped at her eye.

"Tim, you still going to do that for me?" Nate asked his brother.

"I could do it later. I could stick around here for a while if you want me to," Tim said.

"Why would I want you to do that?"

"Okay," Tim said.

"And close the door," Nate said.

Tim left and closed the door behind him.

"Have a seat," Nate said, and lowered himself into his own chair with what looked like some pain.

Daphanie sat, too. "So are you okay?"

"I'm going to be fine. Four bullets can't keep ol' Nate down." He smiled a little.

"What happened? Who did this to you?"

"I don't know," Nate said, not granting Daphanie as much access as he knew she wanted. "The police are looking into it right now, but they haven't found anything yet."

"On the news, I think they said that someone else got shot. Who was that?"

Nate didn't answer right away, but finally said, "My ex-wife."

"The woman you were in bed with that night I came home from England."

"Yeah," Nate said, shame in his voice.

Daphanie looked around the room, noticed there wasn't a single balloon, get-well card, or flower anywhere.

"What happened to us, Nate?"

"No." Nate shook his head. "We're over. No need to talk about that."

"You at least owe me an explanation. You never gave me one."

"Daphanie, I don't mind you visiting. Actually, it's good to see you. But if an explanation is what you came here for, then maybe you should leave, and probably not come back."

Daphanie stared at Nate for a long moment. Nate did not turn his eyes away.

"I'm sorry. You're right," Daphanie said. "I don't know what I was thinking. I won't mention it again."

Nate smiled thinly. "It's all right." He tried to lift himself from his chair, but Daphanie could see the task was painful. Finally, he got to his feet. "It's time that I take my medication. Maybe I should see you another time."

Daphanie stood, walked over, gave Nate a kiss on the cheek. "Take care, and you know if you need anything at all, you can call me."

"I know."

Daphanie was about to step out the door, but halted.

"What room is your ex-wife in? Would you mind if I visited her to say hi?"

"She's in a coma, Daphanie."

"Oh," Daphanie said, feeling foolish. "I'm sorry to hear that."

When Daphanie left Nate's room, she headed in the opposite direction from which she had come.

She walked down the hall to room 385. Daphanie wanted to know if Nate would actually allow her to visit his ex-wife. That was why she had asked. But something had told her he wouldn't. So earlier, after Daphanie had gotten Nate's room number, she had asked what room Monica Kenny was in, as well. The receptionist had given her the number of the door she was now standing in front of.

Daphanie stepped in. She walked over to stand beside Monica's bed. She had only seen pictures of Nate's ex-wife. Looking at her now, Daphanie could see the woman was beautiful. She lay resting peacefully, bandages around her head, sheets pulled up to her chest. Coma, Daphanie thought. She felt sorry for her, knowing there was a chance that Monica would never awaken. Daphanie was tempted to take a look at Monica's chart at the foot of the bed, but she didn't.

She stood there a moment. No one entered the room. No one was monitoring it. Daphanie turned and left.

25

The next day, Lewis exited the train and walked the three blocks down to the Department of Children and Family Services building.

Once inside the door, Lewis stepped into a large room filled with rows of chairs, all of them occupied by women. Most of the women were young; many of them held infants and toddlers in their laps and tried to keep an eye on their older children as they ran through the aisles.

Lewis saw a long counter at the front of the room. The setup looked like bank-teller stations. Women stood behind each of the four stations, behind thick glass. Lewis got into the shortest line. When it was finally Lewis's turn, he stepped up to the window. Before him stood an attractive slender young woman with brown hair. She had shapely lips and hazel eyes. She was beautiful, except for a diagonal two-inch scar on the side of her forehead. It looked as though she had tried to cover it with her bangs, but it was still visible.

"Can I help you?" the woman said, as though she couldn't care less. Her name pin read EVA.

"I need to talk to someone about getting my daughter back."

She slid a card with a number on it into the metal tray before Lewis. "Take this number and—"

It was the same kind of card Lewis had seen all the women in the chairs holding. He looked up in a far corner of the room. A digital counter just ticked off number 78. Lewis glanced down at his card. Number 136.

Lewis dropped the card back into the tray. "I need to speak to somebody now."

"Sir, all these women with their children need to speak—"

"They have their children. Somebody else got mine. I need someone to tell me what to do to get her back."

Eva gave Lewis a sympathetic look. "You're gonna have to see a counselor."

"How long is that gonna take?"

Eva shook her head. "Today is our busiest day. Tomorrow it's—"

"C'mon, Eva," Lewis said. "Just take a minute and help me with this. I wouldn't be asking if this wasn't really important."

Eva looked at her coworkers in the booths on either side of her. She leaned to her left, said something to the blue-eyed woman beside her, then dropped a sign in her window that read BACK IN 5 MINS.

Eva gestured for Lewis to meet her at the door at the far end of the counter.

"Follow me," Eva said.

Lewis stepped through the door and followed the woman. Even in the situation he was in, he could not help admiring her petite, curvy shape. This was the most attractive woman he had laid eyes on since he'd been involved with Monica.

Eva opened an office door, stuck her head in, then pushed the door open all the way. "This office is empty." She walked in, stepped behind the desk, and asked Lewis to have a seat. "Now, what were you saying?"

Lewis told Eva everything. How Layla's mother had died of an overdose. How he had just gotten out of jail, but was not convicted of the crime. He told her how Monica was the woman who had been caring for Layla, but that she was in a coma, and the last time he spoke to her, she said she no longer wanted to be with him.

"But the man she's with now is keeping my daughter from me."

Eva shook her head, sadness on her face. "That's awful."

"So how do I get her back?"

"It should be a very easy fix."

"How?"

"I mean, I'm not a social worker or counselor yet. I'm just an associate. But from what I know, he has no right to have your daughter. She's legally yours, right?"

"Right."

"Okay, give me her birth certificate, and—" Eva began, reaching out across the table.

"I don't have her birth certificate," Lewis said, looking worried. "I need that?"

"Yeah. It's proof."

"But I don't got it," Lewis said, starting to panic.

"It's cool. It's not a problem," Eva said, trying to calm Lewis. "The records building is like fifteen minutes from here. Just go down there, show them your ID, and get a copy. Bring it back here, and someone should at least be able to start the process to help you get your daughter back."

"You ain't playing with me, are you?"

"No." Eva smiled. "It might take a few days. But no, I wouldn't play with you." Eva stood, walked around the desk.

Lewis jumped from his seat and, without thought, threw his arms around her. "I gotta give you a hug for this."

Surprised, Eva said, "Oh, okay."

After the hug, Eva said, "I wish I could do more. If you only knew how few men I see trying to gain custody of their children. It happens, like, never. Most act like they don't even know they have a child."

"Well, that ain't me. I'm going down to that office, get my baby's birth certificate, and I'll be right back."

When Lewis stepped out of the DCFS building, he felt rejuvenated. This mess would be over soon, and he'd have his daughter back.

26

Lewis stepped up to the counter at the Cook County Clerk's Office.

"How may I help you?" an older, dark-haired woman pleasantly asked Lewis.

"I need to get a copy of my daughter's birth certificate."

The woman placed a form on the counter, along with a stubby pencil.

"Fill this form out completely. When you're done, I'll need eight dollars for the certificate. Okay?"

"Okay," Lewis said, smiling.

Lewis did what he was told. When he gave the woman the form and his money, he was told to come back in half an hour to pick up the birth certificate. For those thirty minutes, Lewis waited in the hall on a bench just outside the office. He thought about getting Layla's certificate, doing whatever work had to be done to get her back, and seeing the look on Nate's face when Lewis lifted Layla out of his arms for good. Lewis also couldn't help thinking about Eva. She had been very nice to him. He wondered if she was single.

After exactly thirty minutes, Lewis was at the counter again, the same smile on his face.

"You're back," the dark-haired woman said.

"Yup. Is it ready?"

"Sure." The woman laid an envelope on the counter before Lewis.

"Thanks a lot," Lewis said, after taking the envelope and starting out of the office.

"You might want to check to make sure it's right," the woman called to Lewis.

"Okay," Lewis said, stepping out of the office. He walked down the hall, pulling the birth certificate out of the envelope. It was odd, but he had never seen his own daughter's birth certificate before.

Lewis smiled wider as he looked over the sheet. But then he halted, his eyes narrowing as he read, a frown appearing on his face. He spun around and marched back down to the records office.

"Excuse me," Lewis said. He saw the woman who had helped him, but she was at some other woman's desk holding a conversation.

"Excuse me!" Lewis practically yelled.

The woman walked to the counter, concern on her face. "Yes, is there something wrong?"

"What is this, some kind of joke?" Lewis said, slapping the certificate on the counter. "That ain't my name right there where the father's name's supposed to be."

The woman looked down at the certificate. She looked up at Lewis as though she wanted to apologize. "I don't know what to say."

"Tell me why this form is wrong."

"Sir, I don't know if this form is wrong."

"What?" Lewis said, wanting to reach over the counter and shake the woman by the collar of her shirt. "It is wrong! How did this man, Brian Wilson, get on my daughter's form?"

"Were you at the hospital when your daughter was born, sir?"

"No. But you still ain't tell me how this man's name got on this form."

The woman lowered her eyes and said softly, "The mother tells the hospital the name of the father."

27

Freddy sat in Joni's backyard on an old bench, wracking his brain trying to come up with a plan for escape.

It wasn't that Joni was trying to force him out. She seemed to be loving every minute he was there. She was really getting a kick out of Nathaniel. Freddy didn't know for sure, but he was just about certain she was in the house that very moment, on the floor, playing some game with the boy. After the short time they had been there she was starting to get attached, and that was just one more reason Freddy had to get out of there.

But what would he do? Where would he go? He only had about eighty dollars in cash, and he was afraid to try to pull money out of the ATM for fear the police might be able to track him that way. He would've asked Joni for a few extra bucks, but she'd said her money was running out.

Freddy didn't know anyone else anywhere in the country, so he was practically trapped there.

"What the fuck?" Freddy said, standing from the bench, turning and kicking it, frustrated.

Just then he heard someone banging on the front door of the house.

Could it be the police? Freddy spun in a circle, looking over his shoulder for somewhere to run, somewhere to hide.

There was no garage, but he could hop the back fence, take off running. But what about Joni? What about the boy?

"Joni, open up! I know you're in there!"

The demand came from the front of the house. It was the deep voice of a man. It wasn't the police.

Freddy slowly walked around the side of the house. His gun was upstairs under his mattress.

"Joni, I said open up the fucking—"

"What do you want? I told you not to come around here no more, Sam," Freddy heard Joni answer.

Freddy snuck to the corner of the house, peering around to see a short, squat man with dark skin. He wore a wife-beater shirt, extra-large baggy jeans, and very white sneakers. His chest and arms were muscular, but he had a large belly.

"I told you I was sorry," Sam said. "I ain't gonna let you be playing me like this for too much longer, or—"

"Or what?" Freddy said, stepping around the corner of the house.

Sam turned to see Freddy. "Who the fuck is you?"

"Freddy, please," Joni said, opening the screen door and stepping onto the porch. "You don't—"

"Joni, shhh," Freddy said, a finger to his lips. He redirected his attention to Sam. "I'm an old friend of Joni's. Why you here banging on her door, harassing her like this, when she told you she doesn't want you here anymore?" Freddy had stepped all the way over to the porch steps, placed his foot on the first one.

Sam smiled, walked down the steps, and stood directly in front of Freddy. He was a good four or five inches shorter than Freddy, but his broad stance more than made up for his lack of height. "Did anybody say shit to you, motherfucker?"

Freddy stared into Sam's face, not blinking.

"Hunh?" Sam said. He looked over his shoulder, chuckling. "Joni, did I ask this motherfucker anything?"

Joni stared at both men, looking frightened.

"Tell you what," Sam said. "Why don't you get the fuck out my face, let me deal with my woman, or else, when I'm done with her, I'm gonna deal with you?"

Freddy showed Sam a fake smile and said, "Tell you what. Since you don't know who the hell I am, where I come from, or just how crazy I might be, I'm gonna let you walk away this one time if you leave right now," Freddy said, sliding his right hand into his pocket and slipping his fingers around his car keys.

He would've preferred not to, but if he needed to, without hesitation he would jab the biggest key into Sam's throat and watch him choke on his own blood till he died.

Sam continued to look at Freddy and must have read those intentions. He took a step back, looked again at Joni, and said, "Joni, I'ma be back, and we gonna talk about this. You hear me?" He gave Freddy a hateful look and stepped around him, intentionally brushing Freddy's shoulder. He walked to his aging Impala, climbed in, and drove off.

Freddy watched the car till it turned the corner and disappeared. Afterward, he walked up the steps and waited as Joni stepped into the house, then closed the door behind both of them.

Freddy saw that Nathaniel was on the floor in front of the TV, watching cartoons.

He took Joni's hand, pulled her into the dining room.

"I thought you said you had that under control," Freddy said.

"I do."

"It didn't look like it to me. That's the man that's been putting his hands on you?"

"That ain't none of your business, Freddy."

"It wasn't before. But I'm here now."

Joni chuckled sadly. "But you weren't here then." She turned, was about to walk out the dining room door, but stopped and said, "When you ready to stay awhile, then you can start calling shots. Till then, stay out of my business."

28

Later that evening, Daphanie opened the door, and Trevor walked in carrying a paper shopping bag from Babies"R"Us.

She felt awful about the way she had left things. Trevor had been leaving a barrage of phone, text, and e-mail messages again, none of which she returned. Finally, telling herself that he hadn't asked for any of this, Daphanie called and told him he could drop by.

Trevor stood in the middle of her living room, the bag in his hand, looking around as if it were the first time he'd seen the place.

"I want to thank you for letting me come. I apologize for my outburst in my office. I was just—"

"No need for an apology. I was wrong, too," Daphanie said, reaching for the bag. "What's this?"

Trevor handed her the bag with a smile. "Just a few things I picked up for the baby. Some pants and tops."

"You don't even know the sex yet."

He smiled wider. "Whatever it is, I'll take the other stuff back."

Daphanie pulled the garments out. There were two outfits, shirts and pants. One of which was pink, the other blue.

"Thank you," Daphanie said.

"My pleasure," Trevor said, folding the bag along its creases and tucking it under his arm. "You weren't really serious about . . . you know, me not being in the baby's life, were you?"

Serious as hell then, Daphanie thought. But now she didn't have to worry, considering in a few days there would no longer be any baby. Of course, she didn't tell Trevor that.

She just smiled in his face, and said, "No. I wasn't serious. I was just emotional, you know."

"Oh. Good."

"But I think there is reason for concern regarding your wife," Daphanie said, setting the folded clothes on the coffee table. "How do you expect to handle that? I mean, what if she finds out? Do you even care?"

A pained expression came to Trevor's face. "Of course I care. I love my wife, but . . . but . . ." Trevor turned his back, took steps away from Daphanie.

"But what, Trevor?"

Turning again to her, he said, "What am I supposed to do? I've always wanted a child and she's always known that. The only reason I don't have one is because she doesn't feel like committing the time. And she says I don't know the stress it'll put on her body. I told her I don't give a fuck about stretch marks or a few extra pounds." Trevor looked anguished. "This is something I want, and now I have a chance to have it. Really, what am I supposed to do?"

"You tell me," Daphanie said.

"I'm not going to do what you said, sneak around, keep our child a secret. I don't think I can do it now, so before it's born, I'm just going to have to tell my wife."

"And what if she leaves you?"

"I hope that she won't," Trevor said, pacing. "No. She won't. I know her. She'll accept our child. She will understand that since she wasn't willing, I had to do what I had to do. She'll welcome our child, love it like it is her own."

He's fucking delusional, Daphanie thought, staring at Trevor. One, because he actually believes his wife would do what he's thinking. And two, because he must think, if I really did have the baby, I'd go for that craziness. I'm not gonna go through all the tortuous crap that woman doesn't want to, and allow her to enjoy all the upsides to motherhood. Hell, no!

"That's the plan?" Daphanie said, trying not to laugh.

"Yeah," Trevor said. "What do you think?"

"I think it's a start. Might need a little work, but it's a start," Daphanie said, walking over and giving Trevor a hug. "Thanks for the clothes."

"Thanks for being understanding, and keeping me in our baby's life," Trevor said, hugging her back.

Daphanie walked Trevor to the door, a phony smile glued to her face. When she closed and locked the door behind him, she told herself she knew for sure now. There was no way in hell she was carrying this baby to term.

29

"I want Daddy," Nathaniel said, looking away from another cartoon that played on the television before him. "When can I see my daddy?"

"Soon enough, kid," Freddy said. "Your Auntie Joni was nice enough to buy you that DVD. You need to be watching it," Freddy said, leaning back into the cushions.

He glanced at his wristwatch. It was approaching nine P.M.

Joni walked into the room from the kitchen and saw Nathaniel yawning.

"Awww," she said. "The poor baby is sleepy."

She walked over to Nathaniel, scooped her hands under his arms, and lifted him up to her. "I'm gonna take him up to bed, okay?"

"Good, he was starting to get on my nerves."

"Freddy! Don't say that. You'll hurt his feelings. Now get over here and apologize to him."

Freddy looked up, saw that the boy's bottom lip was poked out.

"Freddy," Joni called again.

Freddy got up, walked over. "Sorry, kid, okay?" he said, rubbing Nathaniel on the head. "Got a lot on my mind. Know what I mean?"

"I'll be back down in a minute," Joni said. As she carried Nathaniel up the stairs, Freddy heard the boy say, "I don't wanna go to bed."

"We'll read you a bedtime story, and you'll fall right off to sleep, baby," Joni told him.

When Freddy heard the old floorboards creaking over his head and was sure the two were upstairs, he grabbed the remote and flipped the channel from cartoons to CNN. He had been doing that since his arrival, trying to see if anything about the shooting had been aired. He sat there on the edge of the sofa for twenty minutes, but no news from Chicago. He was relieved, at least for the moment. When he heard Joni descending the stairs, he quickly switched to another channel. Joni sat and threw her arm behind him, across the spine of the couch, a huge smile on her face.

"What you cheesin' about?"

"Nathaniel. He's an angel."

"Yeah, he's not a bad kid, I guess."

"I wanted one so badly," Joni said softly. "I guess God didn't think I was fit to—"

"Stop it, Joni. You would've been a good mother. Just by the way you take care of Nathaniel, I can see that."

"Really. You think?"

"I know."

Joni gave Freddy an appreciative peck on the lips.

Caught off guard, Freddy just stared at Joni.

She leaned in, kissed him slowly, fully on the lips now. She wrapped both her arms around his neck, sliding closer to him, when he gently pulled away.

"No, don't," he said, as Joni tried to hang on to him.

"Why not? You don't want me 'cause I can't give you kids? You still hung up on Kia?"

"No. It's just not the time. There's too much going on."

"What, Freddy? You never told me, remember?"

"I can't."

"I see. You want me to understand what's going on, you just don't want to tell me."

Freddy sighed. "Yeah. That's right."

A knock came at the door.

Freddy jumped. "Who is that?" he whispered, his eyes wide.

"Don't worry. I'm sure it's cool," Joni said, getting up from the sofa and walking around the corner to the door.

Freddy sat poised to act if he had to. Exactly what he'd do would be determined by who was at the door. He stood slowly, took a step in the door's direction, wishing he had his gun on him.

When the door was opened, Freddy heard a man's voice say, "What's up, girl? I got company, and I need to borrow your cork-screw."

"Hey, Billy," Joni said.

Freddy heard heavy footsteps move quickly toward him. He hurried back to the sofa and sat, trying to look normal.

"Oh," Joni's friend Billy said, walking into the living room and seeing Freddy. "I didn't know you had company." He turned to Joni, looking somewhat embarrassed.

Freddy clenched his teeth, felt his muscles tightening, not at the fact that there was another man in Joni's house, but because that man wore a police officer's uniform.

"Hi, how you doing?" Billy said, stepping forward, extending a limp-wristed hand to Freddy.

Freddy stood, took the man's hand, and shook.

"My name is Billy. I'm Joni's neighbor."

"I'm . . . I'm John," Freddy said.

Billy was six feet tall or so. He looked to weigh over two hundred pounds. Freddy had him by an inch, but the man had easily thirty or forty pounds on Freddy. He was clean-shaven, with black hair that was cut very short to his head. He was a decent-looking guy who couldn't stop smiling.

"Well, I'm not gonna interrupt whatever you two got going on," Billy said, smiling at Joni. "Just came to borrow the corkscrew 'cause I got a little party of my own going on. So nice meeting you, John."

"You, too, Billy," Freddy said.

Billy walked quickly into the kitchen, like he had done it a thousand times before. While Billy rummaged through the kitchen drawers, Freddy stared narrow-eyed at Joni.

Billy walked back into the living room, holding the corkscrew over his head. "Found it. Good night," he said in a sing-songy voice.

The front door was slammed shut. Joni opened her mouth to speak. Freddy lifted a finger to his lips, indicating to her not to say a word.

He waited till he thought Billy was far out of earshot, then said, "Who the hell was that?"

"That's Billy, my friend."

"I can see that. Why didn't you tell me you had a cop living right next door to you?"

"It ain't right next door. He's fifty yards away at least. And how would I know it made a difference, since you ain't telling me nothing?"

"Don't play games, Joni," Freddy warned.

"Besides, he's not a cop. He's just a mall security guard."

"He carry a gun?"

"I said he's a mall security guard. No."

Freddy felt himself calm down the slightest bit. "I'm going up to bed."

30

Lewis sat downstairs in Uncle Henry's living room, in the dark, leaning forward on the sofa, his face in his hands.

It was ten P.M.

This afternoon, Lewis had tried not to go off on the woman at the records office, but when he heard what she said, Lewis couldn't help saying, "You trying to tell me that I ain't the father? Is that what the fuck you trying to say?"

"No, sir," the woman said, slightly rattled. "I'm just saying that the mother put someone else's name on the birth certificate."

Lewis raised his voice again, said a few curse words. Security was called, and Lewis was dragged out of there, yelling and kicking.

Afterward, he hadn't gone back to DCFS to see Eva. What would've been the point if Layla wasn't really his?

But that wasn't true. It couldn't be true, Lewis told himself. He wandered around the streets for the rest of the evening, trying to avoid doing what he knew he had to do now.

Lewis picked his cell phone up from the coffee table.

He flipped it open and the screen lit up a small space in the dark room. He scrolled down his contact list, punched a few buttons, pressed Call, then placed the phone to his ear.

"Salesha," Lewis said, when he heard Selena's mother pick up.

The last time Lewis had seen Salesha, and her other daughter Salonica, was not two months ago, when they came to Chicago from St. Louis trying to take custody of Layla. He couldn't stand either of them, and they didn't like him. They only decided to stop trying to gain custody when Lewis offered them money to leave town. That was the type of women they were.

"Yeah, this Salesha. Who this?"

"It's Lewis."

There was silence on the other end.

"You ain't getting that money back, Lewis, so don't even—"

"I ain't calling for the money. I need for you to tell me something."

"Oh. Well, shoot," Salesha said. "What you wanna know?"

Lewis breathed deeply, exhaled. He closed his eyes, felt the phone shaking in his grasp. "Is Layla my daughter?"

Again there was a moment of silence.

"What you mean, Lewis?"

"You heard what I asked you, Salesha. And don't act like you don't wanna hurt my feelings. Don't lie to me. I need to know the truth."

"Lewis . . ."

"Salesha, just answer the fucking question!" Lewis said, near tears. "Am I Layla's father or not?"

"There were other men," Salesha said softly. "When you were with Selena, she told us there were always other men. And because of that, she ain't know for sure who in the hell the father really was."

31

Nate had been sitting by Monica's bedside, holding her hand for the entire morning and most of the afternoon.

Two hours ago, Dr. Beck had stepped into the room. Nate stood with less pain.

"How are you doing, Mr. Kenny?"

"Fine. I think you can take this IV out of my arm now. I'm tired of taking it everywhere I go."

"How's the pain?"

"Much more manageable. Almost completely gone," he lied.

"Do you want to go back to your room so I can take a look at your incisions, or are you fine here?"

"This is fine," Nate said.

Dr. Beck lifted Nate's gown and peeled back the bandage covering the incision on his thigh. "Someone changed your dressing this morning?"

"Yes."

"It's healing nicely," Dr. Beck said. She looked at the other scars and had the same opinion. "Well, you're recovering faster than we figured. You should be ready to get out of here in a few days."

"I guess. But what about my wife?"

Dr. Beck walked around Monica's bed. She placed her stethoscope into her ears, then placed the dome under Monica's gown and on her chest. She listened for a moment, moved it slightly, then listened again.

Dr. Beck pulled the stethoscope from her ears, pulled a small penlight from her lab coat pocket, leaned over, opened Monica's eyelids, and shone the light in both eyes.

"Well?" Nate said.

"No change."

"Shouldn't she be awake by now?"

"Like I said before, Mr. Kenny, there's no telling when she'll wake up. But as you know, we are constantly monitoring her. If and when it happens, we'll be right here."

An hour ago, Nate had tried to contact the detectives working his case. He called their office, and a female officer told Nate neither Davis or Martins was in. He could try them on their mobile phones if he liked.

"I'll do that, but I want you to take a message for them."

Nate left a message instructing them to call him ASAP, then dialed their cell phones. He got voice mail on both. He hung up the phone after leaving angry messages for both men. He then flipped to a local news channel, where a reporter stood holding a microphone in the face of Detective Martins.

"Yes," Martins said. "That's right. The suspect's name is Freddy Ford. There is a fifty-thousand-dollar reward for any information that leads to the arrest of this man."

The reward was Nate's suggestion, his money, but obviously

it was doing no good. Nate had turned to Monica, feeling help-less. He called his private investigator, told her to bring him some clothes. He had to do more to find Ford.

A soft knock came at the door. Nate knew it was Abbey.

"Come in," he said, releasing Monica's hand and standing.

Abbey stepped in, wearing another dark suit. She held a gar-ment bag draped over one arm.

"Good afternoon, sir."

"Hello, Abbey," Nate said, taking his clothes. "I don't want to do this, but I feel if I don't force them, the police won't do what they're supposed to. I have to be out of here."

"I understand, Mr. Kenny."

"I'm going to my room to dress. I'll speak to my doctor, and then we'll leave," Nate said. "I'll need you to call Waters, let him know we need to talk to Freddy's people."

"Yes, sir."

"And if he offers any resistance, remind him of the deal we made regarding his daughter."

32

Daphanie stood in the large storage room at Reese Pharmaceuticals, where all the drug samples each rep would dispense to doctors were kept. Considering she had to pack her things and get
the hell out in less than two weeks, she had no idea why she was
still going through the motions of calling and visiting doctors.
Maybe because she had plenty of vacation days and knew this
was the last day she had to work before taking those days and
leaving the job early. Daphanie had her shoulder bag with her,
and the small wheeled cart she used to stack the sample cases,
making it easier for her to transport them.

The storage room was nothing but a series of shelves, stacked
full with vials of this liquid drug, boxes of pills of that drug.
There were capsules, topical creams, and ointments—drugs for
every use imaginable.

She wandered through the labyrinth of pharmaceuticals,
looking for an osteoporosis drug.

"Hey," someone said from behind her.

Startled, Daphanie spun around.

"What's up?" It was Parker.

"Oh, just grabbing some Osteoflex samples for the visits I have to make today."

"Osteoflex is in the front of the room. Want me to help you load your cart?" Parker said.

"Would you, please?" Daphanie said.

"How many do you need?"

"Um, three cases should do it," Daphanie said. "You know what? Make it four."

Parker stacked the cases onto Daphanie's cart, clapped the dust off his hands, and said, "So I'm really sorry about . . . you know."

"It's not your fault, Parker. You gave me an out before this happened, I just didn't take it," Daphanie said, showing him a smile.

"Don't worry, you'll find something soon. You're too good for someone not to scoop you up," Parker said.

He was turning to leave when Daphanie stopped him.

"You know, I have some vacation days. I was thinking, instead of having them paid, I'd rather just take the days and leave early. That would make today my last day. What do you think?"

"Awww," Parker said, seeming sincerely disappointed.

He walked back to Daphanie, giving her a friendly hug. "We're going to miss you around here, but I completely understand. Just come by my office, and I can submit the paperwork for you."

33

Freddy stood by Joni's dining room window, looking through the parted curtain. Joni was outside tossing a large rubber ball back and forth to Nathaniel. Joni saw Freddy there and waved. He raised a hand, waved back.

He had been pretending to watch Joni play with the boy, but he was really looking past them, staring at the house where the security guard lived.

Joni said Freddy had no need to fear him, but Freddy couldn't get comfortable with a man who had any relationship whatsoever with the law hanging out just next door.

He thought he had become a little too relaxed over the last few days. It was easy to do because no one was breathing down his neck here in Atlanta. But he knew that hell could've been rising up in Chicago. And he discovered it had been.

This morning, Freddy checked the *Chicago Sun-Times* and *Tribune* Web sites. He keyed in his name, and a story popped up. He read the article and discovered that Nate and Monica were alive. There was a fifty-thousand-dollar reward on his head. That pissed Freddy off. Mr. Kenny didn't have the money to let

Freddy and his mother stay in the house they had lived in all their lives, but now after his ass had been shot, he was giving out a fifty-grand gift certificate for info on Freddy. He was on edge the rest of the morning. But things were going much better in Atlanta than Freddy had imagined. Joni was getting closer and closer to Nathaniel, and she seemed to enjoy Freddy being around.

Joni told him she'd stop talking to that Sam guy. She told him she'd tell Freddy if Sam called her phone or showed up at the house again. But late last night, Freddy had stood at her closed bedroom door, listening. Her voice was hushed, but her tone was harsh, and something told him it was Sam she was talking to. He wanted to forbid her from having any contact with him. But just like Joni said, until Freddy made a commitment to her, he really was in no position to say anything.

Joni smiled now, waved again at Freddy as he stood at the window. He did his best to smile back, then left the window when he heard his name mentioned on the TV. He stood in front of the screen, a scowl on his face. There was a detective on the news, a bald, squared-jawed brother, talking about the bounty that was on Freddy's head. This was bad news.

But it was being aired on WGN, the only Chicago channel that Freddy was able to pick up on Joni's cable. He still hadn't seen anything on CNN or any other national news channels, which led Freddy to believe that the Chicago police didn't know he had left town. The door opened behind him. He quickly clicked off the TV. Things were changing. Freddy thought he was safe, but he knew the police would soon expand their search. He didn't think anyone knew of his connection to Joni in Atlanta, but sometimes things had a way of just getting out. He couldn't afford to wake and see Joni's house surrounded by cop cars. Joni walked up behind Freddy. She was holding Nathaniel's hand. She grabbed Freddy's, too.

"You should've come out with us. We had so much fun, didn't we, Nathaniel?"

"Uh-huh," the boy said, nodding his head.

"Maybe tomorrow," Freddy said.

34

Arriving from the hospital, Abbey pulled her Audi into the drive-way of Nate's house and cut off the ignition. Nate was in the pas-senger seat, on the phone with Detective Davis.

"What have you found out?" Nate asked.

"We tried to speak to Lewis Waters, but he's no longer in custody."

"I know that," Nate said, agitated. "Tell me something I don't know."

"Ford's last address was over at his uncle's house. He was liv-ing there with his mother, and—"

"I'm aware of that, too," Nate said. "Did you speak to her?"

"We spoke to her."

"And?"

"She knows nothing."

"What do you mean, she knows nothing? She's Ford's mother. If anyone were to know about him, it'd be her."

"She said Ford told her nothing. She said she told him not to, because she didn't want to lie to us when we came."

"So she knew you were coming?"

"Yes," Davis said. "Ford told her that."

Nate turned to Abbey, shook his head in disgust. "Have you found out any useful information, Detective Davis?"

Davis did not answer.

"Detective Davis—"

"Mr. Kenny, I can only imagine the pain you're going through, and how important this case is to you, but I'm the detective, not you. If Ford is found, it will be because we find him. So once you take a step back and realize that I don't take orders from you, everything will run much more smoothly. Understand?"

"Good day, Detective Davis," Nate said, disconnecting the call.

"Is everything okay, Mr. Kenny?" Abbey asked.

"Grab my bag out of the trunk, Abbey."

"Yes, sir."

Nate exited the car after Abbey.

Abbey retrieved Nate's bag from the trunk and made her way along the walk toward the front door of the house. Nate stood by the car, staring blankly at his home. The last time he was here, he almost died.

He slowly walked up the path to the front door. Abbey slid her spare key into the lock.

"One moment, Abbey," Nate said, feeling his pulse quicken. "You took care of everything, didn't you?"

"Yes, sir. All the carpeting in the front rooms was replaced, along with the sofa, and the entire house was professionally cleaned."

"Okay. Open the door."

Abbey unlocked the door, pushed it open, and stepped in first. She walked quickly through the first floor, checking every room, then made her way upstairs. When she returned, Nate was standing in the foyer, a look of apprehension on his face.

"It's all clear, sir."

Nate walked down the short hall into the living room. A flashback of the attack entered his mind, but he quickly shut it out. He would not be afraid in his own home.

He sat down on the sofa. "Those detectives are incompetent. We continue to rely on them, Ford will never be found."

"I'm sorry, sir, but there is not a great deal to go on. But I spoke to Lewis Waters, and told him we'll pick him up so we can interview the mother ourselves."

"What makes you think her story will change?" Nate said. "They said she knew nothing."

"Maybe they didn't interview her the right way," Abbey suggested.

"Tomorrow, then. We pay her a visit."

35

Lewis matched the numbers on the scrap of paper he pulled out of his pocket to the address on the run-down house he stood in front of. The house was around the corner and down the block from the apartment Lewis used to share with Selena.

Last night during his conversation with Salesha, Lewis asked her, "Selena ever mention anybody named Brian Wilson?"

"Yeah," Salesha said. "He sounds familiar."

"Did she ever say where he worked, or where he lived?"

Salesha said her daughter told her the man lived somewhere in the neighborhood, around the corner or something.

First thing this morning, Lewis went back to his old neighborhood and questioned anyone hanging on the street corner, sitting on their front porch, or walking down the street. After approaching four people and finding out nothing, Lewis asked a man who looked a few years older than him.

"You know anybody name Brian Wilson live around here?"

The man wore a huge dirty white T-shirt. He was unshaven and smelled bad.

The man said, "You got a cigarette?"

"Ain't got no cigarette," Lewis said.

"Then I guess I don't know no Brian Wilson."

Lewis dug a crumpled five-dollar bill out of his pocket, handed it to the man. "Buy you a pack. You know him now?"

"He live right there," the man said, pointing to the house across the street.

"What?" Lewis said, looking at the run-down old house. "Right there?"

"Yeah."

"Thanks," Lewis said, heading over to the house.

"But he ain't home till, like, six this evening. He at work now. Come back at, like, six, and he'll be home."

"He live there with anybody else?" Lewis asked.

"He got a wife and two kids. Boy and a girl."

Now Lewis stood on Brian Wilson's porch, after rapping on the door. It was six o'clock.

The door swung open and a man stood behind the black steel security door. He wasn't ugly, but he wasn't handsome, either. He was Lewis's complexion, shorter, heavier set, with a wide nose and thin lips.

"Was up?" Brian Wilson said, not opening the security gate.

"I need to talk to you," Lewis said.

"Who are you?"

"We knew the same girl."

"You still ain't answer my question," Brian said.

"Look, we need to talk. So why don't you just step out here so we can do that?"

Brian smiled, chuckled suspiciously. "Yeah, right. This the hood. I ain't no fool," Brian said, about to close the door on Lewis.

"You knew Selena around the corner?" Lewis said.

Brian held the door open. "Naw, I don't know no Selena."

"Yeah, you do. You used to fuck her."

"Look, fool. I don't know what you talking about. And if you don't get off my porch—"

"You gonna what?" Lewis said, practically pressing his nose to the screen of the door.

"I'm gonna slam this door in your face."

"Then I'll just tell your wife and your kids what you was doing around the corner."

Brian looked back into the house over his shoulder, and then looked back at Lewis. He said, "What's this about, man?"

"Step out."

Brian sighed, unlocked the door, then stepped out onto the porch.

"Now what?"

"Did you know Selena?"

"Yeah, I did. So what? She dead now. I heard it was an overdose, something like that."

Lewis pulled out a tiny snapshot of Layla, handed it to Brian. Brian glanced down at it.

"She cute. So what?"

"Is she yours?" Lewis said.

"What?" Brian said, pushing the picture back into Lewis's hand.

"You used to fuck Selena. She had a baby."

"So? I used to fuck a lot of women. That don't mean that every little shit they give birth to is mine."

"It do when your name is on the birth certificate."

Brian stared at Lewis, serious now. Lewis took the certificate out of his back pocket, held it up to Brian. Brian took it, stared wide-eyed at it, shaking his head.

"Naw. I got two kids, and they upstairs. I ain't got no other kids, and you can't make me say I do."

"I ain't here for that," Lewis said. "Selena always told me this child was mine. I just need for you to tell me that if she ain't mine, but yours, you won't want her. That if I tried to adopt her or something, you won't try and stop me."

"Dude, dude! I swear I won't," Brian said. "But you gotta promise me that you never gonna bring this back to me, mention this to my wife or kids."

"I promise. But you might need to sign something. Adoption papers or something."

"Yeah, yeah, whatever the fuck, man. Just let me know, and I'll do it."

36

The door to the small house opened. Mrs. Weatherly smiled, then stepped forward and gave Daphanie a hug.

"Please, come in."

Daphanie followed Mrs. Weatherly into the living room. It was crowded with old floral-printed, plastic-covered furniture.

"Have a seat, Daphanie," Mrs. Weatherly said. "Would you care for some coffee or tea?"

"No, thanks. I'm fine."

Mrs. Weatherly was Nate's housekeeper, his cook, and Nathaniel's nanny. She did everything for Nate and Nathaniel. That is, until Daphanie came on the scene. After that, sometimes Daphanie would take Nathaniel to the park, or to the bookstore, or to lunch. She would spend time with him in the hopes of creating a bond.

Daphanie liked Mrs. Weatherly, and she felt the older, distinguished woman had liked her as well.

Wearing a blue dress with a white lace collar and cuffs, Mrs. Weatherly sat across from Daphanie. She was a small woman with golden skin and graying hair she wore pinned back.

"I hope you don't mind that I called earlier," Daphanie said. "I missed you. I wanted to make sure that you were alright."

Mrs. Weatherly smiled. "I never got a chance to tell you how sorry I was that things ended between the two of you the way they did. I thought you were perfect for Mr. Kenny. But he was my employer, so I wasn't able to—"

"I understand perfectly."

"How is he? Do you know? Tim called and told me that he survived, but I just haven't found the courage to go and visit him."

"He's fine. And I'm sure when you finally see him, he'll understand. But you said he *was* your employer. What exactly do you mean by that?"

Mrs. Weatherly closed her eyes a moment.

"I was resting in the coach house. Maybe I shouldn't have, but I had taken a sleep aid. I hadn't heard the shots, but for some reason I had just woken up, sat straight up in bed. I had gotten this awful feeling that something was terribly wrong. I put on a coat and hurried to the house. When I walked in . . ." Mrs. Weatherly gasped. "There were police and yellow tape. Neither Mr. or Mrs. Kenny were there, but my God, the blood all over the place. Those dear, poor souls. I fainted."

Daphanie got up, sat beside Mrs. Weatherly, wrapped her arm around the woman.

"It's okay. It was a natural reaction."

"I thought I would come here to my sister's house, take a week off. You know, get over the trauma of what happened. But I can't. I've tried. But I can't go back. I've told Mr. Kenny's brother, but I have not told Mr. Kenny yet. I can never go back there."

"He'll need someone to take care of him when he's released from the hospital," Daphanie said. "Someone to watch Nathaniel and Layla. Mrs. Kenny—how is she?"

"She's in a coma. They don't know if she'll wake up." Mrs. Weatherly shook her head. "They're going to need someone to take care of them. I would, but . . . I just can't," Mrs. Weatherly said, lowering her eyes.

Daphanie patted Mrs. Weatherly's hand. "It's okay. It's understandable."

The older woman looked up. "Nate trusted you before. Why don't you do it?"

"I might have to," Daphanie said, acting as though she weren't sure she wanted the responsibility. "Yes. I think I might have to."

37

The next day, Abbey pulled Nate's Mercedes to a halt in front of the large brick house atop the small hill.

"This is it?" Nate said, not looking back at Lewis, who sat in the backseat.

"Yeah, this is where Kia lives."

"And you said she'd talk to us. You're sure?"

"Yeah. I called her yesterday," Lewis said. "She ain't want to, but I convinced her."

"You better not be wasting my time," Nate said, opening the passenger door.

Lewis didn't respond, just opened his door and climbed out of the car. Standing at the front door, after ringing the doorbell, Nate, Lewis, and Abbey waited for someone to answer.

The door opened after a moment. Kia stood in the doorway. She was slender, tall, and beautiful. She looked like a model on her day off, wearing jeans and a T-shirt, with her hair pulled back.

"How are you, Lewis?" Kia said, opening her arms to give him a hug.

"I'm okay," Lewis said, hugging her.

Afterward, she turned around without addressing Nate and Abbey, and said, "You can come in." Kia walked everyone into the large, expensively decorated living room. "You can have a seat if you like."

Lewis sat on the sofa. Nate carefully lowered himself into a chair with Abbey's help, then Abbey took the chair beside him.

Kia sat beside Lewis. She pressed her palms together and placed them between her knees.

"So you're the man that ruined Freddy's life," Kia said, finally eyeing Nate.

"I was trying to help him," Nate said.

"Bullshit," Kia spat. "He was doing fine by himself. He had gotten his real estate license. He and Lewis were going to start their own company. He was getting his life together, and then you came along."

"Ms. Martin, I'm sorry for the way things—"

"We were going to have a baby," Kia said, emotion in her voice.

Lewis placed his arm around her shoulders, pulled her close to him. "It's okay, Kia."

"Like I said, I'm sorry, but—"

"Your apology doesn't do shit for me—or for Freddy. I wish he did kill you!"

"Kia!" Lewis said, staring at her, shocked.

Kia closed her eyes, wiped a tear.

Looking at Nate, Kia said, "That was wrong. I don't wish that. I'm sorry. It's just all that I went through, and now this."

"I understand," Nate said. "And I accept your apology. And after hearing what Lewis told you Freddy did, I'm sure you can understand why I need to find him, why I need to find my son."

"He didn't take your son. Freddy wouldn't do that," Kia said.

"I don't know that for sure. I don't know him like you do. But if you can tell me what he said to you the last time you two spoke . . ."

"I told this to the police already," Kia said.

"Good. Can you tell me now?" Nate said.

Kia sniffed. "A few nights ago, he came by. I could tell something was really wrong. He said he did something bad. That he had to do it to make up for what you did to him."

"That's it?" Nate said.

"That's all he said."

"Did he say where he was going?"

"No."

"Do you know where he was going? Where he could possibly be?"

"The only place I would know Freddy to go would be home. And since that isn't there anymore, I don't know where he is."

An hour later, Nate, Abbey, and Lewis were in the small, dark living room of Freddy's Uncle Henry's home.

Nate was exhausted, and in a fair amount of pain, so he was sitting. Lewis sat as well. Mrs. Ford walked in from getting the glass of water Nate wanted. She handed it to him, then was met by Abbey, who stepped directly in front of her.

On the drive over, Nate had told Abbey that she should be the one who questioned Mrs. Ford.

"Ford's ex-girlfriend did apologize for what she said, but I do believe she would prefer me dead," Nate said. "I imagine his mother has even stronger feelings, so it'd probably be best if you do the questioning."

"Yes, sir," Abbey said as she drove. "What should the tone of the questioning be?"

Nate thought for a moment. "Whatever tone you think will get the information we need."

Now, standing in the living room with Mrs. Ford, Abbey smiled thinly and said, "My name is Abbey Kurt. Like Mr. Waters told you, we've come to you with just a few questions regarding your son."

"Okay," Mrs. Ford said, seeming very nervous.

"Good," Abbey said. "As you know by now, your son is responsible for the shooting of two individuals. The police are trying to find him. He's obviously in hiding. Do you know where he is?"

Nate stared intently into the older woman's eyes, hoping he would be able to tell if she was lying.

"I don't know nothing."

"When was the last time you saw your son?"

"Four nights ago, I think. I don't really remember. It was late, like midnight. He said he had to go. He did something bad. The police would be looking for him. I told him I ain't want to know."

"Where would he go?"

"I don't know. Only friend he had was Lewis, right there, and ya'll ain't talking no more, right?"

Lewis shook his head.

"So you have no idea of where your own son is? That's what you're trying to have us believe?" Abbey said coolly, pacing before Mrs. Ford.

"I ain't trying to have you believe nothing. I'm just telling you what is."

"He hasn't tried to contact you?"

"No."

"You haven't seen him since that night?"

"No."

Abbey stopped her pacing and stood directly in front of Mrs. Ford.

"Do you love your son?"

"What kind of question—"

"Just answer it."

"Yes."

"Even though he killed your husband in his sleep?"

Lewis stood. "How you gonna ask—"

Abbey held up a palm, quieting Lewis.

Mrs. Ford looked shocked, as if thinking that was information that only she knew.

Abbey continued. "I don't have to inform you that your son is a violent, remorseless killer. The police know he has a gun, and they consider him armed and dangerous. There is a good chance they will shoot him on sight when they find him. Is that what you want, Mrs. Ford?" Abbey said, raising her voice.

"No."

"Do you want your only son to be gunned down in the street?"

"No!"

"Then tell us where he is!" Abbey yelled.

"I don't know where he is!" Mrs. Ford cried, tears in her eyes.

"Then when they find him, they will kill him, and they will come and get you, lock you up for obstruction of justice, and you will have nothing. That's what you'll have. Nothing."

"That's enough," Lewis said, stepping over to Freddy's mother, comforting her.

Mrs. Ford dropped her face in her hands, bawling. "I don't know nothing."

Abbey was about to take another run at her when Nate touched her on the arm, shook his head.

Nate stepped over to the sobbing woman. "Mrs. Ford, I'm the man your son shot."

Mrs. Ford looked up, tears running down her face.

"You're the man that took my husband's house from me."

Nate was silent. "Yes. I took your house, then your son came and shot me and my wife, and took my three-year-old son. Wherever he is, whatever he's going through, he's taking my son through it, too."

Mrs. Ford lowered her head. "I'm sorry. Your baby shouldn't be involved in this."

"And I'm sorry for you." In a soft voice, Nate asked, "Is there anything you think you can tell us that will help us find your son and mine? Anything. Even if you don't think it's important."

Mrs. Ford shut her eyes, shook her head.

"Anything, Mrs. Ford."

Finally, Mrs. Ford said, "Right before I stopped him from telling me where he was going, he said he was leaving."

"That's what he said, just like that? He was leaving?" Nate asked compassionately.

"Yeah. Not like he was just leaving home, but like he was going far away. You know, leaving Chicago."

"Thank you, Mrs. Ford," Nate said, reaching into his suit pocket and pulling out his business card. "If your son happens to contact you, do you think you can please let me know?"

Mrs. Ford took the card, wiped tears from her cheeks, but did not answer.

38

It was one A.M. **Freddy** pushed the blankets off himself. He was fully clothed.

He got out of bed. He had not slept at all, knowing what he must do.

He had told Joni good night two hours ago as he was standing outside her bedroom door with her.

"You okay?" Joni had asked, smiling.

"I'm alright."

"Are you having an okay time? Are you glad you came?" Joni was holding his hand again. It was a habit she had picked up over the last day. He didn't hold her hand back, so her grasp on his fingers was weak.

"I'm glad I came."

His answer was not enthusiastic, but it was sincere.

Joni smiled wide, tightened her grip on his fingers. "Why don't you prove it? Sleep in my room tonight."

"I can't, Joni."

"You don't love me anymore?"

"Joni."

"You don't even care about me?"

"You know I care about you, but this isn't the time. I told you that."

"Okay. But you're here now. We're gonna find the time, right?"

Freddy had done his best to smile. "Yeah. Sure."

Freddy pulled the blankets back up now, set the pillow neatly on top of them at the head of the bed.

He quietly snuck out of his room and into Nathaniel's. The boy was sleeping heavily, as usual.

Freddy slid open the dresser drawer and took out only the clothes that Nathaniel had been wearing the day Freddy brought him here. In the drawer, he left the four outfits that Joni had bought for him at the mall. Freddy slipped the tiny pair of jeans onto Nathaniel, sat him up, and stretched the T-shirt over his head.

He lifted Nathaniel from the bed, cradled him in his arms, then carried him out of the room.

Once Freddy laid Nathaniel in the backseat of the car, he climbed into the front and slid the key into the ignition. Without starting the car, he shifted it into neutral. He got behind the car, pushed it down the slight decline of the hill. It rolled a good hundred feet, then came to a stop.

Freddy sadly looked back toward the house, up at Joni's window, then lowered himself into the car. He started it, then drove away.

After driving only ten minutes, Freddy braked at a stoplight. Waiting for it to change green, he realized he still had no plan. He was behind the wheel of his car, the boy in the back, but he had no idea of what direction his car was even pointed in.

Freddy left because he felt that the police and Nate Kenny would find him and take him down. And when they did, they most likely wouldn't care that Joni was innocent, and they would take her down, too. As much as he was trying to fight it, Freddy was developing feelings for the girl again. He couldn't allow himself to let her fall with him. The light turned green. Freddy kept his foot on the brake.

He had less money than when he had left Chicago. He had no other friends. There was nowhere else he could think to go.

He pressed gently on the accelerator and pulled the wheel hard to the left, making a U-turn.

Fifteen minutes later, Freddy walked back through Joni's front door, the boy still sleeping in his arms. All the lights were still off, the house quiet. He was glad Joni had not been awakened. Freddy nudged the door closed with his shoulder, walked across the living room toward the stairs, and mounted them.

"I wish you would've at least told me you were leaving."

It was Joni. When Freddy turned, he barely saw her there, in a corner of the room, sitting.

"Whatever you did must be really bad," Joni said, her face and body cloaked in shadows. "You ain't got nowhere else to go."

39

Daphanie was disappointed after walking into Nate's hospital room the next day and finding nothing but an empty bed. She stepped out of the room, walked down to the nurses' station.

"Was Mr. Kenny moved to another room?" Daphanie asked a nurse with graying hair and glasses.

"The man in 312?"

"Yes."

"No. He discharged himself two days ago."

"Thank you," Daphanie said.

Why hadn't he told her? He could've at least called. She could've given him a ride home. Suddenly Daphanie thought about Monica. Had she awakened? Had Nate taken her home with him?

Daphanie turned and hurried down the hall. When she approached Monica's room, through the glass window in the door she saw that Monica was still there, still in a coma. But there was someone in the room with her. It was a man, brown-skinned, handsome, with unruly black hair.

He was sitting in a bedside chair. With both his hands, he held one of Monica's, his face pressed to it. It looked as though he were praying, or crying. Maybe both. Trying not to be seen, Daphanie stood by the door and watched.

Who was this man? Judging by his younger age, and the way he was dressed, in jeans and a T-shirt, he couldn't have been an acquaintance of Nate's. This had to be Monica's friend. But by the look of grief he was displaying, he looked to be more than just a friend.

After another five minutes, Daphanie saw the man stand. He pushed the chair to the corner of the room, stepped back to the bed, then appeared to be saying something. He wiped at his cheek, then leaned over and kissed Monica lightly on her lips. Yes. He was far more than a friend, Daphanie thought, stepping away from the door and walking off the ward. The door to the elevator she stood by opened and closed three times while she waited for the man to appear. Finally she saw him walking down the hall toward her.

He walked up to the elevator, punched the down button, then stepped back. He smiled briefly at Daphanie, then turned away.

When the elevator door opened, the man allowed Daphanie to enter first, then he stepped on.

On the ground floor, when the door opened again, Daphanie stepped off and allowed the man to walk a few paces into the hospital's lobby before she said, "How do you know Monica Kenny?"

"Who are you?" Lewis said, turning.

"Daphanie Coleman. As of a month ago, I was Nate Kenny's fiancée."

When Lewis heard that, he started speaking hurriedly and harshly about what an evil man Nate was. Daphanie told him that if he didn't mind walking across the street with her to the café there, she would buy him lunch.

Forty-five minutes later, Daphanie had learned everything. From how Lewis and Nate had first met when Lewis plowed into the back of Nate's Bentley, demolishing it, to how Nate had blackmailed Lewis's best friend Freddy and set Lewis up to be sent to prison.

"So Nate knew the man who shot him?" Daphanie said.

"Yes, he knew him," Lewis said, a sandwich and chips before him that he had not touched. "Nate brought all that on himself, and he's acting like the victim."

"And you and Monica were supposed to marry, until Nate came back in the picture?"

"That's right. She was raising my child, but now Nate has her, and won't give her back to me."

"What?" Daphanie said, shocked.

"I tried to get her back, but I couldn't. I'm kinda afraid to, but I think I gotta go to the police."

"No," Daphanie said, not knowing exactly why she said it.

"Why not?"

"I don't know yet. But you still love Monica. I could tell by seeing you in that room with her. You want her back?"

"I do."

"And I want Nate. I think that maybe we just might be able to help each other."

40

Nate walked between the desks at the downtown police precinct, Abbey two steps behind him. He stopped at Davis's and Martins's desks. Only Martins was there, filling in blank lines on a police report.

"Detective Martins," Nate said.

Detective Martins stood up, extending his hand to Nate, and both men shook.

"Davis told me he spoke to you, and I'm sorry this case isn't moving faster, but—"

"You're not going to find Ford in Chicago. He's left."

"How do you know that?"

"I spoke to his mother this morning, and—"

"We spoke to her, and she said she knew nothing."

"She thought it was nothing. Ford is gone, Detective Martins, trust me. Please expand the search to include the entire country, and I'll raise the reward to a hundred thousand dollars. Will you do that?"

"Mr. Kenny, maybe if—"

"Detective Martins, will you do that, or is there someone with more authority I need to speak to?"

"No. I'll go back, speak to the mother again, and do what you've asked."

41

Lewis sat at a table in an Arby's Restaurant. Eva sat across from him eating some curly fries and sipping from a strawberry shake. Lewis hadn't ordered food. He had come back to the DCFS building after meeting that Daphanie woman, hoping Eva took her lunch at that time. He didn't know why he had felt compelled to come back. He knew there was really nothing she could do for him until he found out for sure if Layla was his. He just needed someone to talk to.

"It's like you're the only person I can tell this stuff to right now," Lewis confessed.

"What stuff?" Eva said. "You didn't come back the other day. Is everything alright?"

Lewis looked up at Eva. "I don't know if she's mine."

"If who is yours?"

"Layla. My daughter. I ain't come back because my name wasn't on the birth certificate," Lewis said, dropping his head. "I found the guy who was on it. He don't want nothing to do with Layla."

"You gotta find out if she's yours. You gotta take a paternity—"

"I know, I know. I'll do that tomorrow, I hope."

"Good. Once you get the results, then you can start the process of getting her back."

Lewis looked up sadly. "But what if she ain't mine?"

"When you think about her, about all the time you two have been together, in your heart do you feel like she's yours?"

Lewis thought for a moment, and the answer was an undeniable "Yes."

Eva reached across the table, grabbed Lewis's hand, squeezed it, and smiled.

"Then the test will prove that."

42

Freddy paced back and forth across the living room, worried.

Joni had taken Nathaniel to the mall and the grocery store. That had been five hours ago.

He hadn't wanted her to go. Early this morning, Freddy had woken up to what he thought was talking. He propped himself up on his elbows in bed and listened. His bedroom window was open. He climbed out of bed, walked to the window, and peered out.

It was still dark outside. Freddy wasn't able to make out the words, but he heard the sound of Joni's voice. He knew the other voice belonged to Sam.

He wasn't able to see either of them. They stood under the porch roof. But sitting in front of the house was Sam's old Impala.

By the time Joni stepped back into the house and closed the door, Freddy was standing in the center of the living room, his arms crossed over his chest.

Joni turned, jumped, startled to see Freddy there shaking his head.

"He beat you and you're still talking to his ass. What the fuck, Joni?"

"It's not what you think."

"Oh, really. You two weren't just talking," Freddy said, feeling the slightest bit of jealousy.

"I was telling him I can't see him anymore, because I'm seeing someone else."

"And who is . . ." Freddy caught himself before he finished asking the question, just realizing what she was saying.

"I know we ain't really talk about getting back together. And I know you was just trying to sneak out last night."

"I wasn't trying to sneak out. There's just some things that's happening, that—"

She stepped quickly to him, pressed herself against him.

"Then tell me. You can trust me. I want you back, and it seems to me that you need me. We can be together, right?"

Freddy had wrapped his arms around Joni, realizing just how right she was. He did need her. "Yeah, baby. Maybe."

Now Freddy was standing in the front doorway, looking out the screen door, wondering where in the hell that girl was. He had tried calling her several times on her cell, but all his calls went straight to voice mail.

Freddy was about to walk back into the house and close the door when Joni's black Celica slowly pulled up in front of the house. Freddy pushed through the door and stood on the porch, waiting for Joni to exit with Nathaniel, but she did not. She just sat behind the wheel of the car, staring down at the floor.

"Joni," Freddy called to her. She didn't respond, so Freddy hurried down the steps.

As he approached the car, he saw Nathaniel crying in the passenger seat, slapping his little palms against the glass. Freddy ran around the front of the car, grabbed the driver's-side door handle, and flung the door open.

"Joni, what's wrong? What happened?"

Big dark sunglasses hung on Joni's face as she looked up at him. Freddy could see the redness and the swelling from the fresh bruises around the shades.

"Joni, no," Freddy said, shaking his head. "Please don't tell me that man put his hands on you again."

A tear ran down her puffy, swollen cheek.

"Take the glasses off, Joni."

Joni shook her head, sobbing softly.

"Joni!" Freddy yelled. "Take off the fucking glasses!"

Joni crossed her arms, holding herself, leaning away from Freddy.

"I'm sorry, baby. Please," Freddy said, softening his tone. "I need to see."

Joni slowly pulled the glasses from her eyes to reveal the horrible beating she had taken. Both her eyes were swollen and bruised. Her left eye was practically swollen shut. Her lips were puffy and bloodstained, as well as her nose.

All Freddy could imagine was Sam, as big as he was, standing over Joni, slamming his fists into this poor girl's face over and over again. How could he do that? Freddy thought, his heart aching. Freddy hated to be forced into this corner again, but there would be hell to pay for this. He gently reached into the car and helped Joni out of it. She cringed and moaned a bit. He walked her around to the other side of the car, opened the door for Nathaniel, and then walked both Joni and Nathaniel up the steps and into the house.

43

Nate sat in one of the living room chairs, an end table lamp dimly lit beside him. The rest of the house was dark.

His cell phone sat in his lap. He had just hung up after a phone call with his brother.

"You sure you're okay?" Tim had asked him.

"Yeah. Fine."

"You have something there to eat? I could bring something by."

"No. I had Abbey stop by the grocery store before dropping me off," Nate lied. "I'm good."

"And company? I could come by. You know your nephew is dying to see you. And I could bring Layla. Don't you want to—"

"Tell you the truth, it'd be too much right now, Tim. But I appreciate it," Nate said. He sat there in the chair, wearing slacks, socks, house slippers, and a white collared shirt, a white T-shirt underneath. He stared blankly at the space before him.

"You gonna be ready to take her tomorrow?" Tim asked. "It's no rush, though. She can stay here for as long as you need her to."

"I'll be fine. Everything is in place," Nate lied again.

He had spoken to Mrs. Weatherly today. She apologized pro-fusely, but said she was unable to come back to work for him. He had no one to replace her on such short notice, but he needed to see Layla again. He missed the little girl and was surprised by how much she had grown on him in the short time she had lived there at the house. Without his son and without Monica, Nate thought he'd go crazy before long in that house by himself.

"Yeah, bring her by tomorrow."

Nate looked down at his cell phone now. He picked it up, scrolled through the menu, and punched the button to dial Freddy Ford. The phone rang only once, as it had previously done the several times Nate tried calling this number.

"Leave one," Freddy's voice on the voice mail message demanded.

Nate hated that message after hearing it for something like the tenth time.

"You have my son. Bring him back to me, or tell me where you are. I'll come get him, and . . . and . . . I won't even tell the police. Just give me back my son."

Nate disconnected the call.

He stood from the chair. It was approaching ten P.M. He wasn't sleepy. His stomach growled. There was nothing he could do. There was no food, and he simply was not in the mood to drive himself to the store, or even wait on delivery.

He could go up to his office, search online for any informa-tion that would help find Freddy, but he had already done that for hours today. Besides, Abbey was much better at it than he was, and he knew she was working diligently somewhere that very moment.

Nate had reached over to turn off the lamp when he was startled by the ring of the doorbell. He froze, wondering who it could be. The last time he answered the door . . . Nate shook the thought. He cautiously walked to the door, wrapped his hand around the knob, placed his face close to the door.

"Who is it?" His voice was tentative.

"I'm sorry to come by at this hour," Nate heard a woman say through the door. "It's Daphanie."

Fifteen minutes later, Nate sat with Daphanie at his dining room table. He was eating a turkey sandwich she had made him with mayo, lettuce, and tomato.

When he had opened the door, her arms had been filled with three bags of groceries.

"I wasn't sure. But just in case you hadn't gone shopping," she had said, smiling.

Now, after finishing the first half of the sandwich, Nate took three huge gulps from the glass of orange juice, then looked up at Daphanie, who was sitting in the chair adjacent to him, smiling.

"How did you know I was home?"

"When I came to visit you, one of the nurses told me you checked yourself out. Why did you do it? You sure you're okay?"

"There are things I need to take care of."

"Okay."

"You didn't have to bring me food like this."

"I didn't? All you had in your fridge were condiments. What were you going to have, a ketchup-and-mustard milkshake?"

Nate cracked a smile. "I guess. I really appreciate it, but . . " he began, the smile no longer on his face. "This still doesn't change—"

"Nate," Daphanie said, stopping him. "When I told you I loved you, did you believe me?"

"Yes."

"That's because it was true. You made a decision about who you want to be with. But when you get gunned down in your home, do you think I stop caring about you?"

Looking down at his food, Nate said, "No."

"I respect your decision, and I'll honor it. But I'm not going to lie and say I don't still care about you. You've been hurt, and if you need help, you know I'm here for you. You know that, don't you?"

Nate looked up, nodded his head.

"I need you to know I'm not doing any of this to try to win you back. I just want to be here for you. As a matter of fact, I happen to be on vacation for a while, so . . ."

Nate sighed. So far he had kept Daphanie in the dark. Yes, she had asked who had put him in the hospital, but she didn't push any further when he told her he simply didn't know. Nate was in need right now. He didn't want to have to rush to find someone he trusted to care for Layla, or any of his other matters in the home. Knowing him the way she did, Daphanie was completely aware of that. He wasn't sure if Daphanie was telling him the truth about respecting the decision he had made in choosing Monica, but Nate hadn't known Daphanie to ever lie to him, so he felt he could trust her now. He wouldn't disclose everything, but there was some information she'd have to know, if he was to allow her to help him.

"As a matter of fact," Nate finally said, "I'm expecting someone tomorrow, and right now I don't think I'll be able to take care of her by myself. Can you help me?"

Daphanie smiled. "Of course I can."

44

Joni sat behind the wheel of her car, near tears. Nathaniel lay in the backseat sleeping. It was approaching ten P.M., and it had long been dark.

"Joni," Freddy said from the passenger side of the car. "You gotta take me to him."

"Why?" Joni said. "What are you gonna do to him?"

"Do you really care? Look what he did to your face. Do you see?" Freddy said, jerking the rearview mirror over to show Joni her reflection. She glanced up at herself for a moment, then looked away.

"I don't care what happens to him. I care what happens to you. You got a temper, Freddy. I ain't forget that."

"Start the car, Joni. We're going over there, and I'm letting this motherfucker know that he can't put his hands on you no more, that he can't bring his ass around your house no more."

"And why can't he do that, Freddy?" Joni said, wiping at her eyes.

It took Freddy a moment to say it.

"Because you my girl now."

—

Joni didn't know about the gun nestled in the back of the waist-band of Freddy's jeans. He hoped he didn't have to use it, but he wouldn't hesitate for a second if he needed to. When Joni pulled the Celica up in front of Sam's place, Freddy was happy to see it was a small wooden shotgun house in the middle of nowhere. There was enough distance between his house and the next, blocks away, that a gunshot probably wouldn't be heard.

"What are you gonna do, Freddy?"

"Talk to him," Freddy said, staring up at the house through his window. "Talk to him is all." He turned to Joni. "Wait out here in the car with Nathaniel, you hear me? No matter what you hear, don't come in. And if I ain't out in—"

"What do you mean, if you ain't out?"

"If I ain't out in ten minutes, then leave."

"Freddy, I ain't—"

"Drive off! You hear me?"

"Yes," Joni said.

Freddy leaned over, kissed Joni on the lips, then climbed out of the car. He lifted his seat, reached back, and grabbed the base-ball bat he had found in Joni's basement from off the backseat floor.

"What is that for?" Joni said, seeing the bat for the first time.

"Just in case," Freddy said, closing the door.

He carried the bat close to his leg, trying his best to hide it. Lights were on in the front room of the small house. On the rotting wood porch, Freddy heard a TV playing loudly. Freddy knocked on the door. When there was no answer, he banged much harder three times with the side of his fist. Moments later, Sam was opening the door.

Before he could swing it open all the way, Freddy kicked it, forcing Sam to stumble backward, tripping over his feet and fall-ing to his back.

He was carrying a gun. From the floor, he looked to be try-ing to aim it at Freddy. Freddy rushed over to him, swung the bat, clubbing Sam's hand, knocking the gun away.

Sam cried out in pain, but the sound was nothing compared to the shriek he made, when Freddy whirled the bat over his head and brought it down in an angry chopping motion across Sam's left shin.

Freddy heard the loud crack when he made contact. He swung the bat again, breaking the other leg. He threw the bat aside, straddled Sam, and started pummeling his face with his fist.

"Fucking hit my girl!" Freddy said, feeling his knuckles open up against one of Sam's teeth. "Motherfucker!" Freddy yelled, bashing his fists against the man's blood-covered face six more times.

When Freddy was finished, Sam barely moved. His eyelids were only slightly open, but Freddy saw the man's eyes follow-ing him as he climbed off Sam's body, walked over, and grabbed Sam's gun. Freddy stood over him again, his feet on either side of the beaten man's shoulders. The gun was pointed between his eyes.

"She told you to leave her alone," Freddy said, the gun shak-ing in his hand. "Give me one fucking reason why I shouldn't kill you right now."

"Pluh . . . pluh . . . please," Sam said softly, blood spilling from his lips. "I'll never do it again."

Freddy believed him. But that didn't mean the man shouldn't die. He needed to be held accountable for his fucked-up actions, just like Mr. Kenny did. But Freddy was trying to stop his killing. The cop had had to die because he might have tried to bring Freddy in. This fool posed no real threat to him.

"I ever see you again," Freddy said, bending over and placing the barrel of the gun flush against the man's forehead, "I swear I'll kill you. Understand?"

Sam nodded.

Freddy stepped over the man, stuck Sam's gun in the waistband of his jeans with his own piece. He walked out of the house, down to Joni's car, and climbed in. Blood covered both his fists and stained his forearms.

"Freddy! What did you do?" Joni practically screamed.

"I took care of that shit. Now drive, please."

45

Lewis sat in the passenger seat of Daphanie's car, looking out at the one-story white laboratory building. Layla was in his lap.

"Daddy, where's this?"

"It's nowhere, baby," Lewis said, hating to have to lie to her.

He hated everything about what was going on at this moment. But he was thankful to Daphanie. She called this morning and told Lewis she had a surprise for him. "Tell me where you live, and I'll pick you up," she said, and soon showed up with Layla. After hugging and kissing his daughter, Lewis stopped to ask Daphanie how she had done it.

Daphanie told him everything. "I love Nate, but it's wrong for him to stop you from seeing your daughter," she added.

Lewis was overjoyed to finally be reunited with Layla, but sad as well. "She might not even be mine," Lewis sadly admitted. "I'm gonna have to get a paternity test."

"I know someone at a lab downtown. She'll get you in and out the same day," Daphanie said, after agreeing he needed to do it.

But now, Layla in his lap, Lewis asked, "Why do we have to go in there?"

Daphanie pulled her key from the ignition. "What are you talking about?"

"I have my daughter," Lewis said softly. "I talked to the other man. I know the aunt and the grandmother don't want her. So, I don't need proof. I have her now. I can just keep her."

"No," Daphanie said. "You can't. Nate trusted me with her. I come back without her, then what?"

"Then you tell him her father has her."

"Then everything is ruined. He'll know I know you. He'll never trust me, and I'll never get what I want."

Lewis looked at Layla, kissed her on the forehead.

"I'd be sorry about that. But . . ."

"I see," Daphanie said. "You do that, and you'll be no better than your friend. You'd be just like him, on the run. You would be on the street, constantly looking over your shoulder. Is that any way to raise that little girl?"

"No," Lewis agreed sadly.

"Do this the right way, please. Let's just go in there and take the test," Daphanie said. "Everything will come back the way you know it will, and then you can do this the legal way."

An hour after the lab tech stuck what looked like a long Q-tip in Lewis's and Layla's mouths, taking a DNA sample from both, Lewis, Layla, and Daphanie continued sitting in the waiting room. Lewis stood from his chair for the tenth time.

"I thought you said you knew these people. What's taking them so long?"

"It takes time, Lewis. Just calm down and relax."

"Calm down and relax," Layla mimicked, sitting in the chair between them.

She was flipping through the pages of a *Glamour* magazine.

"Yeah, do what she says," Daphanie said, smiling.

"I can't," Lewis said, sitting again. "What if she's not—"

"Stop it. We'll find out in a few minutes."

"Mr. Waters," Daphanie's friend, a tall woman wearing a lab coat, said from behind the counter.

Lewis stood, staring down at Daphanie. "Go over there and get the results. I don't wanna go."

"Lewis," Daphanie said, standing.

"Please. Just get them, alright? I'll be right here."

"Okay," Daphanie said. She walked over to the counter. Lewis saw her receive an envelope from the woman. The two ladies laughed a little, and Lewis heard Daphanie say, "Thanks, girl. I'll talk to you later."

When she came back, Lewis said, "So?"

"What do you mean, so? They're in the envelope. You have to open it to find out. You want to do that now?"

Lewis lowered himself back into his chair. "Yes."

Daphanie held out the results to him.

"No, you do it," Lewis said.

Daphanie opened the envelope, reached in, and was about to pull out the results when Lewis snatched the envelope from her.

"No! Not now. Not here." He scooped Layla up in his arms and said, "Let's go."

In the car, Lewis sat, Layla in his arms again, the envelope on the dashboard. He stared at it.

"I'm going to start the car now," Daphanie said. "You ready to go?"

"I don't know why I'm tripping about this," Lewis said. "I know what the results gonna be. Layla is mine," he said confidently. "I know she is." He turned Layla in his lap to face him. "You my daughter, right? You my little girl?"

· "Yes, Daddy. I'm your little girl," Layla said.

"That's what I'm talking about," Lewis said, kissing his daughter again. "That's all I need to know." Lewis grabbed the envelope and passed it to Daphanie. "Go on open that up, and tell me what I already know."

"Now, that's how I like to hear you talk."

As Daphanie opened the envelope and pulled the results page out, Lewis held tight to Layla. Yes, he felt confident, but he squeezed her anyway, closed his eyes, and prayed as hard as he could that Layla was his.

With his eyes still closed, his daughter pressed so close to him, he could practically feel her heart beating. Daphanie said, "Okay, let me see, let me see," as she looked over the results.

There was a pause—a moment of silence—but still Lewis didn't open his eyes, just prayed harder. Then he heard Daphanie's voice. It was soft, and sadder than a moment ago.

"God," Daphanie said. "I'm so sorry, Lewis, but this says she's not yours."

46

Nate had been sitting by Monica's bedside, holding her hand as he watched television.

He turned to her. "I spoke to those damn worthless detectives today. They said they still haven't found anything. They said that Ford must've left the state like I suspected. What else is new? But they feel he must know someone, that he must be holed up somewhere, because no one has seen him."

Nate looked up at the television screen.

"Oh, this is a funny part."

Playing on the screen was a DVD he and Monica had watched at least half a dozen times when they were married. It was hilarious. Nate had brought it from the house. He needed to try to laugh in spite of everything.

"Remember this, babe?" Nate said, looking to Monica, praying that she would just wake up at that moment, as he prayed every time he looked at her.

But she wouldn't, not then, not ever, a voice inside his head told him.

"Shut up!" Nate told himself.

The negative thoughts came every now and again, but he had always found the strength to push them back. But with each day that passed, it was becoming harder and harder.

He laid his head on Monica's bed, brought her hand to his lips, and kissed her fingers. He closed his eyes, wanting to do nothing but just lay there with his wife forever. Then Nate felt a movement. It was a twitch from Monica's hand. Nate bolted straight up in his chair, his eyes wide open.

"Baby!" he said, shocked. "Are you waking up?"

He saw her hand twitch again, this time more forcefully.

Nate ran to the door, threw it open, leaned out of it, and yelled to the first person he saw, "Get a doctor! Hurry! I think my wife is waking up!"

He hurried back into the room, a huge smile on his face, but was met with something that tore that smile away. Monica's whole body was jerking, shaking violently in bed, the monitors beside her screaming.

Nate ran to her side, grabbed her hand. There was a white foam oozing from her mouth.

"Someone!" Nate yelled, still clutching tight to Monica's hand, not knowing what else to do, not wanting to leave her side. "Anyone! My wife is having a seizure!"

A doctor, a tall, pale man, ran in, a short nurse behind him. When they saw Monica flailing about in bed, the doctor ordered Nate away from her side. He turned to the nurse. "Get a crash cart in here, *stat*! Call a code blue."

Another nurse raced into the room, followed by someone pushing a crash cart.

The second nurse, a thin woman with freckles, said, "I'm sorry, sir, but you're going to have to step out."

She was trying to pull a curtain across one half of the room.

"But that's my wife," Nate said, hearing the doctor order ten cc's of epinephrine.

"What's he doing? What's going on?" Nate was frantic.

"Sir, you have to leave the room. Please!" The nurse said, pushing him toward the door. "If you want us to save her, you have to leave!"

Half an hour later, Nate was allowed back into Monica's room. He stood on one side of her bed; the tall doctor, whose name was Dr. Paulson, stood on the other.

"We had to connect her to a respirator," the doctor said sadly.

This was another machine that had been pushed into the room. A tube came from it that snaked down Monica's throat. The machine was loud. It pushed air into her lungs, and Nate stood there staring in anguish as he saw her chest inflate and deflate.

"Why did you have to do this to her?"

"She was having trouble breathing on her own. I don't think we'll have to have her on for long, but we'll see."

Nate didn't want to ask the question, but forced himself.

"Does this mean she's worse? Does this mean she'll die?"

Dr. Paulson looked at Nate and said, quite frankly, "Yes, her condition has declined some. But that doesn't necessarily mean she won't wake up and be just fine."

"But the chances of that are worse?" Nate said.

"I'm afraid so."

47

Lewis stood on the porch of the very small house Eva lived in. It was ten-fifteen P.M. She had given Lewis her cell phone number when they had met for lunch, and told him to call her if he ever needed to talk. Tonight he had done that. It had been nine-thirty at night when he had called.

"I'm sorry for it being so late, but I really need to talk to you."

"It's fine. What's on your mind?" Eva said.

"No. In person. Can I come by?"

There was silence.

Finally, Eva said, "I have a four-year-old daughter. She's asleep, and to tell the truth, Lewis, I don't know you that well."

"I don't wanna come in. Just come outside your door. Please, Eva," Lewis begged. "Just ten minutes. I got the test results back, and I just need to talk."

The front door opened. Eva stepped out wearing jeans and a T-shirt. Lewis stood there, his arms at his sides, his eyes red, looking as though he were on the verge of tears.

"Lewis, it's going to be alright," Eva said.

That moment, a tear ran down Lewis's cheek, then another. Eva stepped closer to Lewis, opened her arms.

Lewis threw himself into her, saying, "She's not mine. She's not mine."

"Shhh, shhh, shhh," Eva said, holding Lewis tight.

After ten minutes, Eva and Lewis sat on the porch steps.

Lewis wiped away his tears and said, "She was all I had. Her mother died, then the woman that I thought I was going to marry left me for her ex-husband. I been out of work so many times . . . but Layla was always there. I was a loser at everything else, but I always thought I was a good father. Now I'm not even that."

"You are still that," Eva said, sitting very close to Lewis. "Just because you aren't her biological father doesn't mean you aren't her father. Nothing's changed."

"I have no rights," Lewis said angrily. "That man has Layla, and he doesn't have to give her back to me."

"But you said he would, right?"

"Yeah. There's something I have to do for him. If that works out, I get Layla back," Lewis said. "So if that happens, what can I do? Adopt her?"

Eva sighed heavily. "Adoption is a process. Are you working?"

"No."

"Do you have your own place?"

Lewis shook his head.

"I'm sorry, but no one would let you adopt a child under those circumstances. You have to have a stable household, a steady income."

"Then what would happen to her in the meantime?"

"She would go into foster care."

"Then I could be a foster parent. I could get her that way," Lewis said.

"You couldn't. The same rules apply. You have to be working. You have to have a place of your own where the child can live."

"Then what the fuck's the use?" Lewis said, shooting up from the steps, kicking the one he had just stood from.

Eva looked up at him, unshaken. "You don't have those things now, but you can get them. I wanna help you. There's a records clerk position that hasn't even been posted yet. I'm sure I can get you an interview, put a word in for you. I'm in good with the person that hires there."

"You'd do that for me?" Lewis said, somewhat upbeat.

"You ever been convicted of a crime?"

"Not convicted."

"You got your high school diploma?"

"Yeah."

"Then I can do that for you."

Lewis took Eva's hand, pulling her from the steps.

"Thank you," he said, then gave her a hug.

"It's not necessarily the lawful thing to do, and I'm probably the last person that should be telling you to do this. But when you finally get Layla back, just keep her. Don't tell the city or try to adopt her or foster her or anything. Wait till you have that stable home and income, then look into it. You should have no problem at that point, especially since you've been caring for her all her life."

48

The next day, Daphanie sat in the abortion clinic with several other women. Some of them were as old as Daphanie, others looked as young as fifteen or sixteen and sat with their mothers. One girl cradled a teddy bear in her arms.

"Are you sure you wanna go through with this?" Brownie asked.

She was sitting beside Daphanie, holding her hand, sympathy all over her face.

"If I wasn't sure, would we be here?" Daphanie said.

They had been waiting for only half an hour. Women were being called in relatively quickly, and Daphanie figured she should be next.

"So you aren't scared?" Brownie said.

"I'm thirty-seven years old, and this is my first abortion," Daphanie whispered. "Why wouldn't I be?"

"Then don't do it."

"Stop it! Alright?" Daphanie said, shaking her hand loose from Brownie's.

Daphanie felt a woman's eyes on her. Daphanie turned and gave the woman an evil look till she turned away.

"I'm just saying, there has to be a reason, just one, not to do this."

Why in the hell had she even brought Brownie? But if Daphanie really thought about it, the reason she was getting the abortion wasn't because she didn't want the child. She did want to have a baby. She just knew it would ruin her already very slim chance of getting Nate back. She wasn't willing to risk that. Yes, it was shallow and cold as hell. To sacrifice an unborn child for the chance of getting a man. But what else could she do?

As she sat there watching Brownie shaking her head in disgust, Daphanie would've loved to explain to her best friend that if there was any way that she could keep the baby and still make a play at getting Nate back she would, but— Then, like a kick to the head, the idea struck Daphanie. Hey eyes brightened as she saw the idea develop fully in her mind.

A door opened at the far end of the waiting room. A woman wearing a scrub top and glasses poked her head out and read from a clipboard.

"Daphanie C."

Daphanie didn't even hear the woman.

"Daphanie C.," the woman called again, looking around the room.

"Daphanie," Brownie whispered out of the side of her mouth. "They're calling you."

"Oh," Daphanie said, as if just awakening. She looked over at the woman, grabbed her purse, and stood. She took Brownie's hand. "C'mon."

"Where are we going?"

Daphanie walked Brownie through the waiting room, over to the woman with the clipboard, and with a smile politely said to the woman, "I'm sorry. I won't be doing this. I've changed my mind."

Brownie squeezed Daphanie's hand tight, smiled, and said, "You go, girl," as they walked out the abortion clinic doors.

49

Freddy walked slowly through the aisles of the local Walmart. He wore dark sunglasses and a red baseball cap he had dug out of the trunk of his car.

"Excuse me, can you tell me where you keep hair clippers?" Freddy asked a very young-looking woman in a blue Walmart vest who was popping bubble gum.

"Aisle six," she said, then walked away.

But after she left, Freddy felt that she didn't just walk away, but gave him a long look, actually tried to see who he was through his dark glasses. He followed her down the aisle and around a corner of the store, wondering if she was going to some back office to call the police, alert them that she had found the Chicago shooter. He stopped when he saw the woman step behind the electronics counter and start gossiping with an even younger-looking girlfriend. Calm your ass down, Freddy told himself. He walked over to aisle six. He saw a variety of hair clippers packaged in boxes.

A white woman pushing a round-headed baby in a stroller walked past Freddy. He turned his shoulder, trying not to be seen. No matter how much he tried to tell himself it wasn't true, he was certain everyone was looking at him.

Half an hour ago, sitting on Joni's sofa, watching MSNBC, Freddy had seen a mug shot of himself on the screen. He'd lunged forward, snatched the remote off the coffee table, and thumbed down the volume before his name was announced. Joni was upstairs putting Nathaniel down for a nap. He didn't need her knowing about this yet.

"It is now believed that Ford has fled the Chicago area. There is a one-hundred-thousand-dollar reward for any information leading to this man's arrest," the dark-haired news anchor said.

Freddy clicked off the TV and was up off the sofa. He snatched his keys from the table and hurried upstairs.

Standing in the doorway to Nathaniel's room, Freddy said, "I'm going to Walmart. You need anything?"

His pulse was racing. He tried to sound calm, but he was finding it difficult.

"You okay?" Joni said, looking up from Nathaniel, who was now sleeping.

"Yeah. Why you say that?"

"Just . . . you look . . . I don't know . . . antsy."

"Whatever, girl," Freddy had said, faking a smile. "Need anything, or not?"

"I'm cool. See you when you get back."

Freddy picked up the cheapest set of clippers now and carried them over to the self-checkout. He wanted as little interaction with people as possible. Snatching the receipt from the dispenser, sticking it in his bag, he carried his purchase toward the store's exit. Suddenly he froze when he saw a uniformed officer at the door. The large mustached man in the blue uniform glanced at Freddy, then looked away. Freddy was caught. He thought of turning on his heels and sprinting in the opposite direction. But to where? It was his imagination, he tried telling himself. He was paranoid, that was all. The security guard didn't know who the hell he was.

Freddy forced himself forward. As he neared the exit and the guard, Freddy felt beads of sweat fall from under the brim of the cap. Five feet away, then two. Freddy took a step past the man toward the exit.

"One moment, sir," Freddy heard the guard say to him.

He never thought it would end this way. Freddy thought of making a run for it. He didn't see a gun on the man. But what if he had a concealed one? Freddy knew police today don't hesitate to shoot a black man in the back, especially one wanted for attempted murder. Why would a security guard act any differently?

Freddy turned, actually stuck both his wrists out to the officer, as if waiting for the cuffs to be slapped on him.

"I just need to see your receipt, sir," the guard said, a thin smile on his face.

After getting home, Freddy locked himself in the small upstairs bathroom. He stared at himself in the mirror, looking at the hair that had grown long on his head and face. He plugged the clippers in the outlet on the wall and pressed them to his scalp. Looking at himself afterward, his face cleanly shaven, only a shadow of his hair still on his head, he felt he looked like a different man.

He looked down at all the hair in the basin. He scooped it out, cleaned the bowl, and swept the hair off the floor.

Stepping out of the bathroom, Freddy decided he would go straight to his room and not say anything to Joni as he passed her bedroom.

She would probably badger him again about why he fled Chicago, just like she had done the night he had tried to disappear with Nathaniel.

She had demanded he tell her what was going on.

"It's nothing," Freddy kept saying.

"Why would you sneak out of here like that? Leave me? Take the boy? Do you know how much he means to me now?"

"No."

"I think I love him," Joni had said, smearing a tear from her cheek. "I do love him. What did you do in Chicago? Just tell me."

"I told you, I'll tell you when it's time!" Freddy had yelled, surprised that Nathaniel, still in his arms, did not wake up.

Freddy had turned and climbed the stairs, determined not to say another word about it.

Now, as he tried to sneak past Joni's room, she said, "Hold it. Come back here."

She was lying in her bed watching something on TV, wearing gym shorts and a wife-beater. She had caught a passing glimpse of Freddy. He stopped, stepped back to the door, but didn't walk in.

"What's up with the new look, Mr. Clean?"

Freddy smiled, smoothed a palm over the buzzed crown of his head.

"Nothing. Just wanted a new look. No reason."

Joni gave Freddy a knowing smile. "I think there's a reason." She nodded her head toward the television.

Freddy took a step into the room to get a look. On the screen now was the same mug shot he'd seen of himself earlier. Joni got out of bed, stood, crossed her arms over her breasts.

"I think it's time you tell me your side of the story, 'cause I just heard theirs."

That evening around seven-thirty, Daphanie sat outside in her car. She turned to look over her seat at Layla, who was buckled in the car seat.

After her near-abortion, Daphanie had picked Layla up and they had spent the day together. They had gone to the lakefront and the park and had gotten some ice cream. Daphanie had been hesitant, but she'd even taken Layla to see Lewis again.

He had been still very distraught about the test results, but had been glad to see Layla all the same.

"Layla," Daphanie said now. "Do you remember what I told you?"

The child nodded.

"That you didn't see your daddy today, right? This is the biggest secret in the world, and you're a top-secret spy, and you can't tell anybody about you seeing your daddy, especially Uncle Nate, okay?"

Layla smiled and nodded again. Daphanie got out of the car, opened the back door, and unfastened the belts, pulling Layla out of the car seat. She carried Layla up the walk and the steps, and set her down in front of Nate's door while she slid her key into the lock. Walking into the house, she saw that Nate was already home. He sat in the living room, the evening newspaper opened across his lap.

He stood when he saw Layla and Daphanie, and walked over to them. He picked up the child, gave her a kiss on the cheek.

"So how was your day today?"

"Fine," Layla said.

"What did you do?"

"We went to the park and got some ice cream," Daphanie said, stepping in, answering for Layla. "Then we went to the bookstore, and . . . wow, we had a very exciting day, right, Layla?"

Layla nodded.

"I know she's got to be dog-tired," Daphanie said. "She was nodding off in the car. I can take her up and bathe her, then put her to bed." She eased Layla out of Nate's hands.

"Yeah, okay," Nate said. "Good night, Layla."

"Good night," the child said.

When Daphanie came back downstairs half an hour later, Nate was still sitting in his chair. The flat-panel television over the fireplace was on but muted. The evening news was being aired. Nate's attention was still on the paper.

"Anything in there about the guy you're looking for?" Daphanie asked, walking over and sitting on the sofa next to Nate.

"No."

"On the news?"

"No." He seemed solemn.

"Why would he do that? Take Nathaniel?"

Daphanie knew the answer, even though Nate had not told her. Lewis said it was in retaliation for Freddy's girlfriend aborting his child.

Nate didn't answer. His hand pressed against his side, he stood with a fair amount of pain, turned his back on Daphanie. He just stood there not facing her.

"Nate, are you okay?"

"He . . . he tried to kill me, Daphanie," Nate said, his voice barely a whisper. "He killed his own father. He's taken my son. What makes me think he won't kill Nathaniel? Hasn't already done it?"

"Nate, no!" Daphanie said, springing from the sofa and hurrying over to Nate.

Standing in front of him, she saw the tears spilling over his cheeks.

"All these years I've waited for a child, and when I finally find him, he's taken from me," Nate said, breaking down, weeping. He pressed his hands onto Daphanie's shoulders for support. She felt he would've fallen if she wasn't there.

She helped him over to the sofa, sat him down.

She sat beside him, wrapping her arms around him, pressing his head to her breasts as though he were her child.

"Nathaniel is fine. You'll get him back, Nate."

"You don't know that."

"I do."

"You don't!" Nate said, sitting up, looking angrily at Daphanie. "He could be dead somewhere right now. And then what will I do?"

This wasn't supposed to be the time, Daphanie thought. She hadn't planned exactly when she was going to tell him, but she knew it wasn't going to be this soon.

"You said you always knew you were supposed to be a father."

"Yes."

"God knows that. If Nathaniel doesn't come back to you, he'll give you another child."

Nate looked at Daphanie oddly. "What in the hell are you talking about?"

Daphanie eased away from Nate, stood from the sofa.

"Let me first say again, I respect the decision you made. What I'm about to tell you is in no way an effort to change that."

"Daphanie, just say it."

"Remember all the times we made love, telling ourselves that if we got pregnant, we would welcome the child?"

Daphanie could see Nate's eyes widen, his chest starting to heave in anticipation of what she might say.

"Nate . . . I'm pregnant with your child."

51

Lewis would do something to get Layla back, he thought as he walked up the stairs to Uncle Henry's house. He just didn't know what.

He let himself in the house, closed the door, and yelled, "Moms, I'm home."

He didn't receive a response.

"Moms, you around?"

He walked into the kitchen. Moms was sitting at the table, tears running down her face.

"Moms, what's wrong?"

Lewis heard someone walk up behind him. He spun quickly, ready to defend himself. Freddy's Uncle Henry stood there wearing a denim jacket and jeans. Lewis relaxed.

"Oh, hey, Uncle Henry. You scared me," Lewis said, smiling.

Uncle Henry didn't wear a smile. His face was stoic, and he held out his hand. "Give me the keys."

Lewis placed the ring of keys in Uncle Henry's hand.

"I'm sorry about what happened with—"

"Don't," Uncle Henry said. "It's not my responsibility to clean up the mess you two made."

"But—"

"I tried to help the two of you, and look where that's gotten me. Look where it's gotten my sister. She has nothing, and her son is God knows where."

Lewis turned to Moms, who was wiping tears from her face now with a handkerchief.

"My nephew is no longer welcome in my home, so neither are you," Uncle Henry said. "You can sleep in the garage tonight if you want. But after that, I never want to see you again."

52

Daphanie walked into a dimly lit restaurant on South Wabash. A funky blend of techno and jazz played softly through the establishment. Because of the late hour, there were only a handful of couples at the tables. The bar area was still filled with single men, some of whom glanced Daphanie's way as she walked past them looking for Trevor.

Spotting him at the end of the bar beside an empty seat, she walked over and placed a hand on his shoulder. Trevor smiled, stood up, gave Daphanie a polite hug and peck on the cheek.

"How are you? You look great."

"I'm fine," Daphanie said, sitting.

A dirty-blond bartender was already standing before her, laying a napkin down. "What can I get you?" she asked.

Daphanie wanted a drink, a stiff one, considering what she was here to do. But she was pregnant.

"A Sprite with lemon, please," she said.

"I see you're already getting into the mother-to-be lifestyle. I like that."

"Yeah," Daphanie said, trying to ignore the comment. She

lifted the glass of Sprite the bartender placed in front of her and took a long sip from the straw.

"I had to tell my wife I was playing cards with the guys. She looked at me funny, but I think she believed me. So why did you want to meet?"

Setting her glass down, she looked Trevor in the eyes. He looked so full of hope. This was the happiest she had ever seen him. She was giving him what he had always wanted, but she didn't want him. She wanted Nate.

"Trevor, I did some calculating," Daphanie said, lowering her voice, hoping the music would keep what she was saying out of the ears of the guys sitting on the stools beside her. "I'm sorry to say this, but the baby isn't yours."

Trevor looked shocked, then saddened, then pissed. His eyes narrowed on Daphanie as he leaned in and said, "No. That's not true. You said it was mine. You were sure."

"It's not, Trevor."

"Then whose?"

"The man I was dating before you. It's Nate's baby."

"No," Trevor said, shaking his head. He lifted his glass and downed the last of the brown liquor that sat before him. He snapped at the bartender, "Give me another." Then he turned back to Daphanie and said, "Bullshit. I don't believe you. That's my baby you're carrying."

"Why would I lie?"

"That's my fucking baby!" Trevor yelled.

"Shhhh," Daphanie said. This was the reason she had picked a public spot to meet instead of her place. She didn't need Trevor throwing a tantrum. "Can you keep this our business, and not include the entire fucking bar?"

"Why are you doing this, Daphanie? I'm sorry that guy broke your heart. But he doesn't want you. Trapping him by saying—"

"Fuck you, Trevor. I don't have to trap anyone," Daphanie said, standing from her stool, digging in her purse, and tossing a five-dollar bill on the bar. "You should feel lucky. You don't have to take this to your wife. You're off the hook now."

She turned to go. Trevor grabbed her tight by her arm.

"Let me the fuck go!" Daphanie said.

"I don't want to be off the hook. I want my baby. It's mine, and I'm not letting you get away with this!"

"You don't have a choice," Daphanie said. "Now let me go, or so help me God, you'll regret it for the rest of your life."

Trevor held her for a second longer, then released her. She walked quickly out of the restaurant.

53

Needing to get out, Nate called Abbey over to watch Layla. Half an hour later, Nate was finishing his first scotch on the rocks when Tim walked up and had a seat next to him at the Omni Hotel bar.

"What was so urgent about meeting you out here tonight?" Tim said. "And why are you drinking? That can't be good for—"

"What are you having?" Nate asked Tim, while looking at the bartender standing in front of him.

"Seven Up," Tim said.

"He'll have a Jack and Coke," Nate told the bartender. "And I'll have another one of these. Double it up this time."

"Nate, what's going on? Did you hear anything else about Monica?"

"Her condition is the same," Nate said, staring at his reflection in the mirror that sat behind all the bottles of liquor.

"Then why are we here?"

The bartender returned, setting both drinks down on cardboard coasters. Nate grabbed his drink, held it up to his face.

"Pick up your drink, little brother."

Tim did as he was told.

"A toast," Nate said.

"To what?"

"I'm having a baby," Nate said unceremoniously, bringing the glass to his lips, then taking two long gulps.

"What?"

"Take a drink, Tim, and then I'll tell you."

Tim took a sip of his drink, then set the glass down. "What? Who?"

"It's Daphanie. She told me a little while ago. We had been trying off and on while we were together, but neither of us figured anything would come from it. And now . . ." Nate couldn't help cracking the slightest smile.

"And you seem happy. Your wife is in a coma, your son has been kidnapped, and you fucking seem happy about this."

"Is there anything wrong with that?" Nate said, turning to face Tim on his stool. "All that shit you just mentioned is tearing my life to pieces. I can't be happy about getting news regarding something I wanted all my life?"

Tim was quiet. He sipped from his drink again. "I'm sorry. How did she feel about you telling her she had to get an abortion?"

"I didn't tell her that, and I'm not going to," Nate said.

"And you're going to do what, Nate? Monica is in a coma, and Nathaniel is God knows where!"

"Don't you think I know that? Don't you think I want to get my son back?"

Tim didn't respond for a moment. When he did, he said, "And what about Monica?"

"Will she understand this?" Nate said. "Will she accept it?"

"Will she have to?" Nate stared hard at his brother.

"It's what I've wanted all my life. You know that. Sometimes I think it's the biggest reason that I married Monica. And her not being able to conceive is the reason we got divorced. I have it now, and I'm supposed to throw it away?"

"I don't know, Nate. Just respect the fact that you said you were going to marry her again, that you two have a child, a beautiful future together, if you just don't fuck it up. So considering all that, what are you going to do about this?"

Nate swallowed the last half of his second drink, wincing at its strength. He set the glass down hard on the bar, turned to Tim, and said, "I don't know." He grabbed his keys off the bar and stood. "Come by and pick up Layla tomorrow if you don't mind. I have some things I need to take care of."

54

Last night after Joni saw Freddy's face on TV, after he had shaved off all his hair, Freddy had had no choice but to tell her everything. After his twenty-minute admission, Joni's face had been blank.

"And you brought that here?"

"I told you I was in trouble."

"You ain't say that kinda trouble. What the fuck, Freddy?" Joni said, jumping up, pacing around the room. "Anybody know you're here?"

"I ain't crazy."

"You crazy enough to try to kill somebody." That remark had stung Freddy, and Joni had to have known that.

"Fuck it, Joni. Want me to leave?"

Joni didn't respond.

"I said, do you want me to leave?"

"Do what the fuck you want, Freddy!"

They hadn't spoken a word to each other since. It was late in the night, and only now did a soft knock come at his door. Joni opened the door a bit.

"Can I talk to you?"

"Talk," Freddy said, not looking at her.

"In my room, Freddy," Joni said, leaving the door standing open, then walking away.

Freddy got up and went to Joni's room. When he entered, she was standing, staring at him. She walked over to him, threw her arms around his neck.

"I'm sorry about what I said. You told me why you shot that man. He was the reason your baby died, the reason you and your mother lost your home. You're going through hell right now, and I should've been more understanding."

Freddy didn't respond. He stared away from Joni as she looked in his face.

"Freddy?"

"What?" he said, finally eyeing her.

"I understand why you did it. It was wrong, but I understand." Joni placed her palm to the side of Freddy's face. "You can get through this, and I can help you if you want. But you have to want me."

"What are you talking about?"

"I haven't kept secret how I still feel about you, and I know you loved me once."

"Joni—" Freddy said, attempting to remove her hands from around his neck.

"I said you loved me once. But that doesn't mean it can't happen again, does it?" she said, shyly tilting her face up to give Freddy a peck on the lips.

"Joni, I don't think it's the right time."

"You came here for a reason. You trust me. You trust me with that boy, with your secret, but for me to commit to you, to have your back all the way, I need to know we're gonna be together."

Joni kissed him again. This time a little longer. Freddy relaxed, allowed her to.

"You don't miss me? You don't miss this?" Joni said, pressing her palm to the front of his pants. She felt him growing. "It feels like you do. Show me, Freddy."

It was a bad idea. Nothing good could come from what was already happening. But how much worse can things get? Freddy thought. He was lonely, unloved, and love was what he felt he needed most now.

Freddy pressed his lips against Joni's, kissed her hard. He lifted her up. She wrapped her legs around his waist as he carried her to bed.

The next morning, Lewis stood outside Uncle Henry's house, his cell phone pressed to his ear.

"Hello," Daphanie said, answering his call.

"Daphanie, it's Lewis. I think I'm gonna need a favor."

Half an hour later, Daphanie opened the door to her loft and walked in. Lewis followed her, looking around as he closed the door behind him.

"Lewis, come here," Daphanie said from across the living room.

Lewis followed her down a hallway. She opened a door and clicked on the light in a medium-sized room. There was a bed, a nightstand, and a flat-screen television on top of a dresser.

"Will this do?" Daphanie said, walking in.

Lewis felt ashamed.

"If there was anywhere else I could go—"

"It's okay, Lewis. I understand. We're a team for the moment, remember?" Daphanie smiled. "Now, will this suit you?"

"Yeah," Lewis said, lowering himself to the edge of the bed.

It was approaching noon and Freddy was alone, turning over in Joni's bed. Last night had been better than expected. He hadn't made love to Joni in years, and he had forgotten how good it was—how good she was to him.

If Freddy had ever questioned whether Joni loved him or not, after her actions last night he was now certain.

They'd made love three times, and judging by the way she held him, kissed him, took him in, there was no doubt about how she felt. After the second time, Joni quickly rolled over on her side, away from Freddy.

He turned, too, and leaned over her shoulder to see her face. "You okay?"

He could tell she was crying.

"I don't wanna be by myself anymore, Freddy. If you don't want to be with me, then you should leave right now. Maybe that'd be best."

Freddy rolled onto his back. He didn't want to make this decision, not now. But what else did he have going on? Who else wanted him? He had loved Joni once. He knew he could love her again. The only reason he was probably having trouble now was because he was still stinging over losing Kia.

He rolled back up on his elbow, kissed Joni's shoulder softly. "I ain't going nowhere. I don't wanna be alone no more, either."

They made love again. Freddy fell asleep right afterward, and didn't wake up till a moment ago. He crossed his arms behind his head and looked up at the ceiling. He was actually smiling. Did it take all that he had gone through—losing his mom's home, his girlfriend, his baby, and shooting that bastard Mr. Kenny—to find out that he should've been with Joni all along? He wasn't sure, but that's how things had turned out, and he was happy with that. But he knew they couldn't stay here. With his picture splashed all over the place by now, they had to run.

Freddy had no plan. But he would think of one, and he hoped Joni would be down with it.

A knock came at the front door downstairs.

Freddy ignored it. Joni would get it, he told himself.

After a moment, the knocking came again. And a moment later, again. By then Freddy was dressed. He went down the hall to his room and pulled the gun out from under the mattress.

He thought he remembered a fuzzy image of Joni standing over him, Nathaniel in her arms, saying something about going to the mall. Freddy took the stairs down to the first floor and crept over to the front door. He pushed the curtain back and peered out the corner of the window. Billy, the gay security guard, was knocking again, the corkscrew in his fist.

Freddy pulled open the door. "What's up, man?"

Billy looked surprised to see Freddy. "Oh, Joni's not home? I just wanted to thank her again for the . . ." He held up the corkscrew and waved it.

"Okay, I'll tell her," Freddy said, reaching for the corkscrew.

Billy handed it over, then acted surprised after taking another look at Freddy. "New look, hunh?"

"What are you talking about?" Freddy said, his patience with the man growing short.

"Your hair. Presto-chango! All gone. Why the move to smooth and sexy?"

Why all the fucking questions? Freddy wanted to say.

"Just got tired of it," he said instead. "I'll tell Joni you stopped by."

Freddy closed the door. Then he stood there, staring at the corkscrew. He felt odd about the exchange.

No, he thought, he and Joni definitely could not stay.

57

At home, Daphanie had been watching television when the phone rang. It was Nate, asking if she'd come over. He had been doing some serious thinking and he had to talk to her.

After arriving at his house, Daphanie found herself changing the dressings on Nate's wounds.

"When was the last time you had this done? You should've asked me before now."

"I keep forgetting that you were a nurse," Nate said, as Daphanie applied tape to the bandage that covered his abdominal wound.

"Yup, and it comes in handy every so often."

"How much do I owe you?" Nate asked, trying to make light humor, even though Daphanie knew he was troubled.

"Not a dime. You're actually healing really well. Whoever the surgeon was did a nice job." Daphanie stuck the last piece of tape over the bandage. "There. You can put your shirt back on now."

Nate took his shirt from the hook on the bathroom door, pulled it on, and buttoned it up, leaving the tails hanging out over his slacks. He closed his eyes, then stood there by the door, not moving.

"Nate?" Daphanie said, getting concerned. "You okay?"

"You hear that?"

Daphanie listened, but heard nothing. "No. I don't hear anything."

Nate opened his eyes. "I know. There's nothing but silence here. I've lived this all my life. I don't want to do it anymore."

"What are you talking about, Nate?"

"I hate to say this, but Monica has gotten worse. Sometimes I don't think she's going to—"

"Stop it, Nate! Don't say that."

"No. If it happens, I'm going to have to face it."

Daphanie didn't respond. She had only offered her last reply so it wouldn't seem that she actually would prefer it if Monica didn't survive. And no, it wasn't like she wished for Monica to die to get Nate back. But the damage was already done. And if there was a choice, Daphanie would choose Monica never coming out of that coma.

"I guess you're right," Daphanie said softly.

She walked over, placed a hand to Nate's chest.

"And we're still no closer to finding my son. Daphanie," Nate said, looking sadly at her. "If Nathaniel were alive, wouldn't I know it? Feel it? I'm his father, for God's sake."

"Nate, you're beating yourself up too badly. Everything might turn out just fine."

"But what if it doesn't?" Nate shook his head, exasperated. "You *are* pregnant, right?"

"Yes, Nate. I wouldn't lie to you."

"I don't want to be by myself again. I've always told you how much I wanted to have a child."

"But you have one," Daphanie said.

"I mean a biological child," Nate said. "And yes, Nathaniel is my son, and I love him. But if he doesn't come back, I want this child to be in my life. All the time. I want it here, living with me."

Daphanie gave Nate a confused look. "I'm sorry, Nate, but I won't separate from my child."

"I'm not asking you to."

Daphanie took a step back. "Are you saying what I think you are?"

Nate was staring at Daphanie, then his eyes seemed to glaze over, like he was looking into his own thoughts. He focused on Daphanie again, then said, "We'll get married."

"Oh, my God, Nate!" Daphanie said, wrapping her arms around him, squeezing him as tight as she dared. When she pulled out of the hug, she said, "This is because of the baby, isn't it?"

"Is there a problem with that?"

Daphanie wasn't a fool. Marriage was marriage. Whether his reason was to be with the baby or to be with her, the end result would be the same. She'd be with Nate.

"No. But what if you get Nathaniel back safe and sound?"

"Then we'll have two children to raise."

Daphanie took a moment, swallowed hard, and asked, "And what if your ex-wife wakes up?"

Nate looked Daphanie directly in the eyes and said, "I've always wanted a child that came from me. You're giving me that. Monica never could and never will."

58

Freddy stood by the living room window looking out from behind the curtain. He thought about a disturbing conversation he had had with Joni before they had finally fallen asleep last night.

"We ransom the boy," Joni had said.

It took a moment for what Joni had just told him to sink it.

"What?"

"Five million dollars. You said he was rich, right?"

"Yeah, but I thought you liked Nathaniel," Freddy said. "I thought—"

"We were gonna raise him as our own?" Joni said. "Be a happy family? Yeah, the thought ran through my mind, but what do we need more—a kid that's gonna cost us money or one that will get us money?"

She was right. He continued to listen as Joni asked, "Can you still get in touch with the man?"

"His number was in my phone, but . . ."

"Then maybe we can call the police and—"

"Hell, no," Freddy objected. "Might as well tell them where

they can pick me up." He thought for a moment. "I'll call the jail.
Tell Lewis to contact Kenny."

"Good idea," Joni said. "He'll tell the man we want the money,
that he'll have to bring it here to us, and if there are any police,
then the boy gets it."

Freddy looked at Joni, almost shocked.

"You don't mean that?"

Joni lowered her head, as if ashamed of what she just said.

"No, and yes," she said, looking back up. "I admit, I do love
that little boy. Sometimes I'm so glad you brought him here. But
then again, I hate you for it. He reminds me of what I'll never
have, and that makes it a little easier to do what I know has to be
done. Freddy, we got to be out of here, and he's our only ticket."
She leaned in to him. "You still love me don't you? We're still
gonna be together, right?"

"Yeah," Freddy said sincerely.

"Then I'm prepared to do whatever I must to make sure that
happens," Joni said, looking Freddy dead in the eyes. "You hear
me?"

"Yeah, baby. I hear you. You a ride-or-die bitch, huh?"

"That's right."

"That shit's a turn-on," Freddy had said, hugging Joni, as she
laughed.

Now Freddy watched out the living room window. He was staring down the way at Billy's security car.

The man was sitting in it. Just sitting. But before he got in,
he had been standing outside of it, staring at Joni's house. Since
Billy came by to return the corkscrew, Freddy would peek out
the window just to keep an eye on the guy. Fifteen minutes ago,
Freddy peered out the window to see Billy stepping out of his

house as if he were in a haze. He walked toward the car like something was terribly heavy on his mind. He was looking toward Joni's house, then away again, then back at it. Then he stopped, stood outside the security car, his hand on the handle, just looking over his shoulder. *He knows,* Freddy told himself. *He knows it's me.* He imagined Billy must've been watching TV, eating a sandwich or something, before starting his shift over at the mall, and then Freddy's face was thrown up on the screen again. Billy probably asked himself, *Is that Joni's new boy-friend?* And not being certain, but almost sure, he had stumbled out there to his car, wondering if he should go over and make sure. Freddy figured that was what the man was thinking that moment. But he was in his car, which made Freddy believe that he might just mind his own business and drive on to work. That would be what was best, because Freddy sure didn't want to hurt Billy. He had done enough harm for a while.

The white reverse lights flashed on, and Billy backed out of his driveway. But instead of turning toward the mall, the car turned toward Joni's house. A moment later, the car was pulling into her drive.

Freddy let the curtain fall back over the window. He was glad that Joni had gone to the mall with Nathaniel. If Billy really did know—was coming over to try to make a citizen's arrest or some shit like that—Freddy would have to take care of him. He would have no other choice, he thought as he pulled the gun from the small of his back and walked to answer the knocking at the front door.

"Hey," Billy said, a fake smile on his face. "Joni home yet?"

Yes, he knew for sure, Freddy told himself. He exposed half his body from behind the door. He held the gun behind his back.

"Naw, sorry, Billy. Still gone," Freddy said, trying to meet his false enthusiasm. "But she should be back any second. You wanna come in and wait for her?"

"Yeah, I was thinking the exact same thing."

He must think I'm stupid, Freddy thought, stepping back, opening the door all the way and letting the bigger man in. Freddy pushed the door closed. When it slammed shut, Billy spun around, at the same time drawing a club from his belt like a sword. When he faced Freddy, the wooden club was extended out to his side, like he was about to take a swing. But he froze, for Freddy had his gun pointed between Billy's eyes.

"What the fuck, man?" Freddy said. "Why you gotta mess in business that ain't yours?"

"Then it is you. You shot those people in—"

"Congratulations, but you a security guard. This ain't fa' you. Now I'm gonna have to take care of your ass."

Beads of sweat formed on Billy's bald brown head.

"I called the police. They should be here any minute."

"No, you didn't," Freddy said, calling his bluff. "You ain't even know for sure it was me. You sat out there in your car for like five minutes, wondering if you was even coming over here. 'Sides, if you called the police, in a little hick town like this, the whole department would've been here by now. So shut up and toss me the stick."

Billy did as he was told.

Freddy picked the club up from his feet.

"You lucky I know you Joni's friend, or I'd shoot your ass right here. But what I'm gonna do is walk your big ass downstairs, tie you up till she gets back, and decide what to do with you then. Now move," Freddy said, pointing the gun in the direction of the basement door. It was in the hallway that led to the kitchen.

Billy walked slowly, with his hands up. Freddy was behind him, the club in one hand, the gun in the other, pointed between Billy's shoulder blades. The house phone rang, snatching Freddy's attention way for a split second. When he turned back to Billy, the big man was lunging for him. He grabbed Freddy by the throat, forced him forward, knocking Freddy off balance. The club jumped from Freddy's grasp. Both men fell to the floor. Freddy held tight to the gun, knowing if Billy got hold of it he would probably kill Freddy. Billy grabbed Freddy's gun hand. He banged Freddy's fist to the floor till Freddy could no longer hold on to the gun, which went skidding toward the back door of the house. Once Freddy was unarmed, Billy raised his fist and rained three quick, hateful punches down onto Freddy's face. They rendered Freddy powerless for only a fraction of a second, but it was long enough for Billy to crawl off of Freddy, reach back, grab the club, get to his knees, and raise the stick over his head.

When Freddy regained his senses, he looked up and saw the man holding the club high in the air, a scowl on his face. Freddy knew he was going to die, that he'd be beaten. Poetic justice, Freddy thought, almost conceding to the notion. It was the exact same way he had killed his father. Then Billy yelled, swung the club downward. But before Freddy was struck, he heard three gunshots. He saw three holes open in the center of Billy's chest and belch blood. The man's eyes bulged. His mouth fell open, and blood spilled over his lower lip. Then his body fell. Freddy rolled out of the way. Billy's body hit the hallway floor where Freddy had just been. When Freddy turned around to see where the bullets came from, he saw Joni standing just inside the open back door, his gun grasped tightly in her fists, a blank expression on her face.

59

Daphanie walked up to the front door of her building and was about slide her key in the lock when she felt a presence behind her. She whirled around to see Trevor standing there.

"What are you doing, sneaking up on me?"

"I'm sorry if I startled you, but I've been trying to talk to you. Why won't you return any—"

"Because there's nothing to talk about. I've said everything that needs to be said."

"Maybe, but now something needs to be done."

Daphanie was a little scared. She looked up and down the street to see if there was anyone around who might witness the assault if Trevor actually tried something like that.

"What are you talking about?" Daphanie said, trying to sound brave. "Are you stalking me? I swear I'll call the police."

"I'll stop it. I'll leave you alone, never say another word to you once I know the baby's not mine."

"I told you—"

"With all due respect, Daphanie, your word isn't good enough anymore," Trevor said. "I need proof."

Daphanie chuckled. "Proof. What kind of proof?"

"A DNA test. I've done some checking, and there's a test that can be done on the fetus to see—"

"No. Hell, no!" Daphanie said. "I'm not some fucking lab rat. No one's conducting any experiments on me. I say the baby's not yours, and it's not yours. There's nothing you can do but accept that."

"I don't have to accept anything," Trevor said, confident.

"Yes, you do," Daphanie said, taking a step toward him, pointing her finger in his face. "And if I see you lurking around my place again, I'll go to the police and get a restraining order on your ass. But that'll be after I go to your wife. We clear?"

"I'm not done with this," Trevor said, then turned and walked away.

"But I'm done with you," Daphanie called to him.

She watched him till he climbed into his car, then she unlocked the front door to her building and stepped inside.

60

That night Nate sat in his living room chair, in total darkness, brooding.

Was it right for him to feel happy if he lost his wife? If she never woke up?

He stood from the chair with less pain. Nate was on the road to recovery. It was unfair, he thought. He was shot four times, Monica only once, yet she lay near death.

Nate grabbed his car keys. He had not driven since the shooting, but he could not stand being in that house alone for another moment. Half an hour later, he stood at Tim's front door, ringing the doorbell.

"What are you doing here?" Tim said, after opening the door, surprised to see his brother. "You said you weren't getting Layla till tomorrow."

"I'm not," Nate had said, sadness on his face. "Can you get away?"

Tim had glanced down at his watch. "It's almost eleven o'clock."

"Yes or no?"

Now, when Nate told his brother to pull the car over, Tim parked the car in front of a chain-link fence, behind which the remains of a demolished house sat. Nate pushed open the door and stepped out before Tim even cut the engine.

Tim exited the car and walked up beside Nate, who was staring at the pile of old wood and cinder blocks that once were the foundation.

"Why are we here?" Tim said, his voice low.

"This is what started it all," Nate said, not taking his eyes away from the destruction. "This was Ford's house."

"The place you took and sold?"

"Yes."

Tim was silent for a long moment.

"It's not your fault, Nate. Don't even think it."

Nate quickly turned to him. "Who said I was thinking that?" he said, a tinge of anger in his voice. "I know it's not my fault. I did not shoot my wife, then shoot myself. I didn't take my son Lord knows where. But I have to find him." Nate turned back toward the ruins, walked over to the fence, poked his fingers through the links, then hung on to the fence and stared at the mess that lay before him. "Whatever it takes, I have to find that man and make him pay for what he's done to me, to my family."

Tim stood there, watching his brother, not knowing what to say or do to comfort him.

"Please!" Nate said, throwing his head back, staring up at the night sky. "Help me find him. I'll do whatever. Whatever You want!" he said louder, a single tear spilling from the corner of his eye, running down the side of his face. "Whatever You want, I'll do it. Just help me find him!"

Freddy and Joni drove Billy's security car forty minutes from her house. Nathaniel was in his pajamas, asleep in the backseat. Billy's dead body had been pushed into the large trunk.

"Park right there," Joni said, pointing to a spot under a tree.

In silence, Joni and Freddy exited the car and walked around back. Freddy opened the trunk, pulled out two shovels, and handed one to Joni. Under the dark, star-spotted sky, they dug themselves waist-deep in the soft dirt. It took them more than two hours. Afterward, they dragged Billy's body from the car, carried it to the ditch, and dropped it in. They covered the body with dirt, and with the backs of their shovels they patted the mound down tight.

When they were done, Freddy leaned on the handle of his shovel, looked at Joni, and said, "You did what you had to do. There's no need to feel guilty."

Joni looked back at Freddy, not a trace of guilt on her face. "I don't. Let's go."

At 6:00 A.M. Lewis sat up in bed, covered in sweat. He'd had a dream of Layla screaming, calling him, but all he saw before him was blackness. He ran toward the sound of her voice, yelling for her.

"Layla! Where are you? Layla!"

Her voice became fainter, as though she were being carried off. Then there was no sound at all.

Sitting bolt upright now, his chest heaving, his eyes wide open, Lewis was in bed alone.

He pushed the blankets off and slid out of bed. He picked his jeans up off the carpet and stepped into them. He grabbed his T-shirt, pulled it over his head, and turned to face the mirror that hung over the dresser.

Looking at himself, he felt like a loser. What was he doing? Layla wasn't even his daughter, but he refused to accept that. To hell with what that paper said. He would get a new DNA test. He was confident it would prove otherwise. If it didn't, he would have problems. That would mean Kenny would have damn near just as much right to Layla as he did.

If only there was a way that Lewis could convince Kenny to give Layla back to him. He knew that just having custody of her would help his case greatly.

Just then his cell phone rang in his pocket.

A 404 area code appeared on the screen. He didn't recognize the number, but answered the call anyway.

"Hello."

"I don't know why I called the jail first. I should've figured somehow you was gonna get out."

It was Freddy. Lewis felt his stomach tighten into a burning knot.

"They let me out. There was no one to press charges, seeing as how you shot them."

"Then I guess you owe me one, don't you?"

"I don't owe you a motherfucking thing!" Lewis yelled into the phone. "And if you were—"

"Ho, ho, hold up," Freddy said. "Before you go cursing me out, maybe you might wanna find out why I'm calling."

Lewis calmed himself some, then said, "What the fuck you want?"

"Got a little proposition that I think will help everybody out. But I'm gonna need you to get me in contact with that motherfucker Nate Kenny."

63

Daphanie woke this morning, showered, dressed, and headed straight to Nate's house. There, she made his favorite breakfast—fried eggs, with two slices of tomato on the side, skillet potatoes, and chicken sausage links. It was the breakfast she used to make for him on Sunday mornings when they were together.

Nate appeared in the kitchen doorway, a strained smile on his face. "You know you didn't have to do this."

"I know, but what is the point of having a key if I can't surprise you with a wonderful breakfast?" Daphanie said, pulling out a chair at the table for Nate. "So since I did, why don't you have a seat and enjoy it?"

During the breakfast, Daphanie occasionally looked up at Nate and smiled.

After clearing the dishes, Daphanie sat back down and said, "So, what do you have planned for today? Anything I can help you with?"

Nate was about to answer, but his cell phone rang.

"This is Nate Kenny."

Daphanie watched Nate—saw him frown as he listened.

"I don't have to meet you anywhere. I told you—" he began, but paused to listen after he was interrupted. Finally he said, "Don't play with me. Was it really him?" He paused. "Fine. I'll meet you there in half an hour."

Nate disconnected the call and held the phone in his hand with a look of deep concern on his face.

"A man I know named Lewis Waters . . . he had a lot to do with why Monica and I were shot."

"I thought you said you didn't know why you were shot," Daphanie said, trying to sound surprised.

"I lied. I do know. That was Lewis, and he's spoken to the man that shot me. I need to meet him. Will you go with me?"

Lewis sat in Taylor's, the dimly lit bar where he and Nate had met on three previous occasions. He sat at the back corner table—their table.

The front door opened, letting sunlight into the room when Nate walked in. He made his way to the back of the bar, passing two men who sat on stools drinking beer. Nate stopped in front of the table where Lewis was sitting.

"Tell me what he said."

"You're going to give me back my daughter."

"We've already had this conversation. Until I get Nathaniel back, Layla stays with me. Now tell me!"

Lewis stood from his chair. "He wants to make a deal . . . There's a way you can get Nathaniel back."

"How?"

"I need my daughter back."

"And I told you," Nate said. "You're not getting her. Not for what you told me. This could be some game you're playing. I give you Layla, you take off, and I never see her again. No way."

"Then take me to her. Let me at least see her now, and if this information helps you get your son back, I get Layla."

Nate looked as though he were giving it a moment of thought. "No."

"Fine," Lewis said, getting up and walking around the table, stopping right in front of Nate. He pushed his finger into Nate's chest. "Don't let me see her. But I know where she is and I'm gonna get her back no matter what the fuck you say. You don't know where your son is, and if you play this shit like it's a game, you'll never see him again."

Lewis turned and marched toward the door.

"Wait," Nate said.

The two men walked out to Daphanie's Jaguar. It was parked at the curb.

"Get in the back," Nate said, as he climbed into the passenger seat.

Lewis slid into the backseat of the car. He looked up into the rearview mirror and saw Daphanie's eyes, round, staring at him.

"Daphanie," Nate said. "This is Lewis Waters, the man I told you about earlier."

"Pleased to meet you," Daphanie said, not turning around to look at Lewis.

Nate dug his phone from the breast pocket of his suit, dialed a number, then put the phone to his ear. "Tim, is Layla there? I'm coming over, and I'm bringing Waters with me . . . Yeah. Yeah. I'll see you soon."

Nate disconnected the call, turned to Daphanie, and said, "Can you take us to my brother's? We need to see Layla."

Lewis saw Daphanie take another quick glimpse at him in the rearview.

"Yeah, sure," she said, lowering her eyes, sticking the key in the ignition, and starting the car.

Twenty minutes later, Daphanie parked the car in front of Tim's home, and Nate, Daphanie, and Lewis all exited the car.

They walked up the steps to the front door, Daphanie following the two men.

"You said Ford is waiting for your call, and then he'll call back to talk to me," Nate said.

"That's what he said," Lewis said.

Nate rang the doorbell, and the door was opened almost immediately by Tim. He gave Lewis a hateful glare. It didn't seem to matter to Lewis.

"Where's my daughter?" he said to Tim.

Tim looked at Nate.

"He ain't ask you the motherfucking question," Lewis said, stepping right up in Tim's face. "I did. Where is my daughter?"

Tim still looked toward his brother.

Nate nodded, and Tim turned, started into the house. "This way."

Lewis followed Tim through the living room and dining room, leaving Nate and Daphanie behind. Tim pushed his way through a swinging wooden door and into the kitchen. Layla was sitting with Tim's wife at the kitchen table. The woman immediately stood and stepped in front of Layla, as though she had to protect the child from her own father.

"Is there a problem?" Lewis said.

Tim's wife didn't say anything, just looked at Lewis disapprovingly. She turned to Layla, bent over the child, and said, "I'm going to step out now, but if you need anything, just call. I'll be right outside this room."

When she walked past Lewis, he looked at her like she had lost her mind. He wanted to curse her for acting as though he couldn't be trusted in the room with his own child.

When the door swung closed, a smile spread across Lewis's face. He scooped Layla up in his arms, hugged her tight, and kissed her several times on her cheeks.

"How is Daddy's baby girl?"

"Fine, Daddy."

"They treating you okay? Everything good?"

"Fine, Daddy," Layla said again, smiling in his face.

Five minutes later, Lewis walked out of the kitchen carrying Layla in his arms. Nate, Daphanie, Tim, and his wife were all standing in the living room.

Daphanie was looking at Lewis like she was frightened to death that he would leak their little secret. He paid her no mind.

"I kept my end of the deal," Nate said. "Call Ford now."

Tim whispered something to his wife, and she stepped over to Lewis, holding out her arms. Lewis pulled Layla closer to him.

"Let Cynthia take her," Nate said. "Or do you want her to hear this?"

Lewis hesitantly gave her over to Tim's wife, but as she was taking Layla, Lewis said to his daughter, "If you need anything, just call. I'll be right inside this room."

The woman gave Lewis an attitude-filled look, then carried Layla out of the room.

Lewis watched them disappear behind the door, then turned to the others. He took his cell phone from his pocket. "Are you ready?" he said to Nate.

"As ready as I'll ever be."

64

Freddy sat on the living room sofa. Joni sat beside him, holding Nathaniel in her lap. They sat staring at Freddy's cell phone on the coffee table for almost an hour.

"I thought you said he would call," Joni said.

"He will."

"But it's almost an hour past the time you said."

"He'll call, Joni, alright?" Freddy said, rattled. After a moment, he said, "I'm sorry. I've known Lewis damn near my whole life. If he said he's gonna make something happen, it's gonna happen, okay?"

"Okay," Joni said.

Freddy stood from the sofa, paced across the floor. He went to the window, pulled back the curtain, half expecting to see a line of police cars racing down the road, sirens blaring, lights flashing, coming to get him. He turned, looked back at Joni.

She held that boy in her arms like he was hers. She looked up at Freddy like she trusted him with her life, and he felt bad. What if Lewis had called the police? What if Freddy trusted

Lewis when he shouldn't have? What the fuck was he thinking? He had almost killed Monica, the woman Lewis loved, but he gave the man his phone number. Couldn't Lewis have had the police trace the number? Couldn't they be on their way that very moment? They would find the body, know that Joni had killed that security guard, and she would go to prison for life. Her life would be ruined just for knowing him, just like his mother's, just like Kia's, Lewis's, and everyone else's who knew him. He couldn't let that happen to her. Freddy hurried away from the window, was about to tell Joni to run upstairs, grab as much shit as she could, and throw it into a bag so they could get out of there now. Then the phone rang.

Freddy's pulse slowed as he walked over and stood at the table, looking down at the phone. He picked it up, looked at the number.

"It's him." Freddy smiled at Joni and answered. "Hello."

Joni covered Nathaniel's ears with her palms.

"Freddy, this is Lewis."

"I know. That worthless motherfucker Kenny there?"

"He's right here. You want the number to call him back on?"

"No. We don't gotta do that. Pass him your phone," Freddy ordered.

A moment later, Freddy heard Nate's voice.

"Where's my son?" Nate asked. His tone was firm.

"I took him. Where you think he is? With me."

"You better not have harmed a single hair on his head."

Freddy chuckled. "Or what?

"Or I'll kill you."

Freddy laughed. "You lucky you're still breathing, motherfucker. But since you still alive, you can do me a favor."

"I'm not doing a damn thing till I get my son back!"

"You're going to do exactly what I say, and if you do it per-fect, then I'll think about giving the little shit back to you. You listening?"

"Go ahead," Nate spat.

Freddy looked at Joni, smiled wide, and nodded. "You gonna take a plane to Atlanta. I'll call you back with the flight number. You gonna rent a car and drive it to where I tell you. And you gonna bring a suitcase filled with five million dollars—all one-hundred-dollar bills."

"Five million dollars?" Nate repeated.

"You got a problem with that?"

"No."

"I shouldn't have to tell you this, but I'm gonna let your ass know, just in case. You tell the police about this, you bring them motherfuckers—or anybody else, for that matter—I'm putting a bullet in this boy's peanut head. You hear me, Nate?"

Nate didn't answer, but Freddy could hear the man breath-ing hard.

"I said, you hear me, motherfucker?"

"I want to speak to my son. I wanna know that he's alright."

Freddy pulled the phone from his ear. He walked over to Nathaniel, pulled one of Joni's hands away, and placed the phone to the boy's ear. "Say hello to your daddy."

"Daddy?" Nathaniel said.

"Nathaniel!"

Freddy pulled the phone away.

"Ain't time to get all conversational. You got everything I told you?"

"Five million dollars. You'll tell me when and where later. No police," Nate said, hate in his voice. "I heard you, you sick bastard!"

"Remember all that, and don't try no funny shit if you wanna see your son alive again. You know I'll have no problem doing him," Freddy said, then he slapped the phone closed.

"Well?" Joni said, lowering her hands from Nathaniel's ears.

"He gonna do it, baby," Freddy said, pulling her and Nathaniel off the sofa and wrapping his arms around them both.

"He's gonna do it?" Joni said, smiling excitedly.

"That's right, baby," Freddy yelled. "We gonna be rich!"

65

Nate disconnected the call and handed the phone back to Lewis.

"Well?" Tim said, stepping in front of Nate. "Is Nathaniel okay?"

"He's fine, I suppose."

"What does he want?" Daphanie asked.

"He wants five million dollars to give me my son back. He's in Atlanta. He wants me to bring it to him."

"Good," Tim said, picking the cordless home phone up from an end table. "I'll call the police and—"

"Put that down!" Nate ordered.

"But we know where he is. We can—"

"Put it down! Get the police involved and he said he'll kill Nathaniel."

Daphanie gasped.

"He's bluffing," Tim said.

"Look what he's already tried to do to me," Nate said. He turned to Lewis. "Will he do it? Will he actually kill my child?"

"If he feels he has to. Yeah, he'll do it," Lewis said, staring directly into Nate's eyes. "How does it feel to have someone hold your kid hostage?"

Nate didn't respond, but what Lewis had said cut him deep. He hadn't thought about what Lewis must've been going through till that very moment. There was an awkward silence in the room until Lewis said, "So what are you going to do?"

"He's going to call me back. Tell me which flight he wants me to take and where to meet him."

"And you're not going to include the police?" Tim said. "I think that's a mistake."

Daphanie moved to Nate's side, held his arm, obvious worry on her face. "I think Tim's right."

"Just like you said, he tried to kill you while he was here," Tim said. "What makes you think he won't try again when you go over there?"

"Because I have what he wants."

"And after he gets it—what's to stop him from doing it then?" Daphanie said.

Nate's cell phone started ringing. He answered the call. "This is Nate Kenny."

"Mr. Kenny, this is Dr. Beck. I think you're going to want to get over to the hospital."

Distress came to Nate's face. "Is everything alright?"

"Your wife just woke up. She's asking for you."

66

Daphanie sat behind the wheel of her car as she drove Lewis back to her place.

He sat there, deep in thought.

When Nate received that phone call informing him that Monica was awake, he had seemed so happy. Daphanie had felt whatever ground she had gained with him all but disappeared.

"Tim, grab your keys. You're taking me to the hospital. Monica's awake. I need to be there."

"I'm going with you," Lewis had said.

"No, you're not," Nate said. "I can't stop you from seeing her, but I'm sure as hell not taking you."

"Do you want me to take you?" Daphanie said.

She wanted to be by Nate's side, if for no other reason than to show Monica that she still had competition.

Nate looked at Daphanie, and with compassion said, "I don't think that'd be such a good idea. If you could take him," Nate said, cutting his eyes at Lewis, "wherever he needs to go, I'd really appreciate it. I'll call you later."

"But—"

"Daphanie," Nate had said. "Do this for me, please."

Now, at a stoplight, Daphanie turned to Lewis. "So what happens now?"

"Ain't nothing changed," Lewis said. "Monica's awake now. All you need to do is find out when Nate won't be at the hospital and I'll go and tell her every foul thing that motherfucker has ever done to Freddy, to me, and to her."

Standing in front of Nate and Tim, Dr. Beck said that Monica was off the ventilator and seemed to be doing just fine.

"There's no . . . no brain damage?" Nate said hesitantly, very fearful of the answer.

Dr. Beck smiled. "None whatsoever."

"And when will you be releasing her?" Tim asked.

"We'd like to keep her here for observation for a few more days."

"Whatever you think is best for my wife," Nate said.

"Good," Dr. Beck said. "Well, now that that's all taken care of, I think you might want to go up and see your wife now."

"Yes, I think I will," Nate said, gratefully shaking Dr. Beck's hand.

A few steps from Monica's hospital room door, Nate turned to Tim.

"I'm almost afraid to go in there."

"Why? The doctor said she's fine."

"To think I almost lost her. That a year ago I got her out of my life like she was some object," Nate said.

Tim rested a hand on his brother's shoulder. "That's over now, and you didn't lose her. She's right in that room, waiting on you."

"Right," Nate said, mustering up the courage.

When he walked into the room with Tim behind him, Nate saw Monica sitting up in bed, a couple of pillows propped up behind her back. The tube was gone from her throat and bandages were still around her head, but there were fewer of them. When Nate looked at Monica, he could see her eyes were clear. She recognized him, held out a hand to him, beckoning him toward her.

Nate stopped halfway to the bed—felt he might not be able to hold back the tears that might fall. He walked over, hugged his wife tight, sank his face into the crook of her neck, where he wept. Monica held Nate tight, rubbing his back, looking up at Tim, smiling, happy to see them both.

"I love you," Nate said, his voice muffled.

"I love you, too," Monica said, kissing him on the side of his face.

67

Later that night, Freddy propped himself up above Joni's nude body. She squirmed under him, moaning, her palms on his hips, urging him farther inside of her.

Freddy lowered his face, kissed her full lips, and said, "I love you, baby."

He meant every word. He had let go, realized there was no reason to fight it. Kia was gone. His aborted child was gone. Chicago was in the past. This was his new life, his future, and he realized he loved the idea of starting again with Joni.

"I love you, too, Freddy," Joni said, her lustful eyes barely open. She moaned again. "I always have."

Freddy brought her to orgasm, then climaxed himself. They used no protection. Afterward, Joni lay on her stomach, and Freddy lay on top of her, playing with her earlobe.

"What if somehow what we just got pregnant?" Joni said.

"Maybe we shouldn't talk like that, baby. You know—"

"It's just talk, Freddy. What if?"

"Then we'd have it. You know that."

"Would we be good parents?" Joni asked.

"The best parents," Freddy said, going along.

"PTA parents?"

"I think you going a little too far now," Freddy said, smiling.

"That's okay. We kinda like parents already."

"Joni—"

Joni turned over on her back, beneath Freddy. They lay face-to-face.

"I mean, what if we just kept Nathaniel?"

"Then we'd have no money. Then we couldn't go nowhere. And then we'd get caught, sent to jail, and we wouldn't be able to keep the kid anyway," Freddy said, his voice firm.

"Yeah," Joni said, not looking up at Freddy, but up at the ceiling. She had a dreamy quality in her eyes. "I know what you're saying."

Freddy heard a knock on the door downstairs, which startled him. He looked at the clock on the nightstand: 9:01 P.M.

"Who is that?" Freddy said, lifting himself off Joni.

"I don't know."

"You expecting anyone?" Freddy said, slipping up his jeans.

"No, but I'll go down and answer it."

Joni lifted her robe from off the back of a chair and put it on.

"What if it's about, you know . . . him?"

"I don't think so. It's only been a day. Sometimes he'll take off, go to Alabama or Tennessee with one of his male friends for a couple of days, and no one seems to miss him.

"I'll be right back," Joni said, opening the door. "Then I'm gonna want another go-'round."

She closed the door, left Freddy standing in the middle of the room, feeling very paranoid and vulnerable. He spun in a circle, then hurried to the window. He looked out, then immediately fell away from it at the sight of what he thought was a police car parked in front of the house.

"Fuck!" Freddy spat.

He hurried back to his bed, yanked his gun out from under the mattress, and very carefully opened the bedroom door. He eased his way down the hallway and slowly descended the stairs, his back pressed against the wall.

On the last step, Freddy could hear Joni's conversation. She was speaking to another woman.

"No, I haven't seen him," Joni said. "I know sometimes he'll take off on a road trip with one of his friends."

"Yeah, girl," the woman said. Freddy could tell by her tone that she was a black woman. "I know, but for some reason I got a funny feeling."

Freddy eased off the stairs and made his way into the dining room, holding the gun up. Joni had not seem him yet. She stood in the space of the open door, which was shielding her view of him.

"One of our coworkers' birthday was today. I think Billy had a crush on him and I know he wouldn't have missed it for the world."

"Hmmm. I don't know."

"Billy told me you had a cute guy staying here from out of town. You think maybe he saw something?"

"No," Joni said. "I don't think he would've."

"You think I can come in and ask him?" the woman said.

Freddy's body tightened. He crept closer to the door, stood just behind it. Both his hands were wrapped around the gun. He held it right before his face. Joni must've sensed his presence. She glanced behind the door, saw Freddy there, then immediately frowned.

If they were to have any chance of getting away, he would have to kill the woman, Freddy told himself. It was that simple.

"No, that's not a good idea," Joni said to the woman, but something told Freddy she was really speaking to him.

"Why not? It'll only take a second."

Sweat was starting to accumulate in Freddy's hands as he tightened his fists around the gun. Now! Now was the time.

"He's asleep and he gets grumpy when he's woken up. But I'll ask him tomorrow. I promise. Besides, I'm sure Billy will probably show up or call you by then."

There was no response. Freddy figured the woman probably knew Joni was lying, was considering pushing her way in anyway.

"Okay," Freddy finally heard her say. "You're probably right. Tell Billy, if you see his ass, that I don't appreciate him having me worry like this."

"I'll tell him, girl," Joni said, sounding like she really would see him again.

When the woman climbed into her car, Joni closed the door. She looked at Freddy, relief on her face.

"How the cops know—"

"She wasn't a cop. She's Billy's partner. But it don't matter. We gotta do what we gotta do and get out of here like now."

68

This'll be it, Lewis thought, riding up to the third floor of the hospital the next morning. This will be the moment Monica realizes what a son of a bitch Nate is and leaves him once and for all for me.

Before leaving this morning, her purse on her shoulder, Daphanie had said, "I'm going to pick Nate up now. He didn't tell me where I was taking him, but when I know he'll be away from the hospital for at least a few hours I'll call you, and then you go over there. Got it?"

"Yeah," Lewis had said.

"And when you're done, call me and let me know when you leave."

An hour after Daphanie left, Lewis was showered and dressed, sitting on the living room sofa, his cell phone in hand, waiting for Daphanie's call.

When the phone finally rang, she said, "I'm dropping him at work. He has a meeting, and he doesn't want me to pick him up for two hours."

Lewis had hurried out, jumped a train, and took it straight

to the hospital. Now, as the elevator doors slid open before him, he froze, wondering just what he would say to Monica. Yes, he loved her, and he knew at one time she had loved him, too. But the last time he had seen her, she was cowering from him, holding his daughter like she thought he might hurt her. Monica had called the police on him, was going to press charges, have him sent to prison.

Lewis found himself standing just feet from the entrance to her room.

What should he say to her?

Tell her the truth, Lewis told himself. Yes, he would tell her everything, because knowing that bastard Nate like Lewis did, he knew Monica wouldn't have heard it from him.

It would be over for the two of them, and she would have no choice but to come back to Lewis.

He took a deep breath, exhaled, then walked into the room.

Monica was there, sitting up in bed. The TV was on across the room, and she was in midlaugh, until she saw him. Her face became serious.

"Hi," Lewis said.

"Why are you here?" Monica said, reaching for the intercom for the nurses' station.

"No, wait!" Lewis said. "Can I just talk to you for ten minutes? I have something very important I need to tell you about Nate. About everything. About why you were shot."

Monica looked surprised, then said, "You have ten minutes."

"And that's how I ended up right here," Lewis said, after explaining it all to Monica. From Nate blackmailing Freddy, to Nate keeping Layla from him, to Nate planning to fly to Atlanta to rescue his son. Monica sat there silent in bed, her face emotionless during Lewis's entire telling.

She sat there now, still silent.

Lewis expected some sort of reaction from her. Something. "Well?" he said. "After hearing all that, there's no way that you can stay with him."

"I'm marrying him, Lewis."

"What? After what—"

"I knew about everything you just told me," Monica said. "Nate told me everything."

"He told you what I just told you?" Lewis said, hardly believing Nate would tell that version. The true version.

"Yes. Everything was the same."

"And you're going to marry him. Why?"

Monica let her eyelids fall closed for a moment. When she opened them, she said, "From what the doctors told me, I could've died. If that bullet would've hit a little closer to the center of my brain . . ." She paused a moment before going on. "Life's not promised to anyone. I'm tired of going back and forth, and before this happened to me, Nate was the man I chose to be with, and I'm staying with that decision."

Lewis couldn't believe what he was hearing. He felt himself growing angry. "After what he's done to me. I ain't got no place to live. He's keeping my daughter from me."

"Like I said, he told me all that. My house, it's yours, Lewis. If you want it. Nate will give you the keys and arrange for the paperwork to be transferred into your name."

"And Layla?"

"I'm going to miss her." Monica smiled sadly. "But she should be with her father."

Lewis lowered his head, feeling for some reason he should tell Monica the truth he had recently found out, but decided against it. He looked up sadly at her. "Do you still . . ."

"Don't, Lewis," Monica said. "If you want to know if I loved you, you know the answer is yes. Part of me always will. But I can only be with one of you, and like I said, I made my decision. So if you'd just . . ." She paused, emotion breaking into her voice. "If you'd just leave."

Lewis took what he felt was one last look at Monica, turned, and walked out of her room.

69

Daphanie had just hung up the phone from speaking to Nate. She had been on her way to pick him up, but he told her his meeting would run over by at least an hour.

"Well, I can come back, then."

"Don't bother. I'll call Abbey and have her pick me up. But thanks," Nate said.

Daphanie didn't know why, but she thought she heard more and more distance creeping into Nate's voice each time she spoke to him.

After she hung up the phone, it started ringing a moment later.

"Hello," she answered.

"I'm done." It was Lewis.

"What do you mean? How did it go? Is she going to leave him?"

"No."

"What do you mean, no? Did you tell her everything about—"

"I told her everything. But she said Nate told her first. She said it don't make no damn difference. She's going to stay with him."

Daphanie couldn't believe it. "Even after—"

"After everything. She's going to fucking stay with him. So you might as well forget about whatever plans you had to be with him, because it's over."

"I'll talk to you at home, Lewis," Daphanie said, and hung up on him. She tossed the phone to the passenger seat, grabbed the steering wheel with both hands, and yanked it hard, making a sharp U-turn.

Daphanie sat in the chair across the room from Monica's bed for twenty minutes, just watching her sleep. While there, Daphanie could've done anything she wanted to the woman. She had gotten up and closed the door. She went over to Monica's bed, just stood over her, looking down at her for five minutes, wondering what Nate truly saw in the woman. Monica was lucky, because if Daphanie wanted to hurt her, she could've. But that wasn't the kind of person Daphanie was. She walked back to the door, opened it, and sat back down till Monica awakened. She still had bandages on her head. Daphanie figured her injury had not totally healed.

When Monica finally did wake up, she turned her face toward Daphanie, caught sight of her, and acted as though she had always known she had been there. Monica did not act startled or surprised to see her.

"How are you, Monica?" Daphanie said.

"Outside of having a little headache where the bullet entered my skull, I'm okay, I guess," Monica said, pushing herself up in the bed into a sitting position.

Daphanie stood, pushed her chair closer to Monica's bedside, then sat again and crossed her legs, laying her hands in her
lap. "You're probably wondering who—"

"You're Daphanie Coleman, Nate's ex-girlfriend. He told me
there might be a chance you'd be coming to see me. Nice to meet
you," Monica said, slowly extending a hand.

Daphanie didn't stand to shake Monica's hand. She remained
in her chair, a smirk on her face.

"Is there something I can help you with, Daphanie? Nate
won't be coming for a while. His meeting was—"

"Extended for another hour. I know, he called and told me
that," Daphanie said.

"Yes, I appreciate you being there to cater to his needs while
I'm in here. But rest assured, as soon as I'm out, he won't need
your services anymore," Monica said. "I'll be able to take care of
my fiancé just fine."

Daphanie was speechless. She knew Nate was getting back
with his ex-wife, but he had never mentioned anything about
marrying her.

"Look, Daphanie," Monica said. "I don't want to be mean to
you. You've given me no reason to be. It just is what it is. We had
gotten divorced last year for some silliness. He went his way, and
I went mine. I was in a relationship, and so was he. I know you
loved Nate, probably still do. I can't hold that against you. Nate is
a wonderful man when he wants to be, but now he and I are getting back together," Monica said. "Can I ask you to just respect
that and leave us be?"

Daphanie was seething inside. Why hadn't she held a pillow
over this bitch's head when she'd had the chance? "He was going
to marry me," Daphanie said, her voice small and angry.

"I know. I'm sorry. He told me that."

"We were trying to have a baby."

"I know. Nate told me that, too."

Daphanie stood, shouldered her purse, and stepped to the door. "He's told you pretty much everything about me, hunh?"

"No, Daphanie. He told me *everything* about you."

And this was her opportunity. How sweet would it have been to say, Well, he didn't tell you the part about me being pregnant. But Daphanie knew that would blow to hell all the work she'd done thus far. She would let Nate tell Monica that on his own. After that was done, Daphanie wouldn't have to worry about Monica ever again.

70

Freddy disconnected the call after speaking again to Nate Kenny. He had told the man what flight to be on, and where to drive the rental car.

Freddy and Joni agreed they would meet Nate in front of an old abandoned auto repair shop. Joni said it was half an hour away, right off the interstate, so it would be easy for him to find. It would be perfect.

After the call, Freddy turned to Joni, who was sitting on the sofa next to him, holding Nathaniel in her arms. The child had been dozing for the last fifteen minutes.

"Well, it's done," Freddy said. "Tomorrow at four o'clock."

Joni smiled, but said nothing.

"What?"

She looked lovingly down at Nathaniel, then back up at Freddy. "I love him, Freddy. What if we didn't give him up?"

"We already talked about this. We need the money."

"Maybe we can take the money and still find a way to keep him."

"No, we can't!" Freddy said, standing from the sofa. "Do you hear me? We can't. We made the plan, let's stick to it. Okay?"

"Okay," Joni said, sadness in her voice. "Yeah, okay."

Four hours later, after she and Freddy had been sleeping for nearly an hour, Joni gently climbed out of bed and walked out of her bedroom. She pushed open Nathaniel's door, stepped over to his bed, and stared down at him, smiling. After another few minutes, she leaned over, kissed the boy on the forehead, turned around, and went back to bed.

71

"They came just like you said they would," Monica said the next day, sitting up in her hospital bed.

Holding Monica's hand, Nate said, "I'm sorry. Sorry it all had to come out like this. I did what I did to get you back. I never thought—"

"It's done, Nate," Monica said, sounding as though she understood.

Nate brought her hand to his lips, kissed it. "I love you."

"I love you, too."

"If you only knew what I was going through, thinking I'd lose you."

"You don't have to think about that anymore. I'm back, and I'm not going anywhere." Monica smiled.

"You promise?"

"Of course I do."

"Good," Nate said. He saw something in Monica's eyes. He thought it looked like fear. He knew the reason why it was there.

"I don't want you to go to Atlanta, Nate."

"I don't have a choice."

"Do what Tim is suggesting and call the—"

"Tim can suggest all he wants, and he can be wrong. His son is at home, Monica," Nate said, irritated. He stood from his chair. "The police have supposedly been working on this case since the shooting, and still they have no clue as to where Ford is. I can't trust them with our boy's life."

"Okay," Monica said under her breath, her head lowered.

Nate sat again, stared her in the eye. "Will you trust me on this one thing? Whatever happens, I promise I will bring Nathaniel home safely to you. Will you trust me?"

Monica looked into his eyes for a long moment, blinking back impending tears. "Yes, Nate. I'll trust you."

The next morning, Nate walked down the stairs in his home. A small bag hung over one shoulder, a leather satchel was slung over the other. It contained the five million dollars in cash he was to give to Freddy.

Tim followed down the stairs behind Nate. "Please," he said. "Just let me call the police. I'm sure there's a way they can do it, where Ford won't even know."

At the bottom of the stairs, Nate spun around. Tim stopped abruptly, almost colliding with Nate. They were face-to-face.

"And what if Ford does find out? What if he does know, and kills Nathaniel? Then what?" Nate said, an edge in his voice. "Are you saying that holding on to five million dollars is worth my child's life?"

"No, Nate. You know I'd never say that," Tim said apologetically.

"Then we're ending this conversation," Nate said, turning and heading through the living room toward the front door. He stepped outside, where a limo waited curbside to take Nate to the airport.

"Please, Nate. Reconsider."

Nate turned again to Tim. He extended his hand for his brother to shake. "I'll call you once I have my son."

Nate sat in first class. He cracked the cap on one of the two tiny plastic bottles of scotch the flight attendant had just given him. He poured the contents into a plastic cup, then did the same with the second bottle.

As the last drop poured from the bottle, Nate thought his hand was shaking. He stared at it a moment, and yes, indeed, it was. He set the bottle down and grabbed his hand with the other, massaging it.

His heart was racing. He wiped a hand against his brow and brought back fingertips covered with sweat.

The plane had not even taken off yet and Nate was a wreck.

Get yourself together, he urged himself. Your child's life depends on this.

Nate lifted the plastic cup of alcohol to his lips and kicked it back, gulping it all down in two swallows.

He settled back into his seat, stared aimlessly out the window, and prayed that everything would work out.

Nate set the satchel of money in the trunk of the rental sedan, along with his travel bag. He slammed the trunk closed. He paused for a moment, looking over his shoulder. He had the strange sensation that he was being watched.

He walked around the car, got in, and closed himself inside, locking the doors. He pulled a folded page from the breast pocket of his suit and entered the address Freddy had given him into the car's navigation system.

The device calculated the route to the destination Nate entered.

It would take him forty-five minutes.

Nate started the car, shifted it in gear, then backed out of the parking spot.

"Joni, come on. What are you doing?" Freddy called from the open front door. He looked down at his watch and saw that if they left that very minute, they would only be there five minutes before they were supposed to meet Mr. Kenny. He had told Joni that they should've left an hour ago, just in case something went wrong, like a flat tire or something.

"I'm coming," Joni called from upstairs. "Nathaniel had to use the bathroom one more time."

A moment later, Joni hurried to the front door, Nathaniel smiling in her arms.

Half an hour later, Freddy pulled the car alongside the old abandoned building. There was really nothing else around there except two other big vacant buildings. The windows were knocked out, doors were hanging off the hinges.

Sitting in the car with Joni, the windows down, he noted how unsettling it felt.

"Now, when he pulls up . . ." Freddy said. "I told him you'll be the one getting out of the car and walking over to him, getting the money."

"Okay," Joni said, eagerly accepting the responsibility.

"I would've done it. But as long as he knows I'm still with the boy, he knows he needs to do what we tell him. Know what I'm saying?"

Freddy looked over his shoulder to the backseat, where Nathaniel played with one of the toys that Joni had recently bought him. Freddy reached across Joni's knees, opened the glove compartment of the old car, and grabbed the gun. He held it out to her.

"This here is just for show. Put it in your jeans, raise up your shirt a little so he can see it, just so he knows we mean business, alright?"

"Alright," Joni said. Freddy could see the slightest bit of fear, of doubt, in her eyes.

He placed a hand on her shoulder, leaned in to look closely into her eyes. "You gonna be okay with this?"

Joni swallowed hard. "Yeah." She nodded. "I'm gonna be fine. All I gotta do is this one thing. Get our money, and then we gonna leave this place so we can be together." She smiled.

"That's right. This one thing," Freddy said, taking Joni's hand and squeezing. "And we'll be together, and won't have to worry about nothing." Freddy smiled.

The smile disappeared from his face when he saw a dark-colored sedan turning into the parking lot of the building they had parked beside.

"It's him," Freddy said, feeling a quick rush of adrenaline flow through him. He flashed the headlights twice, as he had told Nate he would.

The sedan stopped, facing Freddy's car, fifty feet away.

—

Nate shifted the car into park. His cell phone rang. He picked it up.

"Hello."

"You got the money?" It was Freddy.

"I got it."

"Anybody in the car with you? 'Cause I ain't playin'. I'll snap this boy's neck like a straw."

"I got it!" Nate said.

"I'm sending my girl over there. You give her the money, and when she brings it back, I'll send your boy."

"No. Send him—"

"Shut up!" Freddy yelled. "You ain't in no position to be making demands. You do what the fuck I say, and hope I give you back this boy. You hear me?"

"Yes," Nate said, trying to keep his anger in check. It'll be over in a moment, he told himself. I'll have Nathaniel and be back on my way to Chicago.

"Get the money. She's coming out," Freddy said.

"Okay, we have movement from the Dodge," Detective Martins said into the radio, while looking through the binoculars. He and Detective Davis, along with officers from both the Chicago Police Department and the Atlanta Police Department, were crouched just inside the third floor of one of the abandoned buildings. They all wore vests, prepared for the worst to happen.

"Who is that?" Tim said, watching through a pair of binoculars he had been given, as Joni exited the car.

"We don't know," Detective Davis said, then spoke into his radio. "Keep an eye on the woman."

"We have a shot," a voice came back through the radio. "Do I take the shot?" It was the voice of an officer inside another of the abandoned buildings. He sat crouched, squinting into the scope of a long-range sniper rifle. He followed Joni as she approached the dark sedan, the crosshairs aimed on her skull.

Nate would be angry about him informing the police about all this, Tim thought. But he knew it was the right thing to do. Moment's after Nate had left for the airport, Tim had called Detective Martins, who had been waiting for his call.

"He just left," Tim said. "Come and get me now."

The police picked up Tim, and Martins, Davis, and three other officers from the CPD boarded a private jet and flew to Atlanta.

They had raced to the address where Nate had told Tim he was meeting Ford, a full hour before the meeting. They had set up in the nearby vacant buildings and waited.

Nate stepped out of the car. He saw the woman approaching him.

"Just going in the trunk for the money," Nate said to the woman.

Nate opened the trunk, pulled out the satchel, and slammed the trunk back down.

Joni was standing directly in front of Nate now. She looked him over, as if she were building an impression. A look of distaste covered her face. "So you're him. The man that's caused Freddy all his pain."

"I have your money. Get my son."

"Open it up."

"It's all there. I don't have to lie to you," Nate said, becoming impatient.

"I said, open the fucking bag," Joni said, lifting the front of her shirt to expose the gun in her waist.

—

"Do you see that?" Tim said, the binoculars pressed hard to his eyes. "She has a gun!"

"We still have a shot," the deep voice came through the radio again.

"Hold!" Martins said, still watching the scene through his binoculars. "Do you hear me? Hold!"

"Holding."

Nate unzipped the satchel, held it open for Joni to see. "Like I said. It's all there."

Freddy sat nervously watching the exchange take place. Nathaniel sat in his lap, Freddy's arm around the boy. "What's taking so fucking long? Just grab the bag and bring it back." He felt that something wasn't right. Freddy looked around at the surrounding buildings, getting the strange feeling that he was being watched.

He saw no one, and nothing unusual. But then—wait. His gaze traveled back. He saw a glimpse of sunlight reflect off of something in a window of one of the buildings.

No! Freddy thought, narrowing his eyes, looking closer. And then . . . there. He saw it. A man's head behind a pair of binoculars.

"Zip it back," Joni said.

Nate did as he was told.

Joni reached out, snatched the bag from him.

"Now give me my son," Nate demanded.

Joni shook her head. "I hate you, and I don't even know you. You don't deserve Nathaniel."

"Give me my son," Nate said again, lunging for Joni.

She whipped the gun from her waist, pointed it at Nate, prepared to pull the trigger.

"No!" Freddy said. He had kicked the car door open, stumbled out of it, and was running toward Nate and Joni when he saw her pull the gun. "Don't do it!" he said, reaching out to her.

"Gun!" Tim heard one of the officers say. Then he heard another officer. "Gun!"

"She has a gun!" Tim yelled at Martins. "She's going to kill my brother."

"We have the shot," the deep voice came again, sounding incredibly calm. "Take the shot?"

"She's going to kill him!" Tim said, yanking on Martins's arm.

"Take the shot!" Martins ordered into the radio.

Nate shut his eyes, gasped, taking what he thought would be his final breath, because he knew this woman shooting him at such close range would definitely kill him. He had been lucky last time, but not again.

Joni was smiling, the gun in her hand, the money in her possession. She had done the one thing she had to do, and she hadn't even given up the boy. Her future quickly played out in her head.

Joni and Freddy married on a Cuban beach, Nathaniel there at their side. They lived in a small villa. Freddy and Joni made love every afternoon, and took long walks on the water's edge with Nathaniel at sunset every evening. It was beautiful. Exactly what she always dreamt of for her life. Then a single shot rang out and echoed among the three abandoned buildings. A tiny red speck appeared in the center of her forehead, and the back of her skull exploded outward.

Freddy was mere feet from Joni when she was shot. He was so close that some of her blood, bone, and brain matter spattered across his face. Her body fell lifeless to the ground before him. He fell to his knees, slid beside her.

"Noooooooooooooo!" he screamed. Grabbing her, pulling her body into his. He took her face into his hands, shook her. Blood and vomit spilled from her mouth. "Joni! Joni!" Freddy cried. Then he felt hands on him, yanking him away from her. There was frenzied movement around him, men's voices yelling, but Freddy stayed focused on Joni's lifeless, open eyes, as the men dragged him farther away from the woman he was supposed to spend the rest of his life with.

Nate stood there in near shock, shaking. Police cars came from everywhere, sirens screaming, skidding to a halt, blowing up dust all around him.

"Did you here me, Nate? Are you alright?" Tim said for the second time, standing in front of his brother.

Nate hadn't seen him till then. His eyes were still on the dead girl. He turned his attention to Tim. "Yeah," he said, feeling as though everything that had just happened were a horrific dream. "I'm okay."

75

Freddy was taken into custody, and would be returned to Chicago to stand trial for the crimes he had committed against Monica and Nate.

It was approaching eight P.M. by the time Nate and Tim were finished with the police in Atlanta and were stepping off the private plane that flew them back to Chicago with Nathaniel.

Detectives Martins and Davis assured Nate that they would make Freddy Ford's prosecution a priority.

"We're sorry this had to happen," Detective Davis said, shaking Nate's hand. Nate was holding Nathaniel in his other arm.

"I'm just glad to have my son back," Nate said gratefully.

At nine P.M., Nate and Tim were out at the park near Tim's house, sharing a bench. Layla and Nathaniel played tag a few feet in front of the two men.

"Those two should be in bed," Tim said.

"Want them to tire themselves out."

"So when are we going to see Monica?"

Nate didn't look at his brother when he said, "I don't know. I'm not sure I'm going to."

"What are you talking about, Nate?"

"There was a lot for me to think about during the trip to Atlanta," Nate said, turning on the bench to face Tim. "What if I never saw Nathaniel again?"

"But that didn't happen."

"But what if it would have? I don't know why it's happening now, but I'm finally being given what I've always wanted. I don't know if I can just—"

Tim stood, shaking his head, waving his hands about. "No. No, don't tell me that you're considering leaving Monica. After everything that the two you have been through, you can't honestly be thinking of abandoning her."

"It's not abandonment," Nate said.

"Then exactly what is it?"

Nate didn't speak for a moment. He really didn't have an answer for his brother. Maybe Tim was right. Nate stood, rested his hands on his brother's shoulders. He tried to smile. "I haven't made up my mind on this, but I feel I'm leaning toward accepting this baby in my life. Will you support me in that decision?"

"You're my brother, Nate. But what you're doing to Monica is—"

"Will I have your support?" Nate said, putting forth effort to keep the smile on his face.

Tim shook his head, forced himself to finally say "Yes."

76

Lewis sat in Mrs. Roberts's office, wearing khaki pants, a button-down shirt, and a tie. He felt crazy, but Eva had told him he had to dress nicely for the interview.

They had just come back from her walking Lewis through the records room. There were stacks of files in there. Hundreds of them would have to be pulled, filed, purged, and refiled every day.

Mrs. Roberts quickly went through the filing system, then gave Lewis one of the folders and said, "Okay, file this in its proper place."

Lewis quickly ran through what she had just taught him and looked at the four-digit number on the side of the file, then the color-coded tab. He walked down one of the aisles, looking for the numbers that came just before and after the number on the file he held. He then slid the file he was holding between the two.

He walked back to Mrs. Roberts for her response.

"Very good," she said.

Afterward, Mrs. Roberts had brought Lewis back to her office, where he sat now.

"Where did you work before?" the tall, graying woman asked, not looking down at the résumé Lewis had hurriedly put together last night.

"At a real estate management company."

"And why did you leave there?"

Lewis thought about lying, but really didn't know what to say. He didn't think he'd get this job anyway, so he thought, what harm could the truth cause?

"The owner was my best friend's uncle. He never really liked me, and when I got into a little trouble, he fired me."

"I see," Mrs. Roberts said, finally looking down at the résumé through her bifocal lenses. "And what kind of trouble was that?"

"With the law. I was taken to jail," Lewis said, preparing himself to be dismissed. "But I wasn't convicted. I really didn't do anything wrong."

"Did it have something to do with you trying to provide for your daughter?"

Surprised that this woman knew about Layla, Lewis said, "Yes, it did."

"Are you still working on getting custody of her?"

Lewis felt slightly violated by all the information this woman knew about him. He figured Eva had to have told her, and had to have had good reason. "Yes, I'm still trying, but it's hard."

"There aren't a lot of men out there trying to do what you're doing."

"That's what Eva keeps telling me."

Mrs. Roberts slid Lewis's résumé into her drawer, then stood from her desk and extended a hand out to Lewis.

Lewis stood and shook the woman's hand.

"Eva thinks you'd be a good fit for this job."

"I think so," Lewis said, praying that this woman thought the same thing.

"To be so young, my niece is a good judge of character," Mrs. Roberts said, still holding Lewis's hand, squeezing it the slightest bit harder now. "She wouldn't be wrong this time, would she?"

"No, ma'am, she wouldn't be."

"I hope not," Mrs. Roberts said, smiling and letting go of Lewis's hand. "We're done here today. I'll talk to Eva and let her know when I'll need you back."

"Need me back for what, Mrs. Roberts?" Lewis said, just wanting to be perfectly clear as to whether he had gotten the job, or if she was still just considering him.

"To fill out all the forms and get your start date. Which means, yes, Lewis Waters, I'm giving you the job."

Half an hour later, sitting at Arby's, Lewis tore into a roast beef sandwich. Arby-Q sauce was all over his cheeks. He smeared it off with a napkin and took a long sip from his Coke.

"I guess I didn't have to tell her about your daughter, but I know how my aunt feels about stuff like that," Eva apologized. "She works there to help kids, and people like you. I knew it might've made a difference."

"Don't even try to apologize. You ain't do nothing wrong," Lewis said, trying to keep the smile from returning to his face, but he could not. He shook his head, smiling even wider.

"What?" Eva said.

"I got a call this morning from the guy I've been telling you about. He's going to be giving Layla back to me."

"Are you serious?" Eva said, scooting out of her side of the booth and standing. "Boy, you better come here and give me a hug!"

Lewis put down his sandwich, slid out of the booth as well, and gave Eva a hug. He held her tight. She felt so wonderful in his arms, he didn't want to let her go. When she did lean out of the hug, he stared at her for a moment. She stared back at him, their noses almost touching, there in the middle of the Arby's Restaurant.

Lewis heard a child somewhere behind them whisper to his mother, "Ooh, they gonna kiss."

Both Lewis and Eva laughed and sat back down.

"That is such good news, Lewis. I know you're happy."

"But that ain't it. They're giving me the house I used to live in. They're gonna sign it over to me, free and clear."

"So you're gonna have a house?" Eva said, even more excited.

"Yup. I'm gonna have my daughter, a house, and a job. All I need now is . . ."

"Is what?" Eva said, sipping from her strawberry shake.

"A good woman."

"Hmmm. I heard those are hard to come by nowadays. You gotta really work for one of those."

"I'm willing to do whatever it takes," Lewis said, smiling.

"Well, if that's the case, I think you might have a pretty decent chance at finding one."

77

Lewis had never been more happy in his life as he walked down the street toward the front door of Daphanie's building. He was waiting on Nate's call to tell him when he would get Layla back, and when the man would sign over the house to him.

As Lewis neared the front door, he saw a tall brown man, mildly resembling Nate Kenny, climb out of a car. He stepped down the sidewalk and stood right before the door to Daphanie's building, his arms crossed over his chest.

Lewis walked toward the door. "Excuse me," he said.

The man didn't move aside, but said, "You're him."

"I don't know what you're talking about, bruh. But if you'd step aside, I need to get by."

"I been watching you with Daphanie," the man said, causing Lewis to freeze and look him in the eye.

"What you mean, you been watching me? Who the fuck are you?" Lewis said, getting defensive.

"That's not your child. It's mine!" the man said, appearing angry.

"What are you talking about?"

"I know Daphanie told you that the baby she's carrying is yours, but it's not. That's my child."

"Ho, ho, hold up," Lewis said. "I think you got me confused with somebody else, man. Just who do you think I am?"

"You're Nate Kenny. Daphanie's ex-boyfriend."

"No, I'm not. My name is Lewis Waters."

The man looked embarrassed, but he also appeared frustrated. "Aw, man. I'm sorry," Trevor said, raking his fingers over his scalp. "It's just this has been tearing at me, and I don't know what to do about it. Sorry, man," he said, stepping backward toward his car.

"Wait!" Lewis said. "I know Nate Kenny. Maybe I can help you."

Around the corner and halfway down the block, Trevor sat with Lewis for half an hour, telling him everything that had happened with Daphanie from the day Nate told her he was getting back with his ex-wife till now.

Lewis sat absorbing it all, trying to decide just what he'd do with this information.

"That's jacked up, man," Lewis said, feeling genuine sympathy for Trevor. "What you gonna do?"

"Daphanie thinks I'm stupid. I know that child is mine. I can feel it in my heart."

"Sometimes your heart can be wrong about those things. Trust me, I know," Lewis said. "You gonna have to get a DNA test, you know."

"I have no problem with that, but I know she won't submit to one," Trevor said. "But you said you know this Nate guy. Can't you tell him about me? Maybe he can convince her to—"

"I don't know, man," Lewis said, knowing how delicate his situation with Nate was. He still had Layla, still had the house that he had yet to sign over to Lewis. "I wanna help you, but I just don't know."

"Any way you could, man. I'd appreciate it," Trevor said sincerely.

Lewis seriously thought about getting up, walking away, and never looking back. But in his efforts to get his daughter back, he had been helped by Eva, even by Daphanie. He couldn't just turn his back on someone who was in a similar situation. "Give me your number and I'll get back to you," Lewis said.

78

Nate decided to drive himself today. When he pulled up to Monica's house, Lewis was sitting on the front steps. He stood and stared down when he saw Nate's car.

Nate stepped out of the car, went around and opened the back passenger side door, reached in, and pulled Layla from her car seat.

When Nate turned around, holding Layla's hand, Lewis halted in the center of the walkway.

Nate released Layla and she ran to her father.

Lewis scooped the little girl up and spun her in his arms.

Nate walked up beside them. He held a folder in his hand.

"How is Monica doing?" Lewis asked.

"We need to go inside and take care of this," Nate said, stepping around Lewis and Layla and heading up the steps.

Nate opened the door to the empty house and closed it once everyone was inside. He walked across the living room, into the dining room to the breakfast bar, where he opened the folder and laid out the pages. He set down the keys to the house and the truck Monica had bought for Lewis as well. "Here are your keys back, and this is a quitclaim form. Sign it, file it downtown, and the house will be transferred into your name."

Lewis set Layla down and walked over to take a look at the form. "That's it?"

"Yeah, that's it," Nate said, slipping a pen from his breast pocket and holding it out to Lewis.

Lewis took it and signed the form. Afterward, he gave the pen back to Nate, uncertainty on his face.

"So I keep the form?" Lewis said.

"You file it at the records office."

"Yeah, okay. Thank you," Lewis said.

Nate just looked at him and sighed. Nate turned, walked over to Layla, then stopped. He turned to Lewis. "How will you afford this? It's paid for, but that doesn't mean you don't have to still pay taxes. It's how Ford lost his house."

"You mean it's how you took it."

Nate paused before saying again, "How will you afford it?"

"Not that it's your business, but I just got a job. I can pay for this."

Nate looked Layla in the eyes. He knew he was going to miss her, but his son was back, and he would be expecting a baby soon. He would get over Layla. He walked the little girl over to her father, gave her to Lewis.

"Thank you," Lewis said again.

Nate didn't respond. He turned, walked toward the door. He was prepared to open it, but he stopped and turned back to Lewis. "You don't deserve her, you know. You don't deserve this house. You don't deserve any of it."

Lewis looked bewildered, like he had no clue as to what Nate was saying.

"Look, we took care of our business," Lewis said. "If you'd just leave and—"

"No. Not until I'm finished," Nate said, stepping back deeper into the room. "You had this beautiful child before, but you lost her, because you don't know the importance of being responsible, or taking care of business, or earning a living. You can't hold on to a job because you're lazy and worthless and don't amount to a damn thing," Nate said, feeling himself becoming even more angry. He thought only for a second to ask himself if he was truly angry at Lewis or at himself. It was because he had sought Lewis out in the beginning. It was Nate who had hired this man, who had brought him into his life with Monica. If he had never done that, he and Monica most likely would've still been married. They would've found Nathaniel, adopted him, and been happy and carefree together.

But Nate had let Lewis into their lives. And because of that, Monica had divorced Nate, lived with Lewis for a year, which led to Nate and Daphanie, and the child that he would ultimately leave Monica again for. It killed him to think about it, but Nate knew he would leave. And that was why he was so angry right now at Lewis.

"I just want you to know that I hate everything about you," Nate said, after stepping right in Lewis's face. "After everything that has happened, you made out good for yourself. But I will be watching you. You're a father again. But if you let this child go without absolutely everything she needs, I promise I will come back here and take her from you again. Understand?"

Lewis held Layla closer to him. He looked at Nate with a murderous gaze, but did not speak a word.

"Good-bye, Lewis Waters," Nate said, as though the man's name sickened him. He turned, then walked out of the house.

79

Two hours later, Lewis and Eva left Layla and Eva's four-year-old daughter, Tammi, to play downstairs in the empty living room.

"So this is where the master bedroom's gonna be," Lewis said, after taking Eva on a tour of the entire house. "Whatcha think? You like it?"

"The house or the bedroom?" Eva said with a sly smile.

"I'm liking you more every day. But you know what I'm talking about."

"It's huge, and it's beautiful, Lewis. It's in a wonderful neighborhood, it has a great school system. What more can you ask for?"

"I can think of one thing," Lewis said, walking past Eva, gently brushing against her, as he made his way to the window. "But I'm gonna wait on that. I don't want to ask too soon. Wouldn't want to scare her away."

"Hmph. She might be braver than you think."

Lewis looked out the window, which offered a view of the front lawn. He turned to Eva, concern on his face.

"What's wrong?" Eva said, reading his expression immediately.

"Can I ask your opinion about something very important?"

"Sure. Anything."

Lewis told Eva about bumping into Trevor, told her every-thing the man had said to him. Lewis told Eva about how evil Nate was to him, and how Lewis still managed to hold his tongue when he wanted nothing more than to spit that newfound infor-mation in Nate's face.

"But even though we're over now, and I feel as though she did me wrong, I don't wanna tell Monica about this, 'cause I know it's gonna hurt her," Lewis said. "She's just coming out of a coma. She's been through enough."

"So what are you asking me, Lewis?" Eva said, standing very close to him.

"Should I tell her anyway? Is it something that she needs to know, even though it's gonna hurt her?"

"I think it's good that you're concerned about her feelings. She doesn't need to go through any more. But," Eva said, slipping her fingers in between Lewis's and holding his hand, "I think that man should know, if he doesn't already, that the baby isn't his."

"But I don't care about him. I hate him, and he hates me. So what difference does it make?"

"You're a bigger man. And if it were you in that situation, wouldn't you want to know?"

Lewis looked away, loosened his grip on Eva's hand.

Eva held tight to him, pulled him closer. She looked in his eyes. "I'd like to think you asked me this because you value my opinion."

"I do."

"Then will you take my advice this one time?"

"I don't know."

Eva took Lewis's face between her palms. "Please?" She rose on her toes and kissed him softly on the lips. "Pretty please?"

"Uhm, I still don't know." Lewis smiled.

Eva kissed him again, this time longer, with more passion. Lewis wrapped his arms around her waist, pulled her close, till he knew she was able to feel how much he wanted her. After a moment, he said, "Okay, I'll take your advice."

Lewis stepped off the hospital elevator and headed down the hall toward Monica's room.

An hour ago, his cell phone had rung.

"Hello," he had answered.

"Lewis?"

It was Monica.

"Yeah?"

"Can you come to the hospital? I need to see you."

"Is everything alright?" Lewis said, starting to panic.

"Yes, I guess. Can you come? Did I catch you in the middle of something?"

"No," Lewis had said. "I'll be there in a little while."

At Monica's door, Lewis knocked softly.

"Come in," Monica said.

Lewis entered to find Monica sitting up in bed, a magazine opened across her lap. She no longer wore the hospital gown, but instead a T-shirt and pajama pants. The bandages were no longer wrapped around her head, and now Lewis could see where they had shaved a small part of her scalp on the side of her head to do the surgery.

"I know, I've seen better days," Monica said, running her fingers over the rest of her hair. "I get out of here tomorrow. I'm going straight to Marlene to get something done to my hair so I look human again."

"You look fine," Lewis said, walking over to the bed and giving Monica a light kiss on the cheek.

"You look pretty good yourself. Is everything okay?"

Lewis couldn't help smiling. "Yeah, things are okay."

"I was hoping you were going to bring Layla."

"I don't want to confuse her."

"Oh," Monica said, looking down at her hands. "Where is she?"

"I left her with a friend."

"A female friend?"

Lewis thought about lying, then told himself he had nothing to hide. It was Monica who had wanted things this way. "Yes."

Monica looked as though she were thinking the situation over in her head, then said, "Good for you, Lewis."

"Why did you call me?"

Monica found the remote in her blankets, pointed it at the TV, and turned the set off. She looked at Lewis with both seriousness and sadness on her face. "Since you have Layla, I'll assume Nate made it back from Atlanta okay."

"Yeah."

"Did he sign over the house and the car to you?"

"Yeah."

"Did he tell you if he got Nathaniel back?"

"Monica," Lewis said. "Shouldn't he have told you all this? Didn't he—"

"Did he tell me if he got Nathaniel back?" Monica said, all of sudden getting emotional. She wiped at her eyes. "No, Lewis, he didn't."

"I'm so sorry, Monica. I'm sure he has a good reason," Lewis said, sitting on the side of Monica's bed and grabbing one of her hands. "He'll come to see you, or call you."

Monica looked up at Lewis. He saw a tear in her eye. "I tried calling Nate I don't know how many times. I called Tim, too, but he hasn't called me back. That's not like him. What's going on?"

Lewis thought he knew exactly what it was. Nate thought he finally had a natural-born child on the way, and he was trying to decide if he still wanted to be with Monica. That is, if he hadn't already decided to get rid of her. Lewis hoped he wasn't right, but he was sure he was.

"Do you know where he is? Maybe something happened to him?" Monica threw herself into Lewis, needing a hug. "Did they catch the man who shot us? Maybe he came to Chicago and—"

"I'm sure he's fine, Monica. Everything will be alright," Lewis said, pulling out of the hug. He held Monica by her arms and looked in her eyes, promising her, "I'll find him, okay?"

"But—"

"But nothing," Lewis said, handing Monica the box of Kleenex he took from the tableside bed. "I'll find him, and make sure he comes and talks to you."

81

Lewis pulled his truck up in front of Nate's house and shifted it
into park.

He pulled out his cell phone and dialed Nate's phone for the
seventh time. Lewis would give him one more opportunity to
answer before he walked up and banged on Nate's door.

Again the phone rang several times, then went to voice mail.

Lewis had left a handful of messages, and they'd gone unan-
swered. No more, he told himself, pushing open the door of the
truck and angrily stepping out and walking up the path to Nate's
house.

There he banged on the door with enough force to knock the
thing off its hinges.

Afterward, Lewis realized he hadn't checked to make sure
that Daphanie wasn't here. If she was, then it would just be much
more of a mess than he intended.

Lewis didn't like the way that Nate was playing Monica. She
had chosen Nate over him, and now the man was acting like
a coward, afraid to face her and tell her what he was going to

do with her. It was wrong, Lewis thought, banging on the door again.

The door opened, an infuriated Nate standing behind it.

"What the hell is wrong with you? I have every right to call the police!" Nate yelled.

"You need to let me in," Lewis said.

"Let you in. What the hell for? I told you I never wanted to see your sorry ass again."

"Nate," Lewis said from behind clenched teeth. "I saw Monica earlier today. She told me you haven't been to see her."

"That is none of your business. Now, if you knew what was best for you, you'd get off my property," Nate said, starting to close the door.

"I know why you haven't seen her," Lewis said into the door as it continued to close. "It's because of Daphanie's baby, isn't it?"

The door's movement halted. Nate opened it again, staring at Lewis with confusion. "What do you know about that? How do you know this?"

"I'm not going to tell you out here on this porch. Let me in."

Nate stepped away from the door. "Come in, then."

Lewis walked into the house, proceeded down the hallway into the living room. He was about to take a seat on the sofa.

"Don't sit down," Nate said. "Just tell me what you have to say, then leave."

Lewis told Nate how he and Daphanie had met, how she was expecting to get Nate back after Lewis told Monica of all the evil things he had done.

"So you were staying with her?" Nate said, anger in his eyes.

"Yes."

"Did the two of you—"

"No. Nothing happened," Lewis said, not knowing why he was trying to ease this man's fears.

"Do you still have interaction with her?"

"No. We don't need each other anymore. I have a place to live, and she feels she got you back from Monica," Lewis said. "And she's right, isn't she?"

"I appreciate you telling me this, but that's none of your business," Nate said, seeming much more calm now. "If you'd leave," Nate said, walking Lewis to the door.

"Things aren't what you think they are, Nate."

"What are you talking about?"

"She's lying to you."

"I don't know what you're saying," Nate said.

Lewis stopped in the hallway. "The other day at Daphanie's house, this man stopped me, thinking I was you. His name is Trevor. That name sound familiar to you?"

"No."

"He's Daphanie's ex-boyfriend."

"So what?"

"The baby that Daphanie's carrying, he swears it's his."

82

Nate stood in the spray and steam of the shower's hot water. His arms were out in front of him, his palms pressed into the shower wall to support him. He dipped his head and let the steaming water run through his hair and over his scalp.

He had not been to see Monica. She had been ringing his cell and home phone. He had even gotten two calls from his secretary at work, telling him that his wife had called and said it was urgent.

Nate ignored all of that.

Tim came by and warned Nate that if he didn't see Monica, tell her something, that Tim was going to do it for him.

He felt horrible right now. He should've told Monica something, but, being honest with himself, he knew plain and simple that he was scared. He knew telling her what he was almost certain he was going to tell her would kill her. And Nate wasn't ready to see that kind of pain done to her.

But he also had to admit that he wasn't entirely sure how things would be with Daphanie. Yes, the six months they'd had together, before he got back with Monica, were fine, almost great.

But throwing a child into the mix, would that change things for the worse, or better?

Bottom line, he had toyed with too many women's lives. He was tired, and ready to settle down, be out of the game once and for all. So if that was the case, why was he hesitating?

This was what he had always wanted, he kept telling himself. Yes, all Monica's things were in his house, considering they were going to get married. But it wasn't like they had gotten married. There would not be another divorce. She was not entitled to anything more than she already had. And little Nathaniel was his child. He, and only he, had adopted the boy. There would be no custody battle.

Nate would walk away from their short reunion losing nothing of what he had. In fact, he would actually be gaining a child. One from his own loins.

Yes, he would do it tomorrow, he thought, a slight smile coming to his face. There was just one more thing he wanted to be certain about, before he gave Monica such awful news.

Nate opened his mouth, let some of the shower collect in it, then spit the water out.

He felt a soft hand on his bare back, then another on his hip, reaching around, taking him between the legs. He felt himself becoming aroused. Nate hadn't had sex since the shooting, but he felt he might be able to tonight.

Nate turned around to face Daphanie. She smiled up at him, the strands of her wet hair plastered to her face.

"This baby is mine, isn't it?" Nate said.

Daphanie smiled, still holding his manhood. "Of course it is," she said. "Now kiss me."

83

The next day Nate stood outside Monica's room. He took in a deep breath, exhaled sorrowfully, then pushed through the door without knocking.

Monica turned around. She wore a warm-up suit and sneakers. It was something Nate had never seen before. He assumed Tabatha might have brought the clothes for her.

Monica gasped, then hurried over as quickly as she could to Nate, hugging him. "Oh, my God. I've been trying to call you. I called Tim, and he wouldn't answer his phone, and I didn't know if you made it back from Atlanta," Monica said nervously. She leaned away from Nate, looked him in the face as if to verify he was real, then kissed him quickly on the lips. "Is everything alright?"

"Yes," Nate said, hating himself for what he was about to do.

"Did you get Nathaniel back? Is he fine?"

"Yes."

"Then why didn't you call me? You had me in this hospital worrying, thinking that something was terribly wrong."

Nate didn't respond, but still held Monica in his arms.

"You know, they're letting me out of here today. I called Tabatha to come pick me up, but since you're here, I can call her back."

Nate let his arms fall from around Monica. Immediately he could tell she knew something was wrong.

"What is it, Nate?" There was worry in her voice.

"I didn't come to take you back home, Monica."

Monica took two steps away from him. "What are you talking about?"

"There's something I have to tell you."

Monica stared at Nate, unblinking. She turned away from him, grabbed a paperback off the bedside table, and slid it into a two-handle cloth bag with the hospital logo on it. "This has something to do with that woman that came here, Daphanie, doesn't it?"

"Yes."

Monica turned back around to face Nate, then sat on the edge of the bed and folded her hands between her knees. "Well . . ."

"She's pregnant, Monica."

Monica closed her eyes and winced as if the words had caused her a physical pain. When she looked back at Nate, she said, "The woman can have an abortion."

"I don't want to abort my baby."

"My baby," Monica echoed him softly, lowering her head. "Then what do you want to do?"

"I want the child. I want it in my life. I want to raise it. It's what I wanted all my adult life, you know that."

"I do," Monica said, looking up. "But how is that going to work for us?"

Nate looked around, wished that they could've been somewhere else other than the hospital room where Monica had nearly died and had just woken up from a coma. "I had a decision to make, Monica. This could not work for us. Either I chose the baby, or I chose us."

"And you chose the baby," Monica said, a tear coming to her eye, which she quickly, angrily swiped away with her hand.

"Yes."

"So you're going to be with that woman? You're leaving me, and you're going to marry that woman?"

"Yes."

Monica dropped her face in her hands. "After everything you've done to me, how you treated me ... offering me to another man, leaving me because I could not give you a child ... I came back to you when you asked. I came back to you. Nate, I almost died for you!" Monica said, raising her voice, tears streaming down her face. "And you tell me that you're leaving me, and it's again because I can't have a child. At least you could've fucking come up with something new!" Monica lowered her head again and openly sobbed.

Nate took a step toward Monica, hoping he could comfort her in some way. She slapped him hard across the face.

"No!" she said. "Don't come near me." She reached for some Kleenex from the table nearby and dabbed at her cheeks. "I shouldn't be crying like this."

"Don't apologize," Nate said, rubbing his cheek.

"I'm not. You aren't worth the tears. You aren't worth shit," Monica said. She blew her nose, balled up the Kleenex, and dropped it into the wastebasket. "Now," she said, looking at Nate, almost as though she hadn't just been crying. "How do I get my things out of your house without running into you or that bitch you're going to marry?"

"Just tell me when you'd like to move and I'll make the house available to you."

Monica sniffled and tried her best to display a smile. "Thank you, Nate. Now get the hell out of my sight."

Nate opened his mouth to say something that he hoped would ease the pain some.

"Don't. Just leave," Monica said.

Nate turned, and was about to step out the door when he bumped into Tabatha walking in.

"Hey, Nate!" Tabatha said. "Where've you been? We've been trying to—"

"Tabatha, no!" Monica said. "Don't talk to him. Nate was just leaving. For good this time."

Lewis didn't have to tell Nate that the baby might not be his. He could've left well enough alone. But Lewis knew what it was like to fall in love with a child he thought was his own, only to find out he had been lied to. Despite all that Nate had put him through, regardless of how much Lewis hated him, Lewis felt that no man deserved to be lied to like that.

Lewis was surprised that Nate actually listened to what he had to say.

"Who is this man?" Nate said. "I don't believe what you're saying. I need to meet him."

Lewis said he'd call him, arrange a meeting, put the two of them together, and let them work things out.

"When?" Nate said.

"I don't know."

"Call him now."

Lewis looked at Nate, sensing that the man was testing him, that he needed proof Lewis wasn't lying. "Fine," Lewis said. He got on his cell phone, called Trevor, and scheduled the meeting for later that evening. After hanging up, Lewis said, "You happy, now?"

"Yes," Nate said.

As Lewis drove away from Nate's house his cell phone rang. He fished it out of his pocket, glanced down at the tiny screen, but did not recognize the number.

"Hello," he said.

"You have a collect call . . ." a recorded voice informed Lewis. ". . . from the Cook County Department of Corrections. Will you accept the charges?"

Lewis paused a moment, pulling the truck to a stop sign. He knew it was Freddy. It could be no one else.

"Yes," Lewis said, clenching his teeth and tightening his grip on the steering wheel.

There was a long moment of silence in which Lewis drove through the stop sign and pulled the truck to the curb, then parked.

"Motherfucker!" Freddy said, actually sounding happy.

"Why are you calling me?"

"What? All the years we known each other, they all of a sudden gone? You ain't been thinking about me? You ain't wonder what happened after you sent your boy Nate Kenny down to Atlanta to get his son?"

"He ain't my boy," Lewis said, but he couldn't deny that he was concerned about what had happened to Freddy. "Tell me."

"Remember fine-ass Joni? The girl I dated before Kia."

"Yeah," Lewis said, remembering her vividly. She was good for Freddy. He was wrong for leaving her. "I remember her."

"I was in Atlanta staying with her. She took me back. She still loved me, man," Freddy said, his voice trailing off. "We was gonna be together. We was gonna get money from that motherfucker Nate, then we was gonna just go off together. But . . . but . . ."

Lewis could hear the emotion in Freddy's voice, making it hard for him to go on. Lewis actually felt sorry for Freddy at that moment.

"But your boy had her shot. That motherfucker had her killed!" Freddy yelled into the phone. "Now she gone. She gone, man." Lewis heard Freddy sniffle through the phone.

"I'm . . . I'm sorry, Lewis said.

"It's cool," Freddy said, forcing an insincere chuckle. "They caught me, and brought me back here. They bringing me up on attempted murder charges and all that shit. I got a good public defender, though. Cute little skinny white chick. She all young and innocent looking. A judge will believe her when she say I'm insane."

"What are you talking about?" Lewis said, sitting up in his seat, attentive.

"Yeah, she got the records from when I did that time in the mental hospital. Me killing my pops, my house getting taken, my baby getting aborted—she gonna say all that triggered some mental shit in me that made me go temporarily insane again."

"You ain't insane!" Lewis said. "You knew exactly what you were doing when you went to kill Nate and Monica."

"I told you, Monica was a mistake," Freddy said. "But yeah, I knew what I was doing. I always do. But they don't know that. She gonna try to get me a year in a mental institution, and then I'll be out."

Lewis was silent. No, he didn't like Freddy being behind bars any more than he liked being there himself, but Freddy had almost killed Nate and Monica.

"You know you deserve worse for what you almost did to them," Lewis said.

Freddy chuckled. "You don't even know half the foul shit I did. Seems like nobody found out yet, 'cause it ain't came back to bite me. Bottom line, if I win this case, I'm gonna be on the streets again in a year, and I think I'm gonna be paying another visit to motherfucker Nate's house."

"You don't even know if you're gonna win. And if you do, that'd be the stupidest move you could make. You'd be right back in jail."

"That's if they caught me. But if they did, it'd be worth it. He played me, so that motherfucker gotta pay."

"Whatever," Lewis said, discounting Freddy's crazy talk. "I gotta go."

"Hold on," Freddy said, pausing. There was silence for a long moment, as if Freddy was thinking. "You played me, too. You know what I'm saying?"

Lewis sat up more in his seat, gripping his phone tighter, knowing he wasn't hearing what he thought he was. "No. What the fuck are you saying?"

"You played me, Lewis. You acted like a little bitch and played me. But don't worry, I got at least a year to spend up in this piece, so I'm gonna think about how to deal with that. You never know, you might have to pay, too."

"What!" Lewis said, yelling into the phone. "Motherfucker, you try to come after me, and—" He heard a click. The line went dead.

"Hello? Hello?" Lewis set the phone on the passenger seat, then stared out the windshield. He told himself right now he had to forget that conversation, otherwise he would be looking over his shoulder, watching the calendar, counting the days till

Freddy was released—if he was released. He couldn't do that. There were too many good things happening to him now for him to worry about that nonsense. He would concentrate on the present and worry about Freddy if and when that crazy mother-fucker found the courage to try to step to him.

"Okay, we'll race as soon as I come back," Nate said two hours later to Nathaniel, who was playing with a pair of his toy cars.

Nate got up off the carpet to answer the doorbell.

When he opened the door, Tabatha stood in front of him. Without warning, she slapped him hard across the face, staggering Nate a few steps backward.

"Monica will be getting her shit on Thursday, motherfucker. Make sure you or that bitch ain't around."

Nate rubbed his stinging face, speechless. He watched as Tabatha glared at him evilly, backed away from his door, then turned and walked to her car, climbed in, and drove off.

Nate sat on a stool in a small bar off Clark Street, having a scotch neat.

"Nate."

Nate turned around to see Lewis and another man, who shared Nate's skin color and had similar features.

"This is Trevor Morgan," Lewis said.

Trevor extended his hand for Nate to shake.

Nate looked at it, then spun back around on his stool. "We aren't here to make friends. What are you having?"

"Whatever's on tap," Trevor said.

"Same here," Lewis said.

They took the stools next to Nate. Lewis sat between the two men.

After their drinks came, Nate took another sip from his glass, then turned halfway on his stool to eye both Lewis and Trevor. "So who are you?" Nate asked Trevor.

"I used to date Daphanie before you."

"Dated." Nate chuckled. "I thought people were supposed to give up dating after they got married."

There was a look on Trevor's face that asked how the man knew this about him.

"He has ways of finding stuff out, man," Lewis said to Trevor.

"I do my research, Mr. Morgan," Nate said. "So you have a wife, but you were dating Daphanie. You don't have any children, but you say she's pregnant now with your child. What makes you think that?"

"Because the day you threw her away, told her you were going back with your ex-wife, we had unprotected sex."

"And Daphanie and I had been having unprotected sex for the four or five months prior to that," Nate said, taking another drink of his scotch. "So what?"

"She told me I was the father."

"She told me the same thing."

"I told him you all gotta get a test done," Lewis said.

"And I told you she won't submit to that. I asked her already," Trevor said. He turned to Nate. "Why don't you ask her?"

"There's no reason, because I know who the father is. Me."

"Then why in the hell did she tell me it was me?" Trevor said.

"Because, like you said, I threw her away. At that time she knew she couldn't be with me. She obviously didn't want to raise a child without a father, so knowing that you would want the child, she told you it was yours."

"That's bullshit," Trevor said.

"You gotta get proof," Lewis said.

"Why?" Nate said. "From my point of view, there's nothing wrong with the situation. Daphanie is with me, and she says the child is mine."

"But what if it's not?" Trevor said. "So she doesn't have to submit to a test now. But I will not leave this alone. When she has that baby, I'll get a fucking court order, and she will have to take the test. And then what will you do if you find out it's not yours?"

Nate downed the last of his drink, flagged down the waiter, and said, "Give me another." He then turned to Trevor. "I don't believe you, going through all this. Do you have any children out there?"

"No. I don't have children," Trevor said, seeming to take offense.

"Have you ever gotten a girl pregnant? Even as a teen?"

Trevor rubbed his chin, thought about it. "No."

"Then what makes you think you're even capable of getting Daphanie pregnant?"

"What the hell are you trying to say?" Trevor said, standing from his stool, trying to move around Lewis. Lewis stood as well, and stepped into Trevor's path.

"I'm saying that you might be sterile," Nate said.

"I'm not. But what about you? Lewis told me you always wanted children, but you don't have any, either. And you said you were having sex with Daphanie for four or five months, and only after I had sex with her one time does she come up pregnant. Maybe you ought to get yourself checked."

Nate slammed his glass down on the bar, spilling half of it. He stood from his chair.

Trevor continued to glare at Nate.

Lewis stood between them. "Hold it. Maybe you both ought to get checked. Since Daphanie ain't taking no test, you might be able to find out what you need to know without her."

Nate and Trevor stared at each other for a moment, then they both sat.

"Will you do that?" Trevor asked. "I just want to find out what's what."

"Only if we use the doctor of my choosing," Nate said.

87

That night, Daphanie had made Nate and Nathaniel dinner. Afterward, she put Nathaniel to bed and came back downstairs to watch TV beside Nate.

She rubbed her belly like she had been with child for eight months. Her stomach was as flat as it had ever been.

"I hope it's a little girl," Daphanie said. "I would love to give Nathaniel a sister. Wouldn't that be wonderful?"

"Yeah," Nate said, staring at the TV, his eyes glazed over. He thought about just coming out with everything. Telling Daphanie that he knew Lewis, that he knew about her scheme, and that he'd had a meeting with Trevor. But if he told her that, he would have to demand that she take the test. She would get defensive. She would deny everything Trevor had said. And she still would not submit to the test.

Her argument would be, how could he marry her if he didn't trust that the child she was carrying was his? She would say something about how him wanting her to take the test would ruin forever what they could have. That would be why she wouldn't take it. And to some degree, Nate would feel she was right about that.

"You thought about names yet, babe?" Daphanie asked.

"Uh, no," Nate said, still deep in his thoughts.

She stood from the sofa, grabbed the glasses that had been filled with juice. "Well, I'm gonna go up to bed."

"No," Nate said, snapping out of his trance. "I have a big day tomorrow. Lots of stuff I have to do. Would you mind heading home tonight?"

Daphanie smiled sadly. "Of course not."

The next day Nate performed the demeaning task of beating off into a plastic cup, then handing it to a lab worker, who tried to look as though she didn't think what she was holding was disgusting.

Nate had been sitting in the waiting room, wearing a suit, his legs crossed, reading an *Esquire* magazine, for a little over an hour now.

Trevor sat in row of chairs against the wall as well, just four empty seats down from Nate.

They had agreed that they wanted to be called into the doctor's office together and have the lab results read to them aloud. It needed to be done that way so they'd both know for sure.

"Mr. Kenny. Mr. Morgan," Dr. Phillips called from behind a counter. "You both can step back."

This was a test for which results would normally take more than a few days, but because of Nate's money and influence, he was able to get personal treatment from the doctor and immediate results.

Nate and Trevor walked through the door that led to the lab area and back offices of the clinic.

Holding two manila folders in his hand, Dr. Phillips walked both men back to his office and had them take seats in front of his desk.

The doctor sat behind his desk and opened both folders, pulling out a single sheet from each and setting them on his desk before them.

"Gentlemen," he said, slipping on a pair of reading glasses. "We have the results here."

Nate swallowed hard. He felt his hands coating over with nervous sweat.

"Whose shall I read first?"

Nate was scared silent.

"I'll go first, Doctor," Trevor said.

Out of the corner of his eye, Nate could see Trevor looking at him, but Nate did not return his stare.

"Okay," Dr. Phillips said. "Mr. Morgan, you're fine. Your sperm count is good. Actually, it's pretty high."

Nate heard Trevor let out a huge sigh.

"Thank you, Doctor," Trevor said, sounding relieved.

"Mr. Kenny," Dr. Phillips said. "You next?"

"Yes."

Dr. Phillips looked down at the lab sheet, then back up at Nate. The doctor removed his glasses, then said, "I'm sorry to inform you, but you have azoospermia."

"What!" Nate said. "What the hell is that?"

"It means the results found no sperm whatsoever in your semen."

88

Dr. Phillips spoke to Nate for another fifteen minutes, and asked if he could do a quick physical exam on him. Nate allowed him to.

After the exam, as Nate zipped up his pants and tucked in his shirt, Dr. Phillips said, "Well, it's one of the things I thought it could've been."

"What's that?" Nate said, very concerned.

Dr. Phillips snapped off the exam gloves and dropped them into a small wastebasket. "It's a condition called varicocele. It usually occurs during puberty, and if left untreated it can cause infertility. Basically, varicocele is an enlarged mass of veins in the spermatic cord in the scrotum. It could cause pressure, oxygen deprivation, heat injury, and toxins, but it hasn't really been determined which of these symptoms causes the infertility."

"So?" Nate said.

"Don't worry. It's an easy fix," Dr. Phillips said. "It's a quick outpatient procedure. I'll tie off the veins, and after a month or two you'll be back to normal."

"You mean I'll be able to have children?"

"That's exactly what I mean," Dr. Phillips said, smiling.

When Nate walked out of the doctor's office and into the parking lot, he saw Trevor stepping out of his car. The man walked over to Nate.

"I'm sorry about your diagnosis."

"It's no big deal," Nate said. "I need some simple surgery, but then I'll be fine."

"That's good," Trevor said, looking up as if checking for rain. "So, this proves the baby is mine, then."

"No," Nate said. "It just proves the baby isn't mine."

"Yeah, I guess," Trevor said. "So what do we do now?"

"We don't do anything," Nate said, fishing his car keys out of his pocket. "This is no longer my problem. And once I let Daphanie know exactly what I think about her, she won't be my problem, either."

"But what am I supposed to do? She won't submit to a test. I know Daphanie, she'll always say the child is yours, even after you tell her it isn't. She'll have the baby and never let me see it."

"Like I said, that's your problem now," Nate said, walking off.

Before going home, Nate stopped to have a few drinks and think about exactly how he would approach Daphanie with this shit.

Half an hour after Nate left the bar, he was standing in the center of his living room. Something didn't feel right. It felt as though someone had been there. Then he remembered, this was the day Monica was supposed to have come to move her things.

Had she actually come and had her things moved that fast?

Nate climbed the stairs, hoping for some reason that she hadn't.

He stepped into their bedroom, and the nightstand they shared when they were married was gone. He walked to the closet, slid open the doors, and one half was bare. All Monica's clothes were gone, her shoes—everything.

Nate walked over to the bed, lowered himself onto the edge of it. He dropped his face into his hands, realizing this time he had lost Monica forever.

89

Daphanie filled Brownie's champagne glass with more sparkling grape juice, then topped off her own glass.

"I wish I weren't pregnant so we could celebrate with the real stuff," Daphanie said with a laugh. "But if I wasn't pregnant, I guess there wouldn't be a need to celebrate." She raised her glass. "Toast!"

"It just doesn't seem right, Daph," Brownie said.

"It was going to be me and Nate anyway, if his wife didn't come back into the picture."

"But she did."

"And I took her right back out of it. All this happened for a reason. Now toast, dammit," Daphanie said, raising her glass again. "To my new life as Nate's wife and mother of his child."

"No," Brownie said, setting down her glass and standing with her purse. "I can't do it. You shouldn't be lying to that man. You can't pull this off. The minute the baby is born, he's going to know."

"How?" Daphanie said, setting down her glass. "Trevor and Nate practically look like brothers. If the baby looks like Nate, why would he even question anything?"

Brownie stood, her arms crossed, shaking her head. "And you don't feel the slightest bit of guilt about any of this?"

Daphanie picked up her glass and took a drink. "Nope. I don't."

"Fine, Daphanie. It's your life. You do as you like," Brownie said, heading toward the door. The buzzer rang before she reached it.

Daphanie walked over, pressed the intercom button. "Who is it?"

"It's Nate."

Daphanie turned to Brownie and took her finger off the intercom button. "Speak of the devil," she said, smiling to Brownie. Pressing the button again, Daphanie said, "What are you doing here, Nate? You never come by unexpected."

"Buzz me up, Daphanie."

"Okay, okay."

"I need to be getting out of here," Brownie said. "I'm not as good as you. That man will take one look at my face and see that something is wrong."

"No. Just stay to say hi, then leave. He'll be up in a sec."

Brownie huffed and shook her head again.

A knock came at the door. Daphanie opened it to see Nate. She gave him a hug and a quick kiss before letting him in.

"Brownie was just leaving, but she stayed to say hi."

"Hey, Nate," Brownie said, quickly glancing at him, then averting her eyes.

"Hello, Brownie," Nate said, walking past her into the living room.

Brownie hugged Daphanie. When she stepped back, she held Daphanie by the shoulders and just stared sadly into her eyes.

Daphanie smiled. "I'll call you later," she said, then closed the door after her friend stepped out.

"Champagne. You're celebrating?" Nate said, pointing to one of the glasses. "Aren't you supposed to be pregnant?"

"Supposed to be?" Daphanie chuckled. "Can't fake a pregnancy. And that's just sparkling grape juice." She walked over to Nate, wrapped her arms around him again. "This is such a surprise. I wasn't expecting to see you till later. What brings you over?"

"Why would you do this?"

Daphanie looked up at Nate. "Do what?"

He pushed her arms from around him. "Tell me that baby is mine, when it's not?"

Daphanie all of sudden felt sick, weak, and frightened. How did he know? Was it Lewis? It could've been, but she didn't think he'd do that. Trevor! She thought. But how in the hell did he get to Nate? She had to pull it together, and now.

Daphanie chuckled. "I don't know what you're talking about, Nate."

"Stop lying to me," Nate said, walking away from her.

"I'm not lying. Whose baby could it be, then, if it's not yours?" Daphanie asked, wanting to see just how much Nate knew.

"Who the hell is Trevor?"

Daphanie shook her head. "Nobody. A guy I used to date before you. But he's married. He's not the father of—"

"You slept with him. We met. He told me you two had sex."

"Yes. The day you dumped me for your ex-wife. I was free, I could have sex with whomever I wanted after you did me like that," Daphanie said spitefully.

"Yes, you could. But it was unprotected sex, and you got pregnant by him."

"Why are you saying that?"

"Because that's what he told me!"

Daphanie walked over to Nate, stood in front of him. "I left him for you. While we were together, he always talked about wanting to have a baby. But he was married. That was ridiculous. He called again, thinking that that one time was going to be more. I told him I was pregnant, and he automatically assumed it was his. I met with him specifically to tell him it wasn't."

Nate turned away from Daphanie again. "I want to believe you, Daphanie."

"You can," she said, walking around him, looking up in his face again.

"Why? Because you'd never lie to me?"

"That's right. What we have is too important to do that. I love you too much for that. And what kind of woman would that make me, to tell you this baby is yours if it's not?"

"That's a good question. A lying, worthless, filthy bitch, I suppose."

"What?" Daphanie said, outraged. "You don't come up in my house, calling—"

"Daphanie, the baby is not mine," Nate said calmly. "It's impossible."

"No, it's not impossible!" Daphanie screamed.

"I'm sterile!" Nate yelled.

Silence.

"I was tested. I saw a doctor. I've most likely been this way since my teens." Nate shook his head sadly, but did not look away from Daphanie. "Why would you do this? Why would you tell me such a lie? I left my wife for this."

"And you left me before this," Daphanie said unapologetically. "We were trying to have a baby. We were going to get married. I didn't take the work transfer I would've taken because you said I'd be fine—now I'm out of work. Do you know how hard it'll be for me to find another job, with the economy the way it is now?"

"So you lie about a child that's not even mine to get what you want."

"I deserve it!" Daphanie screamed. "I deserve you, what we had. The life we were going to have. I didn't do anything wrong."

Nate stood in front of her, not saying a word.

Daphanie rushed to him, grabbed him by his suit jacket lapels. "So it's his. But he doesn't ever have to know it. You can raise it like it's your own. You're doing that with Nathaniel. Just do it—"

"Let go of me," Nate said, his voice calm.

"Nate, just listen to me."

"Let go of me," he said more firmly, a rage in his eyes that Daphanie did not want to test.

She released him.

"I'm going to walk out this door. I'm doing you a favor now by letting this end right here. Normally I would not drop this till I got revenge by ruining everything in your life. I'm trying to change because I see where that's gotten me." Nate raised a finger to Daphanie's face. "But don't ever try to contact me again, or I'll forget what I just said and you will be very sorry."

The next night, Nate sat at his dining room table by himself. It was going on nine P.M. The lights were low. In the living room, the flat-screen was on, but the volume was muted.

He had played with Nathaniel before bed. Nate had bathed him, told him a bedtime story, then sat at the edge of his bed till the boy had fallen off to sleep.

Nate then prepared his dinner, the food he was eating now— a cold-cut sandwich, some chips, carrot sticks, and a glass of milk.

He had eaten a quarter of the sandwich. He held the uneaten half in his hand and stared at the space before him.

He sat in total silence.

Monica sat on the steps of Tabatha's front porch, staring up at the sky. It was night. The stars were out, and the weather was warm. She had gotten all her hair cut to the length the hair had grown to around the area of her surgery. It was short and wavy and framed her face nicely, although she didn't think so.

She cupped a glass half full of red wine in both her palms.

Monica heard the screen door open behind her, but paid no mind to it.

She felt Tabatha standing behind her.

Tabatha had put Roland in charge of the store for the past few days, because she wanted to stay home with Monica. Monica knew this was Tabatha's way of getting free days off, and she thought it was sweet that the assistant manager didn't complain.

Tabatha sat beside Monica on the second step. She held her refilled glass of wine.

"Forget about him, girl. I'm telling you, Nate's not worth your thoughts."

"I'm forgetting," Monica said, still looking skyward. "But

it's hard. I gave up Lewis, and now he's found someone else. He looks happy."

"Girl, you gave him up because you didn't want him," Tabatha said. "He was wrong for you from the very first day Nate picked him, which shows you how right Nate was for you. If Nate really knew you, he would've picked someone who was really rich and caring and handsome, and then none of this would've happened."

Monica turned to Tabatha, chuckling. "If you're trying to make me laugh, it's not working."

"It's working a little bit." Tabatha took a sip of her wine. She threw an arm around Monica's shoulder. "Time. It does heal all wounds. Even the Nate-inflicted kind."

Monica took a slow drink from her glass. "You think he's thinking about me right now?"

"Don't, sweetheart. Don't put yourself there."

"But . . . but we were going to get married again. I was living there. We had finally gotten the child that we always wanted," Monica said, getting emotional, feeling herself wanting to cry.

"Don't, Monica. It's over," Tabatha said, setting down her glass, turning to Monica, and hugging her. "It's over now, and you never have to think or worry about him again."

Monica grabbed tight to Tabatha, dropped her face onto her best friend's shoulder, and cried.

A car rolled up in front of Tabatha's house. It was a large black Mercedes. Nate was behind the wheel.

"I don't believe this motherfucker," Tabatha said under her breath. She stood as the car door opened and Nate climbed out. As he walked around the Mercedes, Tabatha descended the first step, pointing at Nate. "Don't you even think about it."

Monica was still sitting, wiping her eyes with her sleeve.

"I need to speak to Monica," Nate said.

"Get the fuck away from here!" Tabatha yelled, stepping down to the sidewalk. "You have done her enough harm. Just go!"

"Monica," Nate said, looking past Tabatha. "Just let me have a word with you. One minute."

"Did you hear what I said? Leave my fucking premises!" Tabatha said.

"No. Wait," Monica said, her voice soft.

"Monica, just let him go," Tabatha said, turning to Monica.

"I want to hear what he has to say," Monica said, sniffling.

"Are you sure?"

Monica nodded.

Nate slowly walked toward the steps, passing Tabatha cautiously. "Can I speak to you in private?" Nate asked.

"No," Monica said. "Tabatha can stay."

"This has nothing to do with her," Nate said. "This is between us."

"There is no us!" Monica screamed at Nate from the steps. She lowered her voice and continued, "That ended the day you got that bitch pregnant. If you have something to say, you can say it in front of Tabatha. If not, drive the fuck home."

"That's right," Tabatha said from behind Nate.

Nate looked over his shoulder, gave the evil eye to Tabatha, then turned back to Monica. "Things weren't supposed to happen this way. We were fine. We were going to get married, remember? Everything we went through to get back together, we just can't throw that away now."

"Our marriage was shit the day we got married, Nate. I just didn't know it then."

"That's not true," Nate said. "That's not true. We were good, and we can be again."

Monica chuckled sadly. "And how is that? You have a baby on the way. You want that baby in your life, you want to raise it. Isn't that what you told me?"

"I know. But I changed my mind. You cannot blame me for getting her pregnant. We weren't together then. It just happened. But I thought about losing you, and I realized that child is not worth it. We already have our family, right? Nathaniel misses you so much. All he does is ask about you."

Monica missed the little boy, too.

"You have a child coming, Nate. I could never give you one. I will always be in the woman's shadow," Monica said. "I couldn't do it."

Nate closed his eyes, sighed heavily, then opened them again. "I haven't been totally honest with you."

"When have you ever?" Tabatha said.

"The child is not mine."

"What?" Monica said. "How do you know?"

"We had a test done. The child is not mine," Nate said. "I swear. You can check. It's not."

Monica just stared at Nate. What did this mean? The baby wasn't his. He was asking her back. If she said yes, she would see little Nathaniel again. She and Nate would get married, and things would go back to the way they were.

"Monica, you ain't actually listening to what he has to say, are you?" Tabatha said, now standing right in front of Monica.

"Tabatha, no one asked for your opinion on this," Nate said.

"Fuck you, Nate! I'm talking to Monica," Tabatha said. She turned back to Monica. "Please don't make this same mistake again. Just tell him no."

"She can answer for herself, Tabatha," Nate said.

"I said—" Tabatha began.

"He's right," Monica said, interrupting. "I can answer for myself."

Monica stood. "So what are you offering, Nate?"

Tabatha shook her head.

"Come back," Nate said. "Come back, and things will be exactly the way they were."

"Really!" Monica said, faking enthusiasm. "You mean like when you were fucking your secretary Tori. Or maybe like when you were taking pills to make you impotent so I would go out and sleep with the man you paid to seduce me, so you could divorce me. It would be like that again? And would you be the same loving man? The man that blackmailed Lewis, that stole his best friend's house from him and his mother. Would you be the man that forced Freddy Ford to come to our house and try to kill us both and kidnap Nathaniel? Would I be so lucky to be married to the man that would not come to see me while I was still in the hospital, and when you did, it was to tell me that you were leaving me once again, because you got some other woman pregnant, and you'd rather be with that child and her mother than with me? But hold it, that was before you found out the kid wasn't really yours. But now that you have that little bit of infor-mation, now you can come back to me, and actually expect me to take you back," Monica said. "Nate, I have one thing to say to you. You must be out of your fucking mind."

"There you go!" Tabatha screamed. "Hallelujah! That's my girl!"

"Nate, I've given you all I had to give you. My love, my devo-tion. Lord knows I would've given you a child if He would've let me. And I almost gave my life being with you, but He didn't want that to happen, either. So now I'm through. I have nothing left to give you, but most important, I have nothing more I want to give you. Now if you'd please do as Tabatha said, and leave her fucking premises."

Nate looked as though there was something he wanted to say, but he remained silent. He turned toward his car, stopped, turned to face Monica and Tabatha again. He opened his mouth as though to comment, but again said nothing. He finally turned, walked back to the Mercedes, climbed in, and drove off.

Tabatha ran to Monica, threw her arms around her, screaming, "You finally did it, girl! You did it!"

Monica smiled, looking in the direction the car had disappeared in, and with pride said, "Yes, I did."

Daphanie had spent the last three days searching online for pharmaceutical representative positions. There were absolutely none. Unemployment payments would last her six months. Her health insurance would run out in the same amount of time. She was pregnant. What the hell was she going to do?

She had retirement she would have to draw from, because her savings were a joke.

All of this because Trevor couldn't leave well enough alone and had to open his huge mouth.

Fine, Daphanie thought. He wants the world to know about his baby, then everyone should know.

Daphanie pushed open her car door and climbed out.

She had gotten her hair done yesterday. It would be the last time, she told herself, till she found another job. But for now it looked marvelous.

She wore a pair of skintight jeans. They hugged her ass and thighs perfectly. Again, in not too many weeks she'd be saying good-bye to those.

Her makeup was perfect. She was gorgeous, she told herself, as she climbed the steps of the middle-class home.

She dug in her purse, pulled out her compact, checked herself in the tiny mirror, and dabbed a bit of powder on her nose for good measure.

She dropped the case back into her purse, then rang the doorbell.

After a few moments, the door was opened.

A mild-looking, somewhat pudgy woman stood in the doorway.

Daphanie didn't speak, just smiled at her, her lips covered in bright red lipstick.

"Can I help you?" the woman said.

"Yes, Mrs. Morgan, you can," Daphanie said in her sweetest voice. "I just want to introduce myself. My name is Daphanie Coleman, and I'm your husband's baby's mama."

Epilogue

Two weeks had passed, and Nate sat in his backyard watching Nathaniel play with the new puppy he had gotten him. The boy had begged Nate till he had no choice but to give in.

Everything was fine. Nate had gone back to work, and he enjoyed being there.

Nate had found a new woman to take care of the boy and the house. Her name was Ms. Langford. She was older, had never been married, and had been a nanny and housekeeper for most of her adult life. She was working out fine.

Evenings for Nate were somewhat lonely, but Nate no longer thought about Monica. He knew they were finally done with each other. He had no intention of trying to appeal to her once again to take him back.

Sitting in his backyard, drinking a glass of homemade lemonade thanks to Ms. Langford, Nate smiled at Nathaniel, and thought that, yes, everything was just fine.

But there was something gnawing at Nate. A feeling that he could not get rid of, no matter how much he tried.

It was a feeling of victimization.

He had been lied to, used, and that did not sit well with Nate.

Even though he had told Daphanie he would not seek revenge for what she had done to him, that promise was not sitting well with Nate. It went against every belief he held, kept him up some nights and waking poorly rested.

For the last two weeks, he had fought the urge to do anything about this, but now he was pulling out his cell phone. Nate scrolled through the call list, highlighted the name he wanted to dial, then punched the Call button.

After the third ring, Trevor Morgan answered.

Nate had a brief conversation with him. Trevor informed Nate how Daphanie had shown up at his front door, told his wife all about the child.

Nate had never known Daphanie to be the type of person she was revealed to be now. It was a good thing he had not married her.

Trevor told Nate that Daphanie had only spoken to him once since then, to assure him he'd never see the baby a day in his life.

That afternoon, Nate left Nathaniel with Ms. Langford and took a trip to the jewelry store.

Two hours later, he stood in Daphanie's living room.

She was surprised to see him, but happy.

Nate said he had a change of heart and lowered himself to one knee, opening the box containing the ring he had just bought, and proposed to her.

Daphanie tearfully accepted.

As they sat together later, holding each other, sharing some wine, Nate carefully informed Daphanie that there were conditions to his proposal.

She told Nate she would do whatever she had to.

Nate told her that he could not marry her as long as she was mother to another man's child.

Daphanie asked Nate what she was to do.

He did not believe in abortion. He did not want Daphanie to kill the child. Nate told her that he would marry her only if after she gave birth to the baby, she signed over full custody, with absolutely no rights or visits on her part, to the father of the baby.

Nate had already had the surgery to correct his fertility problem, and the doctor had already given him a clean bill of health.

Nate promised, as soon as they were married, they could have a child of their own.

Daphanie looked conflicted.

Nate stood, told her he would leave, give her as much time as she needed to think it over. He knew he was asking a lot of her, but he told her he wouldn't have it any other way.

At two-thirty that morning, Nate's bedside phone rang. It was Daphanie. She told him it would be hard, but she would do it.

What she wanted most was a life with Nate, and as long as he promised he would give her a child, she would do whatever he asked of her.

During the pregnancy, Daphanie spent the majority of her time at Nate's place. She wanted to sell her loft. But the housing market was horrible, and Nate suggested she hold on to it, until prices climbed enough so she wouldn't lose on her investment.

Daphanie didn't bother searching for a job, but stayed at home, enjoying her pregnancy. Nate said there was no need for her to work. He was fine with her being home. He told her that if she liked, she could occupy some of her time with the planning of their wedding. One evening, he even brought home an armful of bridal magazines.

He told her the event could be as big or as small as she preferred. But he was leaning on the side of a large society event. They could leak news to the paper, have their photo in *JET* magazine, let the world know. Daphanie was excited.

So until she gave birth, Daphanie had been busy planning her wedding with Nate. She whittled down the guest list to five hundred of their closest family and friends.

Daphanie had gotten word that their photo would definitely run in the forthcoming issue of *JET*, and she had even spoken to the producer of the new BET show *Million Dollar Brides*. They were going to have a camera crew at the wedding to shoot the entire gala. It would be wonderful.

Two days after Daphanie was released from the hospital, she, Nate, and the new baby (it was Nate's suggestion that Daphanie not give the child a name) met Trevor at his home. They were accompanied by two of Nate's attorneys. Trevor had his lawyer there as well.

Trevor's wife was no longer in the home. They had been divorced after she received Daphanie's news.

After the contract was looked over thoroughly by all three attorneys, Trevor signed his name, and the document was passed to Daphanie.

Nate held the baby in his arms.

Daphanie looked down at the form, then over at the child. She hesitated.

Nate smiled at Daphanie, assured her that in no time they'd be married. She would have him at her side for the rest of his life, and they would have a baby, maybe two or three, of their own.

Daphanie seemed contented with that thought. Her hand shaking a bit, she signed the form giving Trevor full custody of the baby.

Nate handed the child over to Trevor. Trevor thanked Nate, and the meeting was over.

The wedding would take place one week later.

The day before the wedding, it was the talk of the town. It

was to be held on the top floor of the beautiful Harold Washington Public Library downtown on State Street and Congress Parkway. With its ancient architecture, marble floors, and ceilings that stretched seemingly a hundred feet overhead, she knew she had picked the perfect place.

The night before the wedding, Nate and Daphanie sat in the bar of the Drake Hotel. They had separate suites there, and Nate had even put up all of Daphanie's family from California in rooms there as well.

In the bar, at a corner table, a candle burning between them, Nate and Daphanie held hands and stared lovingly into each other's eyes.

Daphanie said this was like a dream come true.

Nate assured her it was just the beginning. They had the rest of their lives together to experience that dream.

He stood, leaned over the table, and kissed her lips deeply. Daphanie melted.

Nate told her he loved her dearly. He kissed her hand, then told her the next time he'd see her would be at the altar. He said good-bye to her, calling her Mrs. Kenny.

Daphanie smiled so hard her face almost started hurting, as she watched Nate walk out of the bar. That night she dreamed of the rest of her life with Nate.

The next day, Saturday, the wedding was to start at two P.M. sharp.

When the clock struck two, all five hundred seats in the library hall were taken. Half a dozen photographers stood at strategic spots in the big room, prepared to start snapping photos. The camera crew from *Million Dollar Brides* were stationed through the room as well. And the groom, Nate Kenny, was nowhere to be found.

Daphanie sat in her dressing room, fully made up, wearing her wedding gown, dialing Nate's cell phone for the tenth time.

Her bridal party, as well as her mother, stood around her, comforting her.

Her calls kept going to his voice mail. Daphanie wondered if he was okay, if he might have gotten into a serious accident on the way there.

At two-thirty, all the guest were still seated, but they were getting restless, asking questions. The *Million Dollar Brides* crew were contemplating leaving, the library coordinator was already pressuring Daphanie to either start the wedding or end it already.

Daphanie was frustrated and angry, and asked if everyone could just leave the dressing room so she could decide what she needed to do.

She sat in front of the mirror, staring at herself, trying not to cry for fear of running her mascara.

A knock came at the door.

It must be Nate. Daphanie said come in, and quickly pulled herself together.

When the door opened, it wasn't Nate, but his ex-wife, Monica.

She wore a simple black and white dress with black pumps. Her hair was medium-length and naturally curly. She looked far better than she had when she was in the hospital.

All that aside, Daphanie wondered what in the hell this woman was doing at her wedding, and she asked her exactly that.

Monica told Daphanie that Nate had come to her after he had found out the child was not his. He had told Monica that Daphanie had lied to him. Monica told Daphanie that Nate hadn't taken well to that, and months later when Monica saw the announcement in *JET* magazine, she knew something was up.

Daphanie asked Monica what she meant by that.

Monica told Daphanie if she knew her ex-husband like she thought she did, this entire wedding was a joke.

Daphanie told Monica about all the money that had been spent, that her entire family was in town to witness this.

Monica chuckled and told Daphanie that Nate would spend as much money, as much time, and as much of himself as it took to get revenge against someone who'd done him wrong. And it looked like she had gotten it, Monica told Daphanie.

Monica turned toward the door, smiling, and was about to exit when she heard Daphanie break down and start to cry as if in agony.

Monica turned back to her and asked her what was wrong.

Daphanie told Monica that Nate had made her sign away custody of her baby to the father. She asked Monica if that was part of his plan for revenge as well.

Monica told Daphanie yes. Looking down at Daphanie sadly, Monica said she thought Daphanie deserved some of what she had gotten, but no mother deserved to have her baby swindled from her.

Monica walked over to Daphanie, wrapped her arms around her to comfort her, and told her that if she wanted, she would help Daphanie do whatever she needed to get her child back.

Nate looked down at his watch. It was three P.M. He was satisfied that Daphanie had been sufficiently humiliated by now.

"You want to hold him?" Trevor said, holding out the infant to Nate.

Nate smiled and took the baby in his arms. "Wow, he's a big one for only a couple of weeks old. Do you have everything you need to take care of him?"

"The universe works in strange ways," Trevor said. "The woman I've been dating for the last few months just happens to be a nurse who works in the nursery unit. She's already in love with the little guy, and said she'd help me with whatever I need."

Nate looked down at the smiling baby. He smiled back. "You name him yet?"

"Yeah," Trevor said. "If it wasn't for you, I wouldn't have him. So I named him Nate."

Nate looked up, surprised. "That's *my* son's name, too."

"I hope you don't mind."

Nate thought about it a minute. "Nate," he said to himself and to the baby. "No, Nate's a good name."